"Cantore is a former cop, and her experience shows in this wonderful series debut. The characters are well-drawn and believable, and the suspenseful plot is thick with tension. Fans of Lynette Eason, Dee Henderson, or DiAnn Mills and readers who like crime fiction without gratuitous violence and sex will appreciate discovering a new writer."
LIBRARY JOURNAL

"Cantore provides a detailed and intimate account of a homicide investigation in an enjoyable read that's more crime than Christian."
PUBLISHERS WEEKLY

"Set in a busy West Coast city, the story's twists will keep readers eagerly reading and guessing. . . . I enjoyed every chapter. *Accused* is a brisk and action-filled book with enjoyable characters and a good dose of mystery. . . . I look forward to more books in this series."
MOLLY ANDERSON, www.ChristianBookPreviews.com

"*Accused* was a wonderfully paced, action-packed mystery. . . . [Carly] is clearly a competent detective, an intelligent woman, and a compassionate partner. This is definitely a series I will be revisiting."
MIN JUNG, FreshFiction.com

"*Accused* by Janice Cantore is full of suspense. Although it is nearly 400 pages, it was a book I just could not put down and could not read each page fast enough!"

"The plot takes unexpected twists and turns, which quickly grabs the reader's attention and holds it tightly until the end. . . . The characters are realistic with flaws as well as good qualities, and the author did a marvelous job of weaving a plot so complex that the reader is left wondering who can be trusted right along with Carly."

"This was a great read. There was just enough action and mystery to keep me turning page after page. . . . Strong conflict and well-written characters; you won't want to put this one down!"

"I started reading this novel and couldn't put it down. From the beginning of the book to the end, there is action, suspense, crime, red herrings, and thoughts of a spiritual nature. . . . I hope to be able to read more from this author."

ABDUCTED

PACIFIC COAST JUSTICE SERIES NO. 2

ABDUCTED

Janice Cantore

Tyndale House Publishers, Inc.
Carol Stream, Illinois

Visit Tyndale online at www.tyndale.com.

Visit Janice Cantore's website at www.janicecantore.com.

TYNDALE and Tyndale's quill logo are registered trademarks of Tyndale House Publishers, Inc.

Abducted

Designed by Stephen Vosloo

Edited by Erin E. Smith

Published in association with the literary agency of D. C. Jacobson & Associates LLC, an Author Management Company. www.dcjacobson.com.

Scripture taken from the New King James Version.® Copyright © 1982 by Thomas Nelson, Inc. Used by permission. All rights reserved.

Library of Congress Cataloging-in-Publication Data

Cantore, Janice.
    Abducted / Janice Cantore.
      p. cm. — (Pacific Coast justice ; 2)
    ISBN 978-1-4143-5848-2 (sc)
    1. Policewomen—Fiction. 2. Missing children—Investigation--Fiction. I. Title.
PS3603.A588A64 2012
813'.6—dc23   2012006398

Printed in the United States of America

18   17   16   15   14   13   12
7   6   5   4   3   2   1

Dedicated to my brother Dan and his wife, Sandy.

No matter what, they have always been an inspiration

and an encouragement to me. Love you both.

Acknowledgments

Thanks to my agent, Don Jacobson, for always being positive, to Jan Stob and Erin Smith for all of their help and support, and to Tyndale for allowing me to be part of a team.

1

"I CAN'T BELIEVE it still feels like eighty degrees outside. It's three o'clock in the morning." Carly Edwards bit back a yawn and waved one hand outside the patrol car as she drove up Las Playas Boulevard. The smell of hot pavement permeated the air, and Carly squirmed at the feeling of her undershirt plastered to her body under the stiff Kevlar vest.

"What's the matter? You miss your afternoon shift in juvenile, sitting in air-conditioned comfort?" asked Joe King, her partner, riding shotgun. They'd agreed long ago that the AC was a no-no in the black-and-white while on patrol. Officers needed to hear what was going on outside the car, and that was impossible with the windows up and the AC blowing.

"No way!" She shot a glare at Joe only to find him grinning. "Ha-ha. No matter how hot it gets—or how cold, for that matter—I'll still love graveyard patrol."

Joe settled into his seat. "Well, it's good to have you back. Bet you wish you'd cut your hair. You're probably hot right now."

Running a hand behind her neck, Carly nodded. "I wish I had scissors with me." The hot weather served as a reminder: she needed to cut her hair. No matter how she tied her thick mop back, it was just too hot. She smiled in the semidarkness. *Small price to pay for being back where I want to be.* She turned the car down an alley and slowed, listening and watching while garages and dark backyards rolled by. The radio stayed quiet.

"I was talking to Todd the other day . . . ," Carly said.

"Which one? Todd in detectives or Todd out at the academy?"

"Academy, the department historian. Did you know that back in the thirties and forties, they used to call black-and-whites 'prowl cars'? Don't you think that's a great name? Especially for us working graves. That's what we do—*prowl.*"

"Yeah, I like that. Prowling for prowlers," Joe agreed. "Especially this time of the morning—we prowl through empty streets looking for bad guys."

Carly nodded and checked her watch. "Let's do some prowling over at Memorial Hospital. The watch report said there was an uptick in car burgs in the hospital lot. I promised Andrea we'd give the area some extra attention. Maybe we'll get lucky and catch an auto burglar."

"Ah, Andrea the wild woman. Sometimes I wonder how the two of you live together; you're so different."

"So what are you trying to say? I'm boring?" Carly pulled out of the alley and onto a main thoroughfare.

"No, you're just more down-to-earth. You have to admit, Andrea is a player."

"She may be a player, but she's been a good friend. I don't know what I would have done if she hadn't been there for me after the divorce." She shrugged and kept her eyes moving, watching the dark street and quiet businesses. "I've known her since we were five."

Joe grunted. "I'm glad the match works for you."

Carly steered the car toward the hospital and punched the accelerator, enjoying the speed and the empty city streets but distracted by the subject of her roommate. "I will admit, though, there has been some friction between us lately. She's not happy Nick and I are talking about reconciling." Carly frowned and chewed on her bottom lip. *In fact, it seems to make Andrea downright angry.*

"Maybe she's afraid you'll get hurt again."

Carly slowed the unit as they reached the hospital parking lot. She cast a sidelong glance at Joe. He was looking out his window.

"Is it just Andrea who's afraid for me, or does that go for you, too?" She clicked off the headlights and settled into a five-mile-per-hour crawl through the sparsely filled lot, watching carefully for any movement.

"Yeah, I guess it goes for me, too. I like Nick and everything—he's a great cop—but I remember how much he hurt you. Are you sure you want to take that chance again?"

Simultaneously they turned to face one another. Carly read the concern in his eyes before she turned back to concentrate on the lot. But instead of seeing cars, she began replaying the first date she'd had with Nick after he was released from the hospital. He'd decided to court her as though they'd just met and to treat her with a respect and tenderness that took her breath away. "I'll prove I'm a new man, worthy of your trust and admiration, a trust I'll never betray again," he'd said just before he kissed her good night. As his lips touched hers, his words warmed her heart and she forgot about all the bad baggage in their history.

"I've told you, I believe he's changed," Carly said to Joe. "I've changed too. We're Christians now." She wished the conviction in her voice would infuse her heart. Inside, she winced because Nick had been distant lately. A couple of weeks after that wonderful date, he began pulling away, and she was at a loss as to why. *And we've been through so much.* The last sixteen months flashed through Carly's mind: Nick's affair, their split, the murder case that brought them back together, and the shooting that left Nick with a gimpy hip.

"Well," Joe said, "all I know is that Nick is lucky you'll give him the time of day, let alone a reconciliation."

"I'd be happy to explain the Christian . . ." Something

caught her eye. She stopped the unit. They were in the last parking row, facing the security building on the fringe of the hospital's property.

"You see something?" Joe shifted forward in his seat.

"Yes, I'm sure I saw a light flash across the window there." She pointed to the left side of the building in front of them.

The pair stared into the darkness at the small, one-story building, the only noise the steady hum of the Chevy's engine and an occasional squeak of leather gear.

"Look! Did you see it?" Carly hissed the question in an excited whisper as her heart rate quickened. She turned the car off.

"I saw it." Joe picked up the radio mike. "Adam-7, show us out at Memorial Hospital, possible burglary in progress in the security offices on the southwest portion of the parking lot."

He replaced the mike, and they both waited to hear the dispatcher acknowledge the transmission. Several units answered to assist. Carly nodded to Joe, and they quietly got out of the car.

"I saw it twice more," she whispered without taking her eyes off the building. "You go north; I'll take south."

They parted and came at the building from different directions, each using the few cars and trees in the lot for cover. As Carly approached the southeast corner, a car parked on the side of the building came into view. The vehicle was tucked away where a vehicle didn't belong, in an enclosure reserved for Dumpsters.

When she cleared the corner of the building, more of the

car became visible, and she could make out a faint silhouette of someone behind the wheel. Frowning, she squinted, trying to see better in the darkness. If there was someone behind the wheel, he or she was short. A kid?

She jerked her radio from its holder. Whoever it was, he didn't belong here, and she could read the license plate.

"Adam-7, there's a car—"

The car's engine roared to life. In a cacophony of grinding gears and squealing tires, it lurched backward, straight for Carly.

"Carly!" Joe called her name as she dove into a planter, out of the car's path but still close enough to feel its exhaust as the driver ground the gears into first and screeched forward, away from the lot. Carly fumbled for her radio while Joe ran to her side.

She held a hand up to indicate she was okay and keyed her radio to hail dispatch. "Adam-7, we have a possible burglary suspect fleeing from our location, now northbound on California Ave. It's a small, gray, compact vehicle, license plate 3-Tom-King-Adam-4-6-3."

The taillights sped north toward the freeway.

"Are you okay?" Joe leaned down to help her out of the bushes.

"Yeah, just a few scratches." Carly brushed her uniform off and found no significant damage, only a muddy knee.

The sound of sirens split the air, and the radio told them assisting units had picked up the fleeing vehicle and were now in pursuit.

"I hope they get him," Carly sighed, more than a little disappointed they weren't in a car speeding after the burglar. She jerked a thumb toward the building and spoke in a soft tone to Joe. "Whoever had the light on in there did not have time to get in that car."

Joe nodded in agreement. "Let's finish checking the building."

Carly kept one ear tuned to the pursuit on the radio while she and Joe turned their attention to the security building.

"Look." Joe pointed with one hand and drew his weapon with the other. There was a screen on the ground under an open window. If someone had climbed into the building through this window, then that person was still inside.

The partners lowered the volume on their radios. Carly drew her gun and stepped to one side of the garbage enclosure while Joe took the other end.

From her position she had a clear view of the window. Patiently she watched. Joe was closer to the building, and she could see him straining to hear if there was someone moving around inside. In a few minutes their vigilance was rewarded, and Joe signaled her that he'd heard something. Carly tightened the grip on her gun.

A bag appeared in the window. Gloved hands shoved the bag out. It dropped to the ground and landed softly near the screen.

Carly looked at Joe and held a finger to her lips. They both trained their weapons on the opening. A man poked his head out the window and looked to the left and the right.

Carly held her breath, but she knew she and Joe were well concealed. The man then pushed his entire torso out the window. Head down, he twisted and swung his legs to the left out the long, thin opening. With a push, a little twist, and a whispered curse, the burglar let go of the sill and dropped the short distance to the ground next to the bag. His back was to Carly and Joe, and when he turned, Joe made their presence known.

"Police! Keep your hands where we can see them." Their flashlights pinned the man in strong, bright light.

The burglar jumped and raised his hands in the air. "Don't shoot; don't shoot! I got nothing!"

Carly sensed a combination of fear and surprise in the man's voice. *He thought we'd left to chase his buddy.*

Two assisting units roared into the lot, and the area was awash in more light from both headlights and spotlights. Joe and Carly took the man into custody. Carly led him to their patrol car while Joe contacted hospital security to open the building so they could conduct a thorough search.

Sweat poured down the crook's face. He smelled like a noxious mixture of cigarettes and dirty sweat socks. She leaned him against the patrol car and emptied his pockets on the hood on the off chance there was something from the security offices on his person. All she found was a filthy nylon wallet, a pack of cigarettes, a lighter, and some change. Once certain he wasn't in possession of anything else, she seated him in the back of the unit. Next, she emptied the contents of the bag he'd thrown out the window. Turning on the spotlight, she illuminated everything and surveyed what the thief had seen fit to steal.

The bag was full of papers, spreadsheets. Carly frowned, muttering, "This makes no sense." There were no valuable trinkets, just papers with names and times. As she read more carefully, she saw that the sheets were schedules outlining the strength and positioning of hospital security personnel. She looked back at the crook in the car, and he looked away. He was a skinny, dirty man with the ruined teeth of a speed freak. Carly opened his wallet and retrieved a driver's license. His name was Stanley Harper, and he was thirty years old, a resident of Las Playas.

She sat in the passenger seat of the patrol car and keyed Stanley's information into the computer to check for warrants. Her search brought up two hits.

"Mr. Harper, did you know you have two outstanding traffic warrants?" Carly spoke to the man through the custody cage, looking over her left shoulder while she talked. "And you just got off parole for—surprise of surprises—burglary. Doesn't look like you've learned your lesson."

"I ain't saying nothing. I want to call my lawyer."

Carly flinched at words she hated to hear. Now she couldn't ask him about the spreadsheets.

"You know the drill. As soon as you're processed, you can call Santa Claus if you want."

"My lawyer will do. I'll be out before you finish your paperwork."

2

CARLY TAPPED HER FOOT impatiently, mentally lambasting the elevator for being so slow. She and Joe had skipped breakfast, hurried, and finished the arrest report for Stanley Harper in record time, only two minutes past end of watch. Now, dressed and ready to go, she fretted she'd be late for Nick's therapy session because the department's elevators were archaic. When the car finally slid to a stop, she hopped in and pounded the down button. Thankfully, the car made the trip to the lobby floor without any extra stops.

"Carly!" Gary, the security officer working the lobby desk, waved a hand to catch her attention as soon as she stepped out of the elevator.

"What's up?" she asked from the hallway, slowing but not stopping on her way to the back door.

"Can you help me with this lawyer? His client is that burglar you just arrested."

"What? Harper's lawyer is already here?" This news hit with a jolt and brought Carly to a halt. She'd thought Harper's comment was strictly bad-guy bravado.

"Yeah. Can you please talk to him?" Gary pleaded. "He's really being a jerk, and he won't listen to me because I'm not a *police officer*."

Carly checked her watch. "I'm late for an appointment."

The expression on Gary's face changed her mind. She rolled her eyes. "Okay, okay, I'll give it a few minutes."

He held his hands together as if praying and mouthed the words *thank you*. She followed him to the front counter and was immediately sorry. The lawyer was Thomas Caswell, a nasty private defense attorney who was famous for getting obviously guilty clients off on technicalities. Though she'd never faced him in court, Carly knew his tactics in trial: attack the officer instead of the evidence in order to plant doubt in the minds of jurors. The slimiest and wealthiest of crooks hired Caswell.

"And who are you?" the attorney snapped when Carly appeared at the counter. She faced him in a T-shirt, shorts, and flip-flops.

"I'm one of the arresting officers. Is there something I can help you with?"

"I want your name and badge number." He pulled out

a pad and pen. Carly resisted the urge to tell him it was on the arrest report and gave him the information. He asked her to spell her last name twice. "Now—" when he finished writing, he looked down his nose at her, a tone of superiority lacing his voice—"I want to bail my client, Stanley Harper, out. This young man was giving me a lot of nonsense about a records clearance."

"It's not nonsense. Your client has to clear records before he can be bailed out. I'm sure you know what we're talking about because it's routine for all arrestees. It means Cal-ID has to assure us he doesn't have any more warrants other than the ones we've already found." Carly looked at Gary, who raised four fingers. "That should be in about four hours."

"This is outrageous! I want the watch commander. My client is being unfairly persecuted." Caswell was average height and bony thin, but his facial features were soft. His jowls shook when he spoke.

"Mr. Caswell, it's no use bullying. You've been around long enough to know we have no control over how long Cal-ID takes. Why don't you save everyone a lot of grief, go have some breakfast, and come back in a few hours. Then you can bail your client out." She hoped she had succeeded in keeping the antagonism out of her voice and crossed her arms to regard the lawyer.

"Officer Edwards, I—" He stopped, looked her up and down as if measuring her resolve, then checked his watch. "I do have an engagement to attend to. But this isn't over, not by a long shot. I intend to make this treatment known to your internal affairs department." He bent to pick up his briefcase and then marched out of the building. If the front doors weren't automatic, Carly was sure he would have slammed them.

"Thank you, Carly. I owe you big-time." Gary ran a hand across his brow and blew out a breath of relief. "Do you think he's serious about making a complaint?"

Carly shrugged. "Let him—we're right." The clock at the other end of the lobby caught her eye. "Oh no! I've got to go!" She sprinted out the back door of the station, across the hot parking lot awash in early-morning sun, and leaped into her car.

How will he be today? The question blared in Carly's thoughts as she rushed to her ex-husband's physical therapy session. She tapped the steering wheel and groaned when traffic slowed. The heat of the day added fuel to her anxiety, bringing it to full boil. *Joe and Andrea think I'm crazy for caring; for that matter, a lot of people think I'm crazy. But Nick matters to me, and I want to see him back on his feet.*

Four months ago, a .45-caliber slug had broken his femur, and the injury—although never life threatening—was quickly becoming lifestyle threatening. One setback after another dogged his recovery, from infections to reinjuries to mistakes in therapy. Now he faced the serious threat of not being able to be a police officer again. Carly's mind screamed unvoiced questions. *What will that do to him? What will that do to us?*

"Hey, Carly, how you doing?" Keith, the head therapist, greeted her as she ran into the office.

"Late! Is Nick already in the pool?"

"Relax; we got delayed too." He held his hands up to slow her down. "He just finished up with his stretching and weight exercises."

She let out her breath in a whoosh and wiped sweat from her forehead. "Great! I was really afraid he'd start without me. I'll go change; tell him I'll see him in the water."

Carly relaxed and pushed open the locker room door, thankful for the blast of air-conditioning. As she changed into her swimsuit, she prayed for wisdom and patience. Her natural inclination when Nick tried to push her away was to push back, to get in his face and find out what the problem was. Carly hated beating around the bush and tiptoeing around her ex. But something told her trying to shake him out of the funk he was in wouldn't help; it would only make things worse. Being patient went against the grain, but instinctively Carly guessed that was the best way to handle Nick at the moment.

He always spent five minutes in the warm whirlpool before climbing into the big pool to swim. He was just getting out of the warm water when Carly stepped out of the locker room. Inwardly she flinched when she saw his painful struggle to move. The hip didn't want to flex, which resulted in a stiff, awkward gait. Nick was an athlete, and until the injury, Carly had only known him to move with a fluid, natural grace. And she'd never known him to be without a cheerful optimism that she loved. He smiled and laughed easily, as easily as he'd catch a fly ball in a softball game or deliver a spike in a game of volleyball. Until now.

Watching his stilted gait broke her heart, and it was a struggle to stay positive when the cheerful vibrancy she was used to seeing in the man was missing. His hip injury had turned him from an optimist to a pessimist overnight. She concentrated on the face: the blue eyes, strong jaw, and classically handsome features that always made her heart flutter. He'd once posed for a recruiting poster, and the guys teasingly called him Officer *GQ*. Carly, in happier times, called him her *GQ* hubby.

"Hey, are you ready for a tough five thousand meters today?" Carly inhaled the familiar and welcome scent of pool chlorine and smiled her best smile—an honest one because it was good to see Nick, even under the circumstances.

"Hi!" Nick smiled in return, pausing his walk to the pool. Carly liked to think his face lit up, but she could tell he was hurting. It was probably pain she saw in his eyes. "I thought maybe you wouldn't make it today."

"I wouldn't miss this for the world. We gotta get you back in shape!" She clapped like a cheerleader, then told him about her night, the arrest of Stanley Harper, and the encounter with Caswell, imitating the attorney's highbrow tone.

Nick actually laughed. "You do that pretty good. I've dealt with that guy before. He's a bully. He likes to make noise and scare people, especially when he's standing on shaky ground." His face brightened for a moment as he warmed up into cop mode. "Maybe his client was planning on burgling the hospital, probably to steal drugs. I've heard a lot of rumors that Caswell is as shady as his clients are. But nothing sticks to him; it's like he's Teflon. Did they catch the guy who took off in the car?"

"No, that was the only bummer. We didn't have a helicopter up, and the sheriff couldn't send one to assist. The driver was smart—headed north on the freeway, then got off and doubled back on streets. Our units lost him somewhere near the city limits. The car is registered to Harper, an old address, so that didn't really help us. You think the attorney is in on something shady with Harper?"

"I wouldn't put anything past that guy. It will be interesting to see how he tries to plead the case, what technicality he uses to get his client off." He fell silent as he stepped into the pool.

Carly knew how much Nick missed being out in the field as a working cop. As it was, he was working half days reviewing reports, and while he didn't complain, she knew it was probably tedious for him. Few cops liked being shut up inside with paperwork. She followed him into the pool, and together they stretched their shoulders out before starting laps. Carly prayed while they stretched, thanking God that a little of the old Nick seemed to be with her in the pool today. She finished her prayer for his physical healing and asked God to strengthen their relationship.

As usual, Nick pounded the water. It seemed as though he tried to pound out the stiffness by punishing himself. He normally worked to finish a swim maxed and exhausted. She followed his lead, content to stay within a body length of the possessed man. Though Nick kicked at only half his normal ability, Carly still worked hard keeping up with him. And she was no slouch in the water. Several of her junior college swimming records still stood, seemingly unbreakable. The five thousand meters went quickly.

"Hey, you want to go get some lunch?" Carly asked after they had finished and cooled down. Nick was paddling lazy circles on his back. She bet he was delaying his exit from the pool. In the water he wasn't as affected by the hip.

"Aren't you tired?"

"Well, yeah. But I have to eat, too. Joe and I missed breakfast because we were booking the burglar."

He was silent for a minute, and Carly knew he was going to say no. She bit her lip in frustration and swallowed the whine that nearly escaped. He fell back into the silent and depressed man too quickly for her to adjust. It was so out of character for him, she wasn't certain how to approach it. *Do I insist, push him, point out how difficult he's being, or do I just give him time? He's hurting; I can see that. Would I be cheerful and upbeat if I couldn't walk without the assistance of a cane?*

Carly ducked underwater to smooth her hair back out of her face. When she came up, she admitted to herself that if she were in Nick's place, she'd be a pain and a half. *Maybe I don't know how to deal with him now, but I'll learn. He's worth it.*

"Thanks, but I think I'm going to hang out for a rubdown. You should probably go home and get to bed. You have to work tonight." He gave her a half smile.

"Okay, I guess. How about a rain check?"

"Sure. Maybe we'll do something when you're off." When

he swam toward the other end of the pool, she followed, heartened by the suggestion.

Keith was waiting at that end of the pool. He always stretched Nick out after the swim and, if Nick was particularly sore, set him up with ice packs.

Carly followed Nick out of the pool and grabbed her towel as Keith and Nick talked. The last thing she heard Nick say as she entered the locker room was that he felt a little better. The words cheered her up, but the tone of his voice nagged. He was frustrated, and she could only wonder why the man who'd told her that faith in God and patience could overcome any obstacle seemed to have forgotten what he wanted her to learn.

3

BY THE TIME Carly pulled into her parking space, fatigue had settled like a heavy weight on her shoulders. She figured it probably hit so hard all at once because she was hungry as well as tired, but she didn't know what she felt like eating. Yawning, she climbed out of her car and headed for her apartment.

Andrea was just coming back with the dog. They had an agreement: if Carly wasn't home before Andrea went to work, Andi would give Maddie a quick stretch of the legs. As usual, her roommate looked like she'd stepped out of a fashion magazine for nurses. The colorful scrubs she wore were pressed and wrinkle-free, and Andi's hair and makeup were perfect, unaffected by the heat.

"Thanks, Andi," Carly said as she took the leash. "Appreciate it. I'm beat."

Andrea shrugged but said nothing.

They walked into the apartment, and Carly heard the shower running.

"You leave the water on?" she asked as she bent down to unhook the leash.

"Nope," Andi said with a wave of her hand. "That's my friend. We slept in, so he's showering now and then he'll leave. I have to go. I'm late." She slung her purse over her shoulder and headed toward the door.

Carly frowned as fatigue gave way to crankiness. They'd had a discussion the other day about Andi bringing men home. She'd promised to make it a rare occurrence and to be discreet. "Andi, you know I hate it when you bring these guys home. Come on, it's creepy."

Andrea's eyes narrowed. "Don't start with me, Miss Goody Two-shoes. We just got up late. He'll be gone as soon as he showers. And it's my apartment too!" With that, she slammed the door and was gone.

Carly sighed and brought a hand to her forehead. "That went well, didn't it?" she said to Maddie. Then she heard the shower stop. Shaking her head, she hurried into her room, not wanting to face the "guest" when he left. This was between her and Andrea, no one else. And Andrea's attitude lately puzzled her almost as much as Nick's did. She and Andrea had been roommates in college, more than ten years ago now, before Carly was accepted to the academy.

I don't remember friction like this back then, she thought. But then Andrea was not as wild where men were concerned; she was committed to doing well in school. She'd had to move back in with her mother, who'd been in a horrific car accident, about the same time Carly started the academy. They'd planned to become roommates again sometime, but Carly met and married Nick before Andi could leave her mother.

An arrow-sharp shot pierced her thoughts; maybe Andrea was jealous of Nick. She dismissed the thought with a shudder. True friends weren't jealous like that, and Carly considered Andi a true friend.

She took a shower to cool off in more ways than one and got into bed. She switched from pondering Andi to worrying about Nick and their relationship, and that kept her awake for a bit. But fatigue eventually won, and she slept through the hot day, waking up with just enough time to eat and get to work.

• • •

That night, still tired and stressed about Nick, and a little annoyed at Andrea, Carly perked up at the sight of a bedraggled burglary detective standing in front of the locker room door. She knew he should be home in bed—his end of watch would have been six in the afternoon—so he was waiting to talk to her. Something was up with the Harper case.

"Hey, Weaver, past your bedtime, isn't it? Or do you always loiter outside women's locker rooms at 9:30 p.m.?"

"You people who work this shift are sick. I mean it, certifiably 5150." He lurched forward and put a hand in the elevator to hold the door open. She bet the lump in his lower lip concealed a wad of chewing tobacco.

Carly grinned and set her bag down. "Someone's got to do it. I assume you wanted to talk to me about Harper."

"10-4. I heard you got into it with his slime bag attorney."

She raised her eyebrows and nodded. It never ceased to amaze her how fast information sped around the station. "It was no big deal. Has Harper already been bailed?"

"Nope." It was Weaver's turn to grin. "We called bail deviation and got a bail enhancement because of the puke's priors and because it was a hospital. Deviation upped it to one million pending his arraignment." He paused to spit into a paper cup. "Caswell went ballistic. Anyway, I was wondering if you could tell me anything about the one that got away. Did you get a good enough look at him to pick his picture out?"

"No, sorry. I only saw the back of his head."

"Could you tell if he was black or white?" The elevator tried to close, and he shoved the door back.

She thought for a minute, trying to picture the guy in her mind. "If I had to guess, I'd say white and short. I thought maybe it might have been a kid, but I really didn't get much of a look. He almost ran me over. Why is this a big deal? All Harper took was paperwork."

"Yeah, but it was security paperwork. My sarge is convinced the guy had a bigger job planned. Harper is not the brightest bulb on the tree, but his sheet tells me he's a proficient thief.

We think we may be able to clear several other burglaries with him and his partner. That's why I'm here so late and why I'm getting overtime this weekend; I've been reviewing a boatload of open burglaries. Why else would Caswell turn purple over a two-bit hype loser like Harper?"

Nick's comments ran through her mind. "You're the second person I've talked to today who seems to think Caswell is less than on the level."

"He's scum. And in case you didn't notice, he dresses real sharp, meaning he charges big fees. Where would Harper get the bucks to hire him, much less the moxie to get him out of bed so early in the morning?" Weaver moved the lump in his lower lip to his left cheek. "Lieutenant Jacobs talked to my sergeant; he wants us to look at this real careful. He wants to go higher than detective lieutenant and is really on top of things." He stepped into the elevator and released the door. "If you remember anything, call me," he said, tossing Carly a two-fingered salute as the door closed.

Carly dressed quickly and considered Weaver's information. It wouldn't surprise her if Caswell was crooked, but it would seem that with Harper in jail, whatever plan he'd had was ruined. The security paperwork was safely stowed in evidence. So what if the other guy got away? But then she knew Jacobs, or Jake as he was called, from her academy class. He had great instincts. Even ten years ago her classmates recognized something in him, and everyone bet he'd be chief one day. If he thought there was something more to this, he was probably right.

After squad meeting, she and Joe checked out a car quickly and went to work. The radio was busy, and they soon found themselves traveling from call to call, one end of their beat to the other. Neighbor disputes, noise complaints, and all-around bad tempers dominated the night. Carly forgot all about Caswell, Weaver, and Harper. It was close to three in the morning before things quieted down.

"He's getting so big, he'll be a linebacker, I'm sure," Joe proudly bragged about his four-month-old son, Adam Joseph, or A.J. "Christy and I can't believe how alert he is. He recognizes all kinds of things; it's just amazing."

"What are you going to do if he doesn't like football? Maybe he'll like tennis or golf," Carly teased. She loved the fact that Joe was a devoted father, found it touching.

"Of course he'll like football," Joe continued, refusing to be baited. "His reflexes are great. He'll be quick and strong."

Carly laughed. "You are so funny. I guess it's true what they say—that to a parent, the firstborn is like the only baby ever made."

"Whatever." Joe shrugged. "A.J. is just great, the best thing next to Christy to ever happen to me. I mean it. Wait till you have one of your own."

"That's not likely. I think a dog is all I'll ever be able to handle."

"You'd be a great mom."

And Nick would be a great dad, she thought but didn't say. Kids loved him. It was one area where they couldn't be more different. Nick attracted kids like a magnet and was always able to entertain them, to get down on their level and elicit smiles and giggles, while Carly was never comfortable with children of any age.

"I sure wouldn't want to be a single mom, so I better sort things out with Nick before I start thinking about kids." She frowned in the dark, looking out the car window, remembering the morning swim session. Joe was driving, and the streets were empty. She tried not to think about Nick. Mentioning him now made her stomach flip-flop.

"I was afraid of that." Joe looked over at her, genuine concern in his voice. "I told you last night. He's still backing off?"

"I thought it was just his hip." Carly sighed. "I just don't get it. Two months ago, he was ready for remarriage; now I can't even get him to eat lunch with me."

"Is his hip improving?"

"I think everything is pretty much the same, no change good or bad. I haven't asked Keith, and I'm not sure I want to behind Nick's back. He's just shut me out, Joe, and I don't know what to do."

"Well, I think I have an idea what's bugging him, and I'd bet it's not you."

"Oh? Enlighten me."

"See, the guy's always been a jock. What's he got, four triathlon gold medals from the Police and Fire Games to his credit? Not to mention the fact that he's been the department's Koga guru for as long as I've been here."

Carly nodded and mentally slapped herself because she'd forgotten about Koga, the name of the system the department used for weaponless defense training. Nick had been the head instructor for years and loved it.

"Now he can't even walk—much less train—like he used to," Joe said. "And you're training for that distance race, aren't you? What's it called, the Maui Channel Swim?"

"Well, yeah." She chewed on a thumbnail. Competing in the open-water swim held in Maui every year had long been a dream. After the horrible events that had conspired to bring her and Nick back together, while Nick was in the hospital, he'd encouraged her to send off her application and was 100 percent supportive. He'd read up on how best to prepare for a swim that was likely to include jellyfish stings and a tough, unpredictable current. He was even researching the best boat and captain to hire as a support vessel. She realized that discussing a swim race would seem like a silly thing to most people, but to Carly it was a seed that blossomed in her heart—she and Nick planning something, to be together and to share something special. The way they used to do when they were married.

They rarely spoke of it now.

"But he encouraged me to enter."

"That was before all his therapy problems. Look, I hate to say it, but I understand—he's afraid he'll be half a man."

"I would never look at him that way!"

Joe hiked a shoulder. "Doesn't matter. I bet that's how he's looking at himself. What if it was you, if something happened and they told you you'd never be able to swim again?"

Carly huffed. That thought had occurred to her earlier.

She sometimes felt the need to be in the water as strongly as the need to breathe. A good, hard swim cleared her mind, filled her with energy and ideas.

"Of course," she said finally. "It would bug me, hurt me, but I can't believe I'd shut him out like he's shutting me out."

"You're not a guy."

Carly said nothing as frustration bubbled up. Joe was right: Nick had always been a jock. It's a no-brainer that his lack of mobility would frustrate him. But why did he take it out on her? And if it did become permanent, did that mean they didn't have a chance? The thought froze her heart. *I don't want to let him go. I want him to snap out of it. But what if he can't?*

The emergency beep of their radio split the night and changed the subject. "1-Adam-7."

"Adam-7," Carly answered.

"Adam-7, respond to Memorial Hospital and copy the message being routed to your computer."

"10-4," Carly acknowledged, and she turned her attention to the computer and punched the message button.

Joe started toward the hospital. As passenger, it was Carly's place to read to him what the computer said. But she stayed silent.

"What's up? What are we going to?" Joe asked.

"Well . . ." She hesitated and turned to look at Joe as he cast a questioning glance her way. "It's Christy. She's been admitted to the hospital. They say she's okay, but they don't say what's wrong."

4

CARLY WATCHED THE COLOR drain from Joe's face. He reached down and flipped on the emergency light and siren. Traveling code 3, they were at the hospital a minute later. Joe leaped from the car and Carly ran to keep up with his long strides. Sergeant Barrett, their supervisor, was waiting for them at the emergency room entrance.

"What is it, Sarge? What's happened?" Joe frantically approached the sergeant.

"Calm down. It looks like some kind of allergic reaction. I happened to be here on a station stop when they brought her in, so I had dispatch call you."

"When they brought her in? How did she get here? And why didn't she call me?"

"I guess she felt bad enough to call for paramedics. They brought her and the baby in as a precaution. I can't answer your last question. Try to relax. They're in exam room D."

"Thanks." Joe bolted off into the emergency room.

"Is it serious?" Carly asked the sergeant as Joe disappeared into the hospital.

"I don't know. I know the doctors are running around like they do when things are bad. Maybe you should go in there with him." Sergeant Barrett looked at Carly with tired, worried eyes. Things were probably a lot worse than he let on to her partner.

She hurried after Joe.

"Do you know of any food allergies your wife may have?" an emergency room doctor questioned Joe outside a closed exam room door.

"No, to my knowledge Christy isn't allergic to anything. Can't I see her?" Joe was fidgeting with his gun belt, snapping and unsnapping his keepers.

"Yes, you can see her. They're drawing blood right now; give them a minute."

"Where's the baby? Where's A.J.?"

"He's been taken to pediatrics. He seems fine, perfectly normal. But since your wife is still breast-feeding, we'd like to keep him for observation."

Just then the door opened, and a lab tech rushed out with a rack of blood vials. The doctor motioned for Joe to go in while Carly stayed back in the doorway. She wanted to be there if they needed her but didn't want to intrude.

Christy was pale, and she smiled weakly at the sight of Joe. He bent down and kissed her on the forehead. Carly could hear Christy protest that she was fine, but her voice and appearance were anything but fine. She seemed weak and sounded weaker when she asked about A.J. Joe answered, but Christy appeared not to hear or understand what he was saying to her.

"Officer King?" Another doctor walked in as Joe was stroking Christy's hair.

"Yes?" he answered but didn't take his attention from his wife.

"We're going to admit your wife, so she'll be moved upstairs. Would you like to go see your son while we get her settled?"

Joe looked up from his wife's face to the doctor's, and Carly could see the indecision in his expression. "I hate to leave her, but I do want to see A.J." He leaned down to explain to Christy what was going to happen. He kissed her one more time, then left her in the hands of the medical personnel.

"Do you want me to stay with her while you check on A. J.?" Carly asked.

As Joe considered the question, the doctor spoke up. "You might be in the way. It's best if you stay with Officer King until we get her upstairs."

Carly nodded and followed Joe out of the emergency room and up to pediatrics. Christy's pale face floated in her mind and increased the knot of worry in her stomach.

Upstairs, A.J. looked normal. A nurse was feeding him, or rather trying to feed him, from a bottle. His cry sounded healthy and frustrated. Joe quickly stripped off his uniform shirt and Kevlar vest and took his son. It was a strange, warm sight, the large man in uniform pants, gun belt, and white T-shirt holding the small, squirming baby. She noticed the dots on the little blue sleeper A.J. wore were actually tiny badges. Christy must have made it for him—it looked so unique. Carly brushed back tears, overwhelmed by a flood of emotion and worry. The baby settled down and took the nourishment offered by his father and was soon asleep.

Joe rocked the baby gently. "He doesn't like the bottle, so you have to work to make him take it," he explained to the nurse. "I need to go check on my wife. She should be upstairs by now. What will happen to A.J.?"

"He's only here for observation. So far, he's in perfect health. We won't keep him longer than twenty-four hours." She smiled and took the baby from Joe, laying him gently in a crib.

He thanked her, and Carly could see some tension leave his body. She stayed quiet and walked with Joe to the elevator. He didn't bother to put his uniform shirt or vest back on but rode up holding them in his hand. Christy was up one floor.

"You okay, partner?" Carly asked the pensive, anxious man.

"I don't know. They're being awfully vague, don't you think?"

"Yeah, but they really don't seem to know." Carly was at a loss for words. Her own instincts about the whole situation filled her with dread. The feeling was punctuated when they reached Christy's room. She'd lost consciousness.

Carly and Joe watched as she was hooked up to all manner of machinery. Carly closed her eyes and prayed for her partner's wife and her friend, prayed that a reason would be found for the sickness and, most of all, for a solution.

The doctor danced around Joe's inquiries and said a specialist was on the way. He advised Joe to go home and get some sleep, but Joe refused. With the heart monitor beeping slowly but regularly in the background, Joe handed Carly his gun belt, vest, and uniform shirt and asked her to take them to the station.

"Just ask one of the guys to put them in my locker. Can you bring me my street clothes?"

"Sure. I'll be back quick." She accepted the items and left her worried partner holding his wife's hand.

It was just beginning to get light as Carly drove the patrol unit to the station. Sergeant Barrett told her she could log out even though it was an hour before EOW. While some sergeants were sticklers, insistent that officers never log out a minute before EOW no matter what, Barrett was flexible with early outs. Carly knew before she asked that he'd likely say yes. As she turned in the shotgun she and Joe had been issued at the start of their shift, then signed off their log and changed out of her uniform, she fought a hill of worry threatening to bury her. The urge to talk to Nick was strong, but when she looked at the clock, she knew he'd still be in bed. She decided to wait about twenty minutes and call him when she returned to the hospital. She prayed again, not knowing where Joe and Christy stood with God, but certain he was the right source to go to in the situation.

5

NO CHANGE. Those two chilly words greeted Carly when she returned to the hospital. Though she hadn't been gone that long, she'd hoped the hospital would have been able to determine whatever it was Christy had and at least come up with a plan of attack.

Joe could only shake his head as Carly handed him his clothes. A specialist was there running more tests but still being vague. The bottom line was that no one knew what was wrong with Joe's wife. However, everyone's manner said there was an urgent need to find out. Christy was declining. A.J.'s continued good health was the only positive news.

Officers crowded the hallway offering help. It was one of the things Carly liked best about being a cop. You were part of a family. The blue line always rallied around its own.

"You've got quite a cheering section going," Carly said.

Joe smiled faintly. "Yeah, a couple of guys even volunteered to go get my car so I don't have to worry about it later."

"Good, I'm glad they're here. Make sure you don't hesitate to ask if you need something. Now, go change. I'll hang out till you get back."

Joe nodded and stepped into the bathroom. He emerged in fresh clothes a few minutes later. "Thanks for being here," he said. The circles under his eyes were as dark as the stubble on his chin.

"No problem. Is there anything else I can do?"

He shook his head. "I think I'll be fine. Christy's parents are out of state, but mine should be here soon. I just wish the doctors could tell me something."

"When your parents get here, try and get some sleep. You can't help anyone if you faint from exhaustion." Carly hoped she sounded more like a big sister than a mother.

"I know. Right now I can't close my eyes; stuff is happening too fast. In a little bit I'm going to sit with A.J. for a while. They said if he stays the same, I can take him home tonight. I'd rather take them both home, but I'll settle for A.J."

"Is there anything you need me to get for you—a razor, maybe? Or lunch?"

Joe rubbed his chin and shook his head. "One of the guys is bringing me a shaving kit, and I'm just not hungry right now." He flashed a rueful smile. "I say that knowing my mom will feed me. She thinks food fixes everything."

"Sometimes it does. You know how I feel about pizza."

At that Joe smiled. It was good to see that he could. Carly put a hand on his arm.

Just then his mom and dad arrived. Joe turned and hugged them both. Carly said hello, then listened while Joe explained the situation to them. They had questions, but Joe had no answers.

She waited for an opening and got his attention. "I'm beat. I'm going to go home and take a nap. Call me if anything changes or if you need anything at all, okay?"

"I will. Thanks again for everything." He grabbed her in a hug. She left him at his wife's side, bracketed by his parents, and prayed the doctors would find an answer for Christy soon.

I'm exhausted, she thought as she drove out of the hospital lot. *Probably so exhausted I won't be able to sleep. I'm glad it's the end of the week for us and we don't have to work tonight. All week long, between Nick and the heat, I haven't gotten much sleep.* Saturday was also a therapy-free day, so she didn't have to worry about rushing to the rehab center. She hit Nick's number, and it rang once before she was directed to voice mail.

"It's me. Give me a call when you get a chance."

Keyed up and positive she couldn't drop right off to sleep, Carly decided to stop at her mom's before going home for a nap. The fact that she considered her mother's house a desirable destination was proof that their relationship was better than it had ever been. As Carly struggled with Nick, knowing that she could talk to her mom about it and lean on her was a bright spot in her life. They used to butt heads about any and every little thing, but when Carly found faith, they reconnected. Now they were in sync, and she found that her mother was dear and wise counsel.

Mom's house was still in the process of being remodeled after the fire that destroyed the front half four months ago. A corrupt cop had tossed a Molotov cocktail through the window in an attempt to scare Carly away from an investigation. Carly relished the reality that he was safely behind bars and her mother hadn't been hurt in the attack.

No workers were present today, but the waiting-to-be-stuccoed frame of the living room stood as a reminder of the work in progress. Carly blew out a frustrated breath as she did every time she came by. The remodel was taking so long, she worried her mother was being taken advantage of. But her mom wasn't worried, so Carly kept her mouth shut.

Since two bedrooms, one bath, and the kitchen were inhabitable, Kay chose to stay in the house while the living room, one bedroom, and one bathroom were being redone. Carly found her mother out on the back patio under an umbrella, drinking iced tea with the next-door neighbor, Jack, and using sign language to discuss projected plans for the remodel.

"Morning, Mom." Carly waved at Jack.

His greeting was a smile and a nod.

"Good morning. What a nice surprise!" She stood and gave Carly a hug. "What's wrong? Did something happen at work?"

I don't have to say a word; she always knows. "Not at work, but something happened to Christy." Carly told her mother all she knew about Joe's wife, which wasn't much. Kay listened and signed for Jack.

"I came home planning to nap and then go back to the hospital and see if anything has changed. I didn't mean to interrupt your discussion." Carly nodded to the blueprints on the table.

"Don't be silly; you're not an interruption. We were just talking about the addition I want. You know I'd like to have a room available for troubled kids or people needing temporary shelter. Jack has some ideas to help preserve my privacy."

Jack pointed to the plans and showed Carly his idea.

"I agree with Jack," Carly said. "Adding that wall will give you and any houseguest a greater measure of privacy. Just remember, I want to be able to talk to whoever comes to stay here. And you have to promise—" Carly put her hands on her hips for emphasis—"if I don't approve, it's a no-go."

Jack signed something to Kay.

"Jack says you're being overprotective," Kay explained with a smile. "But I know your frame of reference, so don't worry; you get approval rights before anyone moves in."

"Thanks." Carly yawned and rubbed her eyes. She really didn't like her mother's plan to be a foster mom but knew arguing would get her nowhere. Carly's father had died five years before, and she was glad that Kay was far from being a helpless widow. She was taking foster-parenting classes through the county, and she counseled troubled teens at church. Kay's idea of becoming a foster mom had a lot of support from the church—especially from Jack, who was a deacon. Carly still thought the plan was crazy. The concept of a stranger sharing her mother's house bothered her. She squelched her protest in favor of bringing the focus back to Joe's problem.

"Don't forget to put Christy on the prayer chain." Carly grabbed a chair and pulled it under the umbrella's shade.

"I'll get the word out. Is Nick involved?"

"He doesn't know yet. I called and got his voice mail. If he doesn't call soon, I'll call him again." She accepted the glass of tea Kay handed her. "Have you talked to him lately, Mom?"

"Not for a couple of weeks. He seems to be having a difficult time with his rehabilitation." Her mother settled back into her seat and sipped her own tea.

"That's an understatement. What's wrong with him? He's the one always saying God will work things out. He doesn't seem to believe that about his hip. I can't talk to him anymore." She took a sip and then held the glass to her forehead. The cool liquid was soothing inside and out.

Jack tapped on the table to get Kay's attention and began to sign furiously.

Carly watched as the two conversed. "What's he saying?"

"He says Nick needs time. He might never walk normally again, and he can't accept the prospect of being handicapped. He's afraid to get close to you again, afraid you'll reject him if he's handicapped."

"Has Nick told Jack that?" Carly felt her face flush hotter than it already was from the weather. First Joe with his theory about Nick. And now Jack was telling her the same thing—

that Nick was basically having a panic attack and taking it out on her. If he really believed she'd abandon him, what did that say about how shallow he thought she was?

There was more signing before Kay continued. "He didn't have to say anything. Jack knows the feeling. When he was seventeen, a girlfriend broke his heart, saying she couldn't live with his disability. He knows what Nick is going through and thinks that right now he feels like less of a man. Jack is sure we just need to be patient and let Nick work things out; he'll come around."

"This is silly! Nick should know that it wouldn't matter to me if he never walks right again. I mean, I'd be sad for him, but it wouldn't change my feelings."

"Let him process; let him adjust."

Carly thought for a moment before voicing the question that pierced her. She had, after all, trusted Nick with her heart—*again*. He'd crushed it once. Was she setting herself up for another fall? "What if he doesn't?"

Jack answered her with one definitive gesture, which Kay translated.

"He will."

• • •

The cooling tea and comfort of sitting in her mother's backyard relaxed Carly to the point where she began to nod off. She said her good-byes and headed the two blocks home.

Andrea's space was empty, so Carly assumed she was at work. *At least I won't have to dodge any showering men today.* Carly yawned as she walked through the courtyard and waved to Mrs. Shane, the across-the-courtyard neighbor. A widow who'd moved in about three months ago, she liked to sit outside her door in a rocking chair. Carly could count on her being there whenever she got back from work late. Mrs. Shane would go inside for lunch and then be back for a couple of hours in the afternoon. Occasionally she'd stop Carly and ask about her day. Andrea thought the woman was nosy and avoided her. But Carly figured she was just lonely.

Any other day Carly might have struck up a conversation. But today she opened her front door, stepped inside, closed it, and leaned against it, sighing and shaking her head. *I hate having this problem hanging in the air between Andi and me.* It made her glad for the distraction her dog provided. Maddie was at the door, tail wagging and tongue hanging out.

"Ohh, sweetie, I'm glad to see you too." She dropped her equipment bag and fell to her knees to hug the dog. When she got up, she checked the communication chalkboard she and Andi kept on the fridge. Andi had marked "fed" and "walked" for Maddie on the day's date.

Blowing out a breath, she put her hands on her hips and looked at the dog. "I'm too tired right now, but I promise a good walk later, when it's cooler."

Maddie just kept wagging and followed Carly into the bedroom.

Once in her room, she got ready for bed and, in spite of

the drama and turmoil of the morning, fell right to sleep. She slept soundly for about five hours and woke up bathed in sweat. The ceiling fan was ineffective; it was really only pushing around hot air. The apartment did not have AC.

"Bet you're twice as hot as I am." Carly reached down and patted Maddie, who was panting at the end of the bed. It was really a heat wave when it got this bad on the coast. Her apartment was only a block and a half from the beach, and generally there was a cooling ocean breeze. Not today.

She got up, let the dog out on the patio, then took an invigorating cold shower, which helped a little. Two things nagged her mind as she dressed in light shorts and a T-shirt. First, she wondered about Christy and how she was doing. She double-checked her phone, but there was no new message from Joe. Second, Carly thought about Andi. By now, her roommate was halfway through her shift. And it kept bugging Carly that they hadn't talked things out after the tiff about the man in the shower. Normally, Andi didn't stay mad long. But this disagreement about overnight guests was the most serious one they'd ever had.

She pondered the situation as she fixed herself a tuna sandwich. After eating it without really tasting it, she decided to take a stab and call the hospital to talk to Andrea.

Her shift schedule was on the fridge. When Carly checked it, she saw that Andi would be covering in pediatrics, so a call to Andi would probably kill two birds with one stone. It would be easy for her roommate to find out what was up with Christy even from pediatrics. *Hopefully*

Andrea is over her huff and can give me an update without disturbing Joe.

Carly punched in the number for pediatrics. The phone rang several times before someone picked it up.

"Hi, can I speak to Andrea, please?"

"Who's speaking?" The voice was impatient, and it wasn't anyone Carly recognized.

"This is her roommate."

"She's busy right now. Can I take a message?"

"No, no message."

The phone clicked before Carly could say anything else. *That's weird.* She sent Andi a text message, using their code for emergency callback, and waited. Fifteen minutes passed, but the phone didn't ring. Carly paced the small living room and decided that Andrea was pouting. This was irritating. She knew now they needed to sit down and have an uninterrupted conversation about the friction between them. The overnight guest situation had been a sore spot for her for a long time, but Carly had suffered in silence.

I guess because I brought it up, I'm going to have to initiate a peace talk. Too bad it had to all come to a head this weekend. Giving up on Andrea, she hit the speed dial to call up her partner's number.

"As much as I don't want to bug you, I want to know what's going on," she muttered while she typed her text message. This time she was rewarded with a callback.

"How are things going?" she asked, hoping the response would be positive.

"Carly." Joe choked her name out.

Carly felt her stomach cramp. Christy must be worse. "Yeah, how's Christy?"

"Christy's doing better. She's, uh, actually stable now."

Then why do you sound so strange? "Okay, what's the matter, then?"

"Oh, Carly," he sobbed over the phone as his thin layer of composure broke. "Someone's taken A.J. Someone stole my son."

6

SOMEONE STOLE A.J.

As many times as Carly repeated the words, they still didn't make sense. Officers were all over the hospital this morning. How could someone kidnap a baby? And why?

She sped to the hospital and prayed that when she arrived, Joe would tell her it was a terrible mistake and A.J. was safe and sound. But the obvious media presence in the parking lot killed all optimism. To avoid the media, Carly parked on a side street and entered the hospital through the emergency room. In spite of the heat, she shivered when she remembered Joe's voice on the phone. In almost eleven years on the force, Carly could not recall a single kidnapping in her city.

And she wondered, *What do you say to someone whose son was just kidnapped?*

Four uniformed officers hovered around the emergency admitting desk. One of them saw her and hailed.

"Hey, Carly, what's the deal with your partner's wife? Why were she and the kid here in the first place?" Tina asked.

"Don't know. Earlier this morning the doctors couldn't say." Carly sighed. "Have you guys heard any more?"

Tina shook her head. "No, no one is saying much. But they're giving out overtime like candy for guys to watch the entrances and talk to potential witnesses."

"Witnesses?" Hope sprang into Carly's chest. "Did someone see A.J. being taken?"

"We've heard rumors someone saw a volunteer leave with a baby earlier, but nothing is confirmed. They don't want false information going out, so we probably won't hear anything official until all their ducks are in a row. You know how it goes." Tina shrugged.

"Lieutenant Jacobs is planning a press briefing soon," one of the guys added. "Our orders are to watch people leaving. Initially, the hope was that the baby was still inside the hospital. But I think now they know the kid is gone."

"How long ago did they discover the baby was missing?"

"We've been watching this entrance for an hour. If Joe called 911 right away, the baby's been gone about an hour and twenty minutes to two hours."

"Thanks for the information. I pray we find A.J. soon."

They all nodded in agreement, and Carly continued into

the hospital. Over an hour, maybe two. A.J. could be halfway to Santa Barbara by now. A shroud of dread and fear enveloped her as the reality of the kidnapping sank in. She stopped at the elevator to gather her thoughts. *I need to encourage Joe, support him, not scare him.*

The elevator doors opened, and Lieutenant Jacobs and Sergeant Nelson stepped off.

"Hey, I'm glad to see you two." Carly greeted the men and felt her gut unclench slightly. She wanted an update from Jake before the press conference. And the lieutenant wouldn't miss a thing.

"Hey yourself, Trouble." Jacobs smiled, but his eyes told her he was intense and focused. Ever since the murder of Las Playas's last mayor, when for a time there was an all-points bulletin out on Carly, Jacobs had called her Trouble. She rolled her eyes at the nickname and fell into step with the lieutenant.

"I wondered where you were," he said. "I know you and Joe are close."

They stopped at an open waiting room that had obviously been turned into a temporary command post. A tactical unit was poring over diagrams of the hospital, and Soto, the public information officer, was on the phone. From the sound of it, he was giving a statement to a news radio station. Nelson sat down to use the phone. He was the new sergeant in charge of homicide, and homicide handled all kidnappings.

"When I went home to sleep, it was only Christy we were worried about, and Joe's parents had just arrived. What happened?" Carly asked.

"I wish I knew. We just don't have much." Jake rubbed tired eyes. "There were cops all over this hospital. Guys were stopping by all morning, checking up on Joe and Christy. The best we can tell is, between one and two hours ago, someone walked into the nursery, picked up A.J., put a doll in his place, and walked away."

"We're not sure about the time?"

"Yes and no. One or two of the parents who were upstairs with newborns remember a volunteer walking around. We're looking hard at this because there aren't any volunteers assigned to that floor right now. Problem is, about the same time the baby disappeared, one of the sick babies began having problems and most of the staff were involved with that infant. The other parents who were up there with sick children can't tell us much because they were concerned about their own problems."

"But Andrea brags about all the cameras in this place. Security here is tops; surely they picked something up?" Carly feared she sounded hysterical; she swallowed, working to calm down.

"Pete Harris is the assigned investigator. He's reviewing security discs as we speak. Everyone who was on duty in pediatrics was talked to, or will be talked to, and no one saw anything or anyone unusual that is any help . . . so far. I've got officers interviewing everyone who was in the hospital at the time of occurrence. The FBI is sending a couple of agents to help. We'll chase down every lead. I promised Joe our best."

He paused and took a deep breath. "You know what the worst part of this is?"

Carly shook her head.

"Joe was on his way to get A.J. and take him home. He found the stupid doll."

Nelson pulled Jacobs away to deal with something on the phone. Carly left them to their work and went back to the elevator. As she stepped on board, her thoughts went to Andrea. She was working pediatrics; chances were good she'd be in the thick of this investigation. When her phone buzzed with a text message, she looked down and saw it was from Nick. *Nick!* She hit her forehead with her hand. *I forgot to call him back. He probably heard the news from the TV. Oh well,* she thought. *He will have to wait until after I talk to Joe.*

Between the hospital's own security and the LPPD, every floor at Memorial was shut up tight. She hated to think it, but it was typical: the barn door securely shut after the horse had escaped. Most of the guards recognized Carly, but a couple of new guys asked to see her badge. When she reached critical care, she found Joe in a quiet module holding Christy's hand. His beard was darker, and black half circles weighed down his bloodshot eyes. He stood to give Carly a hug and held on tight.

"How's she doing now?" Carly asked in a whisper, looking down at the still-pale form. Joe's parents, seated on the other side of the bed, nodded silently to her.

"She's stable at least. They still don't know what's wrong with her, but she's not getting worse. She isn't conscious, but

I'm almost afraid that's better. I couldn't tell her that A.J. . . ." His voice broke.

"Hang in there, Joe. We'll find him. People don't get away with taking babies from hospitals; you know that." Carly hugged his sagging shoulders.

He sniffed back his tears. "I know what I want to believe: that this is a long, involved nightmare I'm in, and I'll wake up any minute now. I can't—I never would have thought that something so horrible could happen to my family."

"My mom has a lot of people praying for you, Joe."

"Thanks . . . thanks."

His mom, a small woman with a scarf covering her head, came over and took Joe's hand. They talked a little about Christy and what the doctors had ruled out. One of the nurses padded softly into the module and said apologetically that there were really too many people in the room. The gentle shove made Carly tell Joe she'd be close if he needed anything. She left to locate Andrea and find out from her how the investigation was going on the hospital's side.

Glancing back as she left, Carly saw Joe with his mother, huddled close to the pale Christy. Her BlackBerry buzzed again, and this time Nick used 911—the call-back-right-away signal.

Well, I've put it off as long as I can, she thought. Still, she decided to make the call from Andrea's floor and rode the elevator one level down. Cell phone use was discouraged in the hospital, so she found a free phone at the nurses' station and punched in his number.

"It's about time!" Nick was livid. "Were you ever going to call and tell me what was going on with Joe?"

As if his rage traveled through the phone lines and infused Carly, she felt her face flush with indignation. How dare he!

"What is that supposed to mean? Since when am I supposed to check in with you? I called you earlier, and it went to voice mail. I was tired. I went home and fell asleep."

"Five minutes! That's all a phone call would have taken you—five minutes. Is that too much to ask?" Nick sounded uncharacteristically harsh. Carly couldn't recall him ever talking to her that way. She took a deep breath and bit back the sarcastic retort on her tongue. *I don't want to hurt you, Nick.* Even though everyone kept telling her she wasn't the problem, she bristled at being his chosen target. Her pastor's Sunday message came to mind: *"Angry words pierce and the holes can't be patched."*

"Nick, I'm sorry, okay? I meant to call you again and forgot. I was tired. I really can't tell you much more than what you've already seen on the news."

The line was quiet, and Carly took the opportunity to count to ten. She felt the flush slowly recede from her face.

"I'm sorry too—sorry I snapped. I'm not mad at you. I . . . well, I just—" his tone was calmer and a little contrite— "I just want to help; that's all. I hate feeling useless."

Carly relaxed. "I don't know if there is much we can do right now. I haven't talked to Andi yet, but Lieutenant Jacobs is in charge on our end, and you know he's thorough." She twisted some hair around her finger.

"You'll let me know, won't you?"

"Of course I will."

There was a pause; then he thanked her before saying good-bye. Carly replaced the receiver and sat for a minute with her head in her hands. *Why has Nick pulled so far out of my reach? He's put up a wall I don't know how to get around or through, and it scares me as much as A.J.'s being missing.*

"You with us?"

Carly jumped at the sound of Andrea's voice. When she faced her roommate, she saw frustration and fatigue and hoped the anger about their conversation yesterday had dissipated.

"Yeah, I'm here. I was just thinking." She shook away her musings and focused on Andrea. "Hey, what's going on? I thought Memorial's security was the best."

"It is. It just doesn't do any good when it's turned off." Andrea sat down in a chair next to Carly, leaned back, and closed her eyes. "I swear, Carly, it was like Casper the unfriendly ghost was here this afternoon. She—at least we think it's a she—waltzed into the nursery security office, turned off all the cameras, and left with A.J. I've been everywhere, talked to everyone, and this person came and went practically without being seen."

There was something strange in Andrea's body language, but Carly wasn't sure what it was. "Was anything going on here today out of the ordinary that would have distracted security from noting her coming and going?"

"Not a thing," she said with some heat. "We were short

one security officer, but the shortage was downstairs at the information desk. That may have made it easy for someone to come in unnoticed, but not all the rest. I can't believe it."

"Andrea, I think we've got something."

Both women looked up at the sound of a male voice. It was Peter Harris, homicide detective. He smiled and dipped his head to Carly but looked every bit as frustrated as Andi. Carly knew he was on a mission. As part of the same case that earned her the nickname Trouble, Pete Harris had weathered storms of internal investigations after it was discovered his partner of eight years was on the take and involved in three murders. It was his partner who had firebombed Kay Edwards's house. Now the man would hopefully end up serving a life sentence in Folsom Prison. The investigation exonerated Pete and he stayed in homicide, working hard to remove all doubts about his loyalty.

"What? Please tell me you've found a lead on the baby." Andrea stood. Carly shifted anxiously in her seat.

"I wish I could." He put his hands on his hips and sighed. "But we do have something. It's this mysterious volunteer. We finally heard something solid. One of the cafeteria workers coming in to start her shift saw someone dressed in scrubs with a volunteer badge leaving with a baby. I've seen this mysterious volunteer on a couple of the security discs, but she never looks up at the camera. Anyway, the time frame fits, and we have a vague description. Lieutenant Jacobs just put a call in for a sketch artist."

"Good! She won't be able to hide if we get a picture of her on TV, will she?" Andrea relaxed perceptibly.

"That's the hope," Pete said with a nod. "We're still searching all the camera feeds for a clear shot of her face, but there are a lot of discs to review. Anyway, someone is bound to spot a woman who suddenly appears with a baby. A.J. is no newborn; he's four months old."

Carly said nothing. Pete's optimism was comforting, but a question nagged. Why did the woman take the baby in the first place?

"News coverage will make it impossible for the woman to hide." Andrea closed her eyes and rubbed her temples.

"Hang in there; we'll find her." Pete patted Andi's shoulder. "Jake is doing everything he can and making sure we get any and all resources to help the investigation. Which brings me to my next question." He turned toward Carly. "I know you're happy back in your patrol niche, but would you consider a brief reassignment to homicide?"

"To work on A.J.'s case?"

"Yep. It might only be grunt work, but we are short-handed. I haven't been assigned a new partner yet, and you know Sergeant Nelson is new. It would help to have a little experience poking around."

"Anything I can do to help, I will."

"Great. I'll run it by Nelson. Give me your cell number."

Carly wrote the number down and handed it to Pete. "How about the lab? Any luck with prints on the doll or anywhere else?" she asked, already ticking off the steps of an investigation in her mind, energized by the opportunity to be actively involved. *Joe is my partner, and I really want to do something for him.*

"Not the doll; it's fabric. But we may get something off the digital recorder in the security office. The volunteer, or whatever she was, knew how to pick a door lock and then how to shut off the cameras. I hope she left a workable print somewhere." He shoved his hands in his pockets. "I'm confident we'll get A.J. back. The media will fill the airwaves with pictures of him, and Nelson will set up tip lines." He looked at Andrea, mouth set with grim determination. "Someone will see something and call. I'm sure of it."

"I hope you're right," Carly said. "Maybe you won't need my services." She still wondered at the vibe she was getting from Andrea and had the distinct impression her roommate was holding something back. But what?

"As soon as I hear from Nelson, I'll text you, one way or the other."

7

"I'M FINISHED, PETE." The lab tech stepped out of the security office, set her kit on a chair, and arranged everything before closing it up. "I did pull off a couple of good prints. I'm heading to the station to process what I have." She handed a cloth doll in a plastic bag to Harris. "You recovered the doll, so I'm signing it back to you to place into evidence."

"Thanks. And let me know if you find anything—even if it looks insignificant." Pete took the doll, and the technician left. He turned back to Carly and Andrea. "Things are looking up. I'm sure she'll come up with something."

Andrea threw her head back and sighed. "This person was smart. She knew someone dressed as a volunteer carrying a doll or a baby wouldn't attract anyone's attention—it would be normal—so even if someone saw her, they might not remember." She frowned, and her lips quivered as she leaned against a counter and watched Harris.

"You're right; and she took care that nothing was disturbed except A.J. She came in carrying something and left carrying something else. And all we get is this doll." Pete held up the bag the tech had handed him, marked with a red *Evidence* tag. Inside was a simple cloth doll dressed in a blue sleeper.

"Maybe this woman was a volunteer here at one time," Carly said. "Are people fingerprinted and given background checks before they're hired as volunteers?"

Andrea shrugged. "I don't know."

"We'll check that," Pete said. "Either way, I'm hoping for a decent print from the security office. If so, we might get a hit from Cal-ID. Even if she's never been arrested, she's bound to have a driver's license." He fidgeted with the doll. "She was certainly not short on cheek to come up here and snatch a baby. Not even state-of-the-art security stopped her. I hope the hospital takes that into consideration if they try to place blame."

Carly raised her eyebrows at the mention of blame. She hadn't really thought about that, but Pete was right. The hospital would definitely want to hold someone responsible for such a horrific mistake or lapse, whatever it was. She glanced at Andi and hoped her roommate wasn't the one who was culpable.

Pete's BlackBerry screamed—literally; a scream was his ringtone. Homicide gallows humor. He unhooked it from his belt and read the message. "It's Jacobs. Time for the press conference. He wants Joe to go on the air and make a plea for the baby to be returned. I'm going downstairs. Carly, you want to come?"

"Yeah, I do. Joe will need some moral support."

"Meet me in the cafeteria when you're done," Andi said as Carly and Pete got on the elevator.

The press conference was set up in front of the hospital. Carly counted all the local stations and several cable stations present. Jake was at the podium with a prepared statement. Joe was next to his father and Sergeant Nelson. Carly guessed that Joe's mom had stayed with Christy. Harris split off to the other side of the podium while Carly stepped next to Joe and gave his shoulder a reassuring squeeze.

He looked at her and nodded thanks, his expression stern. As Jake finished his statement and motioned for Joe to come to the podium, cameras clicked.

Holding a photo, Joe spoke into the microphone, describing his son and pleading with whoever took him to bring him back safe. Carly swallowed a lump as emotions swelled. Just hours before, Joe had called A.J. the best thing that ever happened to him and Christy. *Oh, God,* she prayed, *please bring him back safe and sound.*

When Joe finished, Jake offered to take questions so Joe didn't have to hang around and could get back to Christy. Carly gave her partner another hug as he headed for the elevator. She went the opposite direction to meet Andrea in the cafeteria.

Grabbing coffee and a bagel, she searched for her roommate and saw her sitting at a table next to the window. As she reached the table, Carly noted the brooding expression that darkened her roommate's face. "What's going on, Andi? You look as if this whole thing was your fault."

Andi tipped her head to one side and ran a finger under her eye before she responded. "I feel responsible. I was senior nurse on the floor, filling in for Marsha Collins. I can't believe someone walked in and did this on my watch."

"Hey, you couldn't know this was going to happen. Whoever did this obviously planned it out carefully." She sat down and took a sip of coffee.

Andrea had a half-eaten turkey sandwich and a soda in front of her. She played with the straw and stared out the window at the simmering, hazy city of Las Playas. Carly savored a few more sips of the hot coffee while Andrea picked at her food halfheartedly.

"How'd the press conference go?"

"Good, I think. Joe made a clear and heartfelt plea."

"I hope it works." Andi would not meet her gaze, and she sounded defeated.

"Really, it's not your fault." Carly wondered at her roommate's attitude. It was unlike her to drown in self-pity. But then she'd never had a kid snatched on her watch before. "I know Joe would never blame you. Besides, I can't believe this woman thinks she can get away with A.J. After this conference airs, his picture will be plastered everywhere. She won't be able to keep him a secret."

"I feel like I should have seen something." Andrea put the remains of her sandwich down and chugged her soda. "It's like having our house burglarized. I feel so violated."

"I can relate to that. I just pray the crook keeps A.J. healthy until we get to him."

Andrea choked on her soda and sputtered at Carly. "I swear you sound just like your mother when you throw in that prayer stuff. That kid will be found through investigation or luck, not because of some hokey prayers." She spit the word *prayers* out with such venom it took Carly by surprise.

"Sorry. I just believe prayer helps. I didn't know it bugged you so much."

"I didn't mean to snap, but it does irritate me. Before Nick came back into your life, that stuff used to bug you too, remember?"

"I do remember, but I've changed."

"And that makes you trust that Nick has changed as well?" Andrea shook her head and leaned back in her seat. "People say they're Christian and tell you they can be trusted, but that doesn't always make it true."

"Are you talking about Nick or someone else?"

Andi closed her eyes. "No one. Forget I said it. I'm just stressed."

Carly considered her roommate, trying to remember if there was someone in Andi's past who'd burned her by saying one thing and doing the opposite.

"You know what happened to me, why I became a Christian. And it really doesn't have anything to do with Nick." Carly paused and searched for the right words. She remembered all too well how much the mention of prayer and God used to bother her. But she had gone through a life-changing experience while investigating the murder of the Las Playas mayor four months previous. A fellow officer, a good friend of Nick's, sacrificed his life for her, and she'd jumped from a speeding boat into the ocean to swim for her life after the mayor's killers threatened to kill her, too. She encountered God on a very basic level, and having given him her life, she knew she'd never be the same again.

Finally, looking across at her brooding roommate, she said, "I just know now that God is real, and prayer is an expression of my faith. The last thing I want to do is irritate you."

"How do you know God is real? You're getting goofy. I can't believe all that stuff." She waved her hand as if waving away a stench. "And Nick is supposed to be this super guy all of a sudden, and he treats you like dirt after you forgave the pig."

"Nick is going through a tough time at the moment. He's frustrated with his therapy."

"So it's okay for him to take it out on you? Wake up! This Christian stuff is making you a doormat. That's what it does to women."

Carly looked out the window and gulped her coffee, welcoming the scalding feeling because she didn't know what to

say. Lately that was exactly what Nick made her feel like—
a doormat. *But that's not God, is it?*

"Look here, my two favorite ladies!"

The roommates turned at the same time as Alex Trejo, a
local newspaper reporter, strolled up.

"How'd you find us down here?" Carly didn't know
whether to be mad or glad. She hadn't noticed Trejo at the
press conference, but then, as the police beat reporter for the
Las Playas Messenger, he'd most likely been there. Maybe he
could be an ally in the search for A.J.

"I have my ways." He grinned. "But I'm on your side;
don't kick me out. Can I join you?"

Andrea stood. "You can sit here, Alex. I've got to get back
to the floor. I'll see you later, Carly. And sorry I snapped. I'm
tired, okay?"

"Don't worry about it. And don't work too hard.
Remember, it wasn't your fault."

"Thanks."

Both Trejo and Carly watched Andrea as she left the cafeteria. Trejo turned back and studied Carly for a minute. He
sat in the chair Andrea had vacated.

"What was up with that? She blame herself for the
kidnapping?"

"I have a mind to check you for tape recorders before I
say anything."

"Edwards!" Trejo leaned back in mock indignation.
"How could you suspect me of subterfuge? I thought we
were friends!"

"Yeah, Alex, you're a friend like a tiger is a pet. You may look docile, but you always have to be watched." Carly offered a wry smile.

Trejo laughed. "Okay, okay. Today I'm really on your side. I want to help get this kid back. I like Joe; you know that. I'll do all I can. Is there anything you can tell me that wasn't said at the presser?"

Carly shook her head and toyed with her coffee cup. "I know as much as you do. Someone posing as a volunteer took my partner's baby. They broke into a secure room to turn off surveillance. We're hoping to match prints, and that's the extent of what I know. And I'm hoping you'll help."

"Again, I'll do anything I can. After all, you and Joe helped me out, kept me from getting my head bashed in. I owe you both. He's got to be torn up. How's his wife?"

Carly remembered Alex getting beaten by two corrupt cops, Drake and Tucker, when he tried to conceal her presence in his house. It was Joe coming to the rescue with the FBI that saved both their lives. "He *is* torn up. Christy is stable but not conscious. I don't think the doctors know what made her sick." She drained the last of her coffee and picked at the remnants of her bagel.

"You certainly ate a nutritious lunch," Trejo observed.

"If you walked through the line here, you noticed that not much is appetizing."

"That's true enough. Hey, why don't you let me buy you dinner? We'll get out of here and head down to the Apex."

"No, that's okay. I'll hang out—"

"And do what?" Trejo cut her off. "Look, there's nothing for you to do, and you know it. I know Joe's parents are here, so he'll be taken care of, and Harris has the investigation. No need for supercop Edwards there. You look like you need to get away from this for a bit. Come on, it's on me. I do owe you."

"Don't you have a story to file about the kidnapping?"

He held up his phone. "There's an app for that. Already sent all the pertinent info; it's up on the website as we speak. I will add more when I get it." He regarded her with raised eyebrows.

"Well . . ." Carly considered the offer and Trejo's earnestness. Maybe it was a good idea to get away from the depressing atmosphere of the hospital. "I'm going to check with Joe first. I can't just leave unless I'm certain there's nothing more I can do."

"Fair enough. I'll be in front where they're tearing down the press conference stage."

They stood and followed the path out of the cafeteria that Andrea had taken a few minutes ago. Carly turned left at the elevators, and Trejo turned right to exit. While she rode the elevator up, she thought about Andrea and hoped they'd be able to sit down and clear the air soon.

When Carly arrived at the critical care floor, Jacobs, Nelson, and Pete were huddled together in the waiting area—discussing the case, she figured.

"Carly." Nelson saw her and waved her over. "Pete asked you about helping out with the invest, right?"

"Yeah, I'm up for it."

"Good. I've got a call into Garrison. Where are you headed now?"

"I was going to see if Joe needed anything."

"He sat down after the conference and fell asleep, couldn't keep his eyes open any longer. We've assigned a black-and-white here for Joe. For the time being, they'll take care of anything he needs. I want to be sure you're close when we get approval for your reassignment."

"Yeah, I will be. I'm just going to grab a late lunch." Carly looked toward Christy's room, not wanting to take Joe away from sleep he needed. Turning back to Nelson, she said, "Tell him I was here, and if you need me for anything at all, call."

"Count on it. Thanks for being available."

Carly nodded and got back on the elevator. As the doors closed, she leaned in one corner, heaviness on her heart, not 100 percent certain leaving was the right thing to do. But, she reminded herself, Trejo could be an important ally here: he was the press, and he excelled at disseminating a message. And Nelson would call if he needed her; of that she was sure. In the back of her mind, a little voice said, *What about Nick?*

Well, what about him? she thought. There wasn't anything to tell him right now, and it was time for a hot meal.

"All set?" Trejo asked as she walked out the front door.

"As set as I can be right now. I guess you make sense for a reporter. I am hungry. But let's not go to the Apex; let's go down to Walt's in the marina instead."

"Great, I'll even drive. Let's go." Alex guided her away from the hospital and to his car.

8

"YOU'RE SCARING ME, EDWARDS."

"What? Why?"

"The frown, the worry lines. They'll find the kid, and you're not missing anything taking time out to eat. You're too quiet. Don't you have faith in your department and coworkers?"

"Of course I do." She folded her arms and turned in her seat to glare at the reporter. "But every minute A.J. is gone is a minute away from parents who love him. I'm allowed to be worried."

"I saw the presser. Joe's appeal was spot-on and heart wrenching."

"Yeah, it was that. Does the ace reporter have ideas about what else can be done?"

"Flattery will get you everywhere. But other than going door to door . . ." He shrugged and looked at her while they waited at a red light. "How soon before this becomes an Amber Alert?"

Carly blew out a breath. "I think we need a vehicle description. I'm not certain if just a description of the kidnapper would do it. But this is definitely a stranger kidnapping; that's obvious."

"Then the ace reporter suggests that as soon as you have the needed information, get that Amber Alert activated." He snapped his fingers rapidly. "Until then, I'd guess that the most effective thing is getting A.J.'s picture out there and beating the bushes for tips."

"I have to agree with you."

"Glad we are on the same page," Trejo said as the light turned green and he turned in to the jam-packed marina parking lot. "Wow, everybody and their mother is down here!"

"That's because this is the only place that's cool, and Walt's is going away soon," Carly observed, leaning her head half out the window to enjoy the cooler temperature. Finally, a refreshing ocean breeze to take the edge off the oppressive heat.

"Don't remind me," Trejo said as he circled the lot three times before he found a spot. He and Carly unfolded themselves from his small sports car and walked along the gangway to Walt's. The restaurant was at the end of an ancient boat dock that would soon be removed so the entire marina could be updated to include shopping, dining, and carnival games. But Walt's and the unique atmosphere of his on-the-water dining would be gone. He didn't want to be part of the upgrade.

Carly and Trejo squeezed through the crowd and found seats at the bar. She ordered a chili dog and fries. He opted for fish-and-chips, and they both asked for frosty milk shakes.

"I haven't eaten down here in ages," Carly said, relishing the cool sea air hitting her face. The hamburger joint offered bar-type seating in a half circle at the end of the dock.

"Me either. You made a good selection. They have the best fries anywhere." Trejo turned sideways, and Carly felt his eyes on her. "You know, a person could hold you responsible for us losing Walt's."

"Me?" she asked, facing him with arched eyebrows.

"Hey, you discovered Correa was dirty. He fled, and then it was uncovered how much money he was stealing and that he was stonewalling the redo." He held his hands up, palms out, as if he'd proved his point.

"So you're saying you'd prefer to have a murderer and embezzler in charge of the harbor and marina so we could keep Walt's?" Carly shook her head. Besides being responsible for embezzling the city's redevelopment funds, Mario Correa, the old harbor superintendent, also shared culpability in the murders of Mayor Teresa Burke and Carly's fellow officer Jeff Hanks.

"Just making an observation. Correa did have enough good taste to like the quaint old style of the marina." His eyes twinkled, and she couldn't help but smile.

"Can we not talk about him? I'll lose my appetite."

"Fair enough." Alex nodded and kept his dark eyes focused her way. "So, Edwards, you staying busy back out on patrol?"

Carly fiddled with her napkin, recognizing that Alex was trying to distract her, keep her from worrying about Joe. She could put on a brave face and spar with him, at least during lunch.

"Yeah, Joe and I work hard. It was great until this nightmare with A.J. We just caught a burglar inside the security office at Memorial." She told him about Stanley Harper and Thomas Caswell, then toasted the event with a draw on the straw of her shake after the server put it down.

"Outstanding. Of course, I already knew you two made a good team. I'm the president of your fan club." His phone jangled with a text, and he picked it up to check the screen. "I have to answer this."

She waved him on, and he bent to the task.

Briefly she thought back to the first time she had anything to do with Trejo. He'd reported on an officer-involved shooting she'd been part of and blasted her, insinuating she had done something wrong and that there was a cover-up. Later, they crossed paths when he covered the investigation into the mayor's murder. She'd hated him because of the way he wrote about the police department in general and her in particular. But circumstances forced her to trust him with some information, and once she got to know the forthright reporter, he'd gained her respect.

Since then, she'd frequently seen Alex in court. All the

defendants arrested in connection with the mayor's murder had been in court recently for various hearings. Carly had been subpoenaed for most of them and testified at a couple of preliminary hearings. Trejo had been subpoenaed for one or two and showed up to report on the others. Court appearances generally involved a lot of waiting around, so she and Trejo had chatted quite a bit.

This was the first time they'd gotten together in a social situation one-on-one, and Carly couldn't help but notice Trejo was a very handsome guy. His thick black hair, combed back, was just long enough to tickle his collar now. It used to be long enough to tie back into a ponytail. He'd told her once in court that he cut the ponytail in case he was called on to testify; he figured a shorter hairstyle would make him more credible. Today he wore a T-shirt and shorts over a lean, muscular build, and his olive-colored skin looked healthy and unblemished. She wondered about his age and guessed it was close to her own.

His text finished, he looked up, and his eyes danced with life. "I'm familiar with Caswell; he's a piece of work."

"Do you know him personally or professionally?"

"Ha." He smiled, showing straight, white teeth. "I've never had to hire him, if that's what you mean."

Carly laughed, and it felt good after all the drama of the day. "No, I didn't mean that. You cover crime; have you covered him in the course of your crime reporting?"

"I've seen him in court, and I've written a few paragraphs about him. He defends people with money. Everyone deserves a competent defense, but I hate it when it seems like rich people can buy their way out of a conviction."

"I agree."

"And Caswell can be personally nasty, the kind of guy a reporter wants to dig dirt on, if you get my drift."

"Yeah, I'm familiar with the dirt you dig."

That brought a laugh from Trejo, followed by an innocent look. "Who, me?" He brought a hand to his chest. "Only the bad guys need to worry about me, not decorated, honest, truth-seeking supercops like Carly Edwards." He grinned, and Carly suddenly felt self-conscious under the reporter's regard. "But I'm surprised you don't know more about the esteemed attorney."

"Me? I've never had to hire a defense attorney."

"Yeah, but he's worked for cops, usually really dirty ones."

"Let's not talk about dirty cops. I hope I've seen all of them I'm going to see in my career." She changed the subject. "How did you sneak into the hospital today? It seemed like I was showing my badge at every corner. And I know they were trying to keep the press contained in one area so patients and visiting family were not disturbed in any way."

"A good reporter never divulges his tactics." He stuck his chin in the air.

The arrival of their meals saved him from answering in more detail. There was a brief silence between them as they arranged their food. Once set, Trejo switched back to his original topic of conversation: Carly. "I don't really want to talk about me, Edwards. I want to know about you."

"I thought we finished with that subject. I'm happy to be back on patrol. End of story." Carly took a big, sloppy bite of her chili dog.

"Ha-ha, not what I meant. Are you seeing anyone right now?" He watched her while she chewed, and she struggled not to choke when she swallowed.

"That's a little off the wall, isn't it?" Carly ran a napkin across her mouth.

"I don't think so. I didn't become a hard-hitting reporter by beating around the bush. I believe in calling them as I see them. We've been palling around in court now for about a month. I think you're cute and smart and interesting. If you're not dating anyone, can we go out sometime?"

When she didn't answer right away, he continued. "I apologize if my timing is bad, but I'm not sorry I told you how I feel."

She found the sparkle in his eyes more than a little disconcerting and was startled at how flattered she felt by his interest. If forced to, she would admit that lately, every time she walked into court, she looked for Alex. His lighthearted banter always dispelled the boredom of waiting. He was funny and upbeat, like the old Nick. Her face flushed hot, and she knew the cause was guilt about Nick.

"You did catch me by surprise. I think you're a nice guy—I mean, for a reporter." She grinned to lighten the mood. "But I am kind of involved with someone right now." Her grin barely hid the churning in her heart. *Why does it sound like I'm trying to convince myself I'm already spoken for?*

"Nick? Your ex?"

"Yeah. We've been talking about reconciliation." *Are we really?* she wondered. It had been two months since their last official "date." He'd developed an infection about then and had to spend the night in the hospital for IV antibiotics. *Talk about invasion of the body snatchers. Nick's been pulling away since then.*

"Well, I'm not completely discouraged. I mean, I don't see a ring. You think maybe we can hang out once in a while outside of court?" He held both hands up in front of him when she looked at him in surprise. "As friends, as friends!" he clarified.

Carly laughed a little nervously, wanting time to think before she responded. She liked Alex, and if Nick were out of the picture, she'd say yes immediately. But in spite of the issues between them right now, Nick *was* in the picture. She took a bite, chewed, swallowed, then answered.

"I'll think about it. I do consider you a friend, so let's finish dinner and then get back to the hospital. Joe is also a friend, and I'm worried about him."

Trejo nodded. Carly busied herself with her food, hoping the subject was closed. But Trejo didn't let the silence last.

"If you don't mind my asking, why did you and Nick get divorced in the first place?"

"Well—" Carly thought carefully about how she wanted to answer—"it's a long story, so I'll just hit the high points. Nick had a brief affair. But he's apologized, and I've forgiven him. We have a lot to work out, but we're both willing."

"Whoa! He cheated on you, and you want him back?" Trejo put his palms on the counter, sat up straight, and looked at Carly with an incredulous expression.

Carly smiled. She was used to that kind of response, especially from people she worked with. Adultery was unpardonable to many on the police force. Law enforcement marriages suffered a high percentage of divorces due to infidelity, and forgiveness often seemed a scarce commodity. "Yeah, Alex, I forgave him. I really believe he's sorry, that it was a huge mistake and he's changed."

Trejo shook his head. "You're more incredible than I first thought. Does he know how lucky he is?"

"I try to remind him now and again." *I just doubt I'm getting through.*

"What did he do to convince you he'd changed?"

"He became a Christian, started going to church, and I could see without a doubt that his lifestyle was different." Carly realized she was telling someone other than close friends and family about Nick's conversion for the first time. Her own had followed shortly thereafter, which was why she was able to forgive him. *Finding Christ changed my life for the better four months ago. And it was Nick who led the way.*

"Do you really think if he's a churchgoer he won't cheat again?" Trejo asked the question in all seriousness. She saw no ridicule in his expression, and it made her bold.

"He's sincere about his commitment to God; I'm sure of that. And church isn't what it's all about. As Christians, we believe the focus is a relationship with God, not a building."

Carly looked down at her plate as her stomach lurched. She *was* sure about Nick's commitment to God but totally unsure about his commitment to her. She felt like she was standing on the narrowest of limbs, over the deepest of gorges, and the limb was breaking. She focused on Trejo's voice.

"I just know that a lot of guys will tell their wives anything so they'll take them back. I've heard the motto for cheating cops is 'It's cheaper to keep her,'" he was saying, "and then they go right back to cheating. My mom and dad went to church every Sunday. Mom said her rosary every night, and still my dad kept girlfriends. I remember in high school wanting to beat his head in because he made her cry. But she always took him back because of the church. I don't know whether there is a God or not, but I do know people use him as an excuse for a lot of things, good and bad."

"I believe there is a God and he's got Nick, so I trust Nick." Carly found Trejo's probing gaze beyond unsettling and reached for her shake.

"I envy faith like that, Edwards. I hope Nick doesn't let you down. Whatever happens, I'll be here for you." Their gazes locked. "And I mean that . . . even if we're never more than just friends."

"Thanks, I appreciate that. Now let's finish dinner and get back to the hospital."

He nodded and grabbed the ketchup bottle. "Your every wish is my command."

They finished up, and Trejo snatched the bill before the server could put it on the counter. Carly realized an argument would get her nowhere, so she simply thanked him and waited outside while he paid. She could admit that the meal had been pleasant; Trejo was good company. But she wanted Nick to be the man in her life, the one she thought of as good company. *What's he doing now? Does he think about me as much as I think about him?*

Thankfully, she wasn't able to dwell on the thought. Trejo bounced out of the restaurant and put a hand on her shoulder, pointing to his car with the other.

"Your chariot awaits."

They chatted companionably about a lot of different things on the way back to the hospital. Alex suggested they exchange numbers and repeated his request that they hang out now and again "as friends." Carly jotted down her number and accepted his business card. In spite of herself, Carly realized she wouldn't mind hanging out with him from time to time but had no clue how Nick would feel about that. When Trejo dropped her off, she found herself thinking about his request and wondering why she left a door open. Why didn't she just say no?

9

BACK IN THE HOSPITAL, things seemed to have quieted down. Joe was resting with Christy, and Andrea was nowhere to be found. Carly was deciding whether or not to go home when her phone buzzed. It was Pete Harris.

"Carly, where are you now?"

"Just got back to the hospital."

"How quick can you be at community relations? We're setting up a volunteer tip center here. Are you ready for a meeting?"

"Meeting? About what?"

"About being loaned to homicide. Jacobs and Garrison are here now."

"All right. Are you sure we have to meet with Garrison?

Can't Sergeant Barrett approve this?" Carly ran her fingers through her hair as she headed out of the hospital, apprehension rumbling in her gut and making her wish she'd eaten something other than a chili dog. She and Captain Garrison got along like rival gang members. *He'll say no just for spite.*

"Nope, it's up to Garrison to sign the temporary release."

"I'm on my way, but I hope this isn't a waste of time. He's just as likely to say no as look at me."

"Don't worry; Jacobs and Nelson are both pitching for you. I really need some experienced help going through these tips. We're spread thin."

The fact that Harris called her experienced help gave her a jolt of confidence as Carly hurried to her car.

• • •

Jacobs opened the meeting by explaining how the investigation was going, what information the press had been given, and his hopes for the tip line. Norman Garrison, the captain in charge of detectives, patrol, and training, listened intently, shooting off questions to Harris now and again. Carly felt tension in the room and wondered if it was solely due to the kidnapping. She'd heard department gossip and knew Jacobs was in line for a promotion and wanted Garrison's job. Jake was ambitious, hardworking, and had a solid reputation, so the captain had good reason to worry that his job was in jeopardy. He'd barely kept his rank after a scathing investigation of the department by the FBI. They'd outlined deficiencies in his supervisory skills but stopped short of recommending demotion. It was under Garrison's watch that the old homicide sergeant and an investigator were found to be part of a smuggling operation and responsible for the murder of three people, including the previous mayor. The scenario of him being moved to the records division while Jake was promoted to his spot was not far-fetched.

Since Carly was responsible for uncovering the corrupt cops, Garrison treated her as if she were the cause of all his problems. She knew from personal experience that Garrison could be territorial and petty. She wondered if he'd smack Jake down just because he could or if he'd play it safe, give him everything he wanted—and if something went wrong, be sure to hang all the blame on Jake. She squirmed in her seat and thought about how much she hated politics and posturing.

"And you're certain you need Officer Edwards's services on this investigation?" Garrison asked Sergeant Nelson, nodding in Carly's direction but not looking at her.

"Yes, sir. You know we're a little short in homicide. Carly's a hard worker; we can use her to run down leads." Nelson smiled at Carly across the conference table.

Carly tried to read Garrison and found it impossible; the man was stone.

"Sergeant Nelson and I have discussed this at length," Jacobs jumped in. "Detective Harris has yet to be assigned a partner, and Nelson has his plate full learning his job and interviewing applicants for the open position. Even though Carly has never worked homicide, she's an experienced officer and she knows how to interview."

There was silence for a few minutes. *The captain is probably trying to think of a way to say no,* Carly thought.

"Okay, I'll sign off on it," Garrison finally acquiesced, but he kept his gaze on Jacobs. "There's a great deal of publicity surrounding this case; kidnappings are hot stories. I want a first-class, professional investigation conducted by all parties involved; is that understood?" He stood to leave.

"Of course. And we will get the kid back," Jacobs assured him.

Garrison left the room.

"Well, Trouble, you're in." Jake smiled at Carly.

"Great. Where do I start?"

"How about with me?" Harris asked. "Let's get a car and pick a neighborhood to walk."

"I'm ready."

...

Since the tip line wouldn't be up and running right away—it would take time for the information on A.J. to be broadcast and for people to be made aware of the situation before they could call in—Nelson and Jacobs worked out a grid search pattern in the neighborhoods around the hospital for several teams to walk and knock on doors. The hospital's parking structure was under video surveillance, but it was often difficult to see the driver in the digital recordings, and no one could say for sure they saw someone resembling the kidnapper drive out. So Jake was operating on the theory that she either walked to the hospital or parked on a side street.

Carly and Pete were assigned a grid on the south side of the hospital, a neighborhood of small, older homes. It was a gritty area but not a problem one. Carly had handled a few calls over the years there, usually disputes or burglaries. She didn't consider it high crime and didn't hold out much hope they'd uncover a lead, but she was happy to walk the neighborhood with Pete.

By the time they hit the pavement, people were settling in for a Saturday night. Carly thought about this—if these people were home now, they were likely home when the kidnapping happened. The chances of a witness were good.

"Hi, I'm Investigator Harris; this is Officer Edwards." Pete used the same introduction every time. "We're investigating a kidnapping from the hospital and have a few questions to ask."

Some people were wary at first, but once they realized they were not suspects, they loosened up. Carly filled out a card on each residence with the names of the people who lived there and those they spoke to. She also noted if no one was home at an address because they would have to be contacted later. Everyone cooperated and tried to be helpful, but in spite of the odds that they'd find a good witness, they came up empty. No one had noticed anything out of the ordinary.

"This is a quiet neighborhood" was a comment Pete and Carly heard over and over.

By the time they'd finished a couple of hours later, Carly's feet hurt and her heart was heavy, knowing that every minute that passed, A.J. could be farther away.

10

SUNDAY MORNING Carly woke stiff and bleary-eyed. She'd slept a total of five hours the day before and then had gotten home around three in the morning after the walk and talks. She was happy to help, but when she'd heard Nick was on the team, she'd hoped to work some with him. As it turned out, she'd had precious little time with him. They'd crossed paths briefly when she and Harris had returned to the station. There, the phones were quiet and everyone started talking police work. Detectives, patrol officers, and dispatchers joined in, and talk and tactics had bounced around the room for hours. Nick was more animated than she'd seen him in a while. If it weren't for the fact that A.J. was missing, the night would have been an enjoyable law enforcement bull session.

Yawning, Carly shuffled to the patio door and let Maddie out, then went to the front door to pick up the morning paper. A.J. was front page, and there was even a composite of the kidnapper. "Police Officer's Infant Kidnapped from Hospital" was Alex's headline. She studied the drawing. It was generic, but it was something. As she started coffee, she noticed that Andi wasn't home. Carly wasn't certain she'd been home at all that night.

Don't have the energy for that, she thought as she picked up the phone to tell her mother about A.J. and that she would miss church that morning. But the phone buzzed before she could punch a number. It was her mom, and Carly smiled, thinking she'd probably waited too long to let her mother know what was happening. But Mom would understand.

"Hi, Mom."

"I read the paper, and I've seen the news. What on earth? Joe's baby was taken from the hospital?"

Carly pinched the bridge of her nose and told her mother what was going on with the search for A.J.

"I know you're busy, but how is Joe? First his wife, and now this."

"He's holding up, but this is hard."

Kay sighed. "I'll get the meals ministry going for him and tell Jonah about the situation. He'll probably open the church for a continuous prayer vigil."

"That would be great."

"Will I see you at church this morning?"

"No, I don't think I'll make it. I'm going in to work on my own time to do what I can."

"I understand. Keep me updated if you're able."

• • •

The command post had moved to community relations, and the office was buzzing with activity Sunday morning. Local news had just broadcast the story, and Carly was glad to see more people manning the phones. Joining the officers and dispatchers donating their time were members of Las Playas Search and Rescue, a civilian group of volunteers. They were gearing up to walk neighborhoods; Carly considered doing the same again. But first she wanted to find Nick—and that was the only hitch in the scene, since Nick was nowhere to be found. He'd left earlier than she had last night, promising to be back this morning.

"Hey, how's everyone doing?" Carly smiled.

"We're okay, but no good news so far." Jeanie, a dispatcher, greeted Carly and motioned her to an empty chair. "Nick said to tell you hi if you came in. He left because his hip was cramping."

"Thanks." At least that question was answered. "Have you been getting a lot of calls?" Carly took a seat and settled in. She was tired; answering phones would be the best choice this morning.

"Yeah, but we're getting a lot of kooks, too. Every time the radio or TV broadcasts the information, the lines light up. We're to page Sergeant Nelson if we get anything that sounds good."

Jeanie left Carly to wait for the phone to ring. On one wall of the room were four televisions, all on local channels, with the sound muted. Carly guessed they were waiting for broadcasts of A.J.'s information, but it was Sunday and there were cartoons on. The phone in front of her rang and she answered, doing her best to ignore the TVs and listen carefully, hoping for a tip that would lead her to A.J.

Carly stayed moderately busy fielding phone calls until lunch. Nothing sounded to her like legitimate information, but she copied everything down. Around one o'clock, Pete Harris showed up with several pizzas donated by a local restaurant. He looked as tired as she felt, and she knew he'd been working with very little sleep.

"How's it going? Anything good?" He pulled up a chair and set a pizza between them.

"Not so far."

"Well, maybe things will pick up. I hope you like sausage and pepperoni."

"There is no such thing as bad pizza." She grabbed a napkin and a slice of pizza. Pete was already munching on his. "You look tired. No luck with any tips you followed?" she asked before biting into her slice.

He shook his head and swallowed. "Nope. I ran down about a dozen with Nelson. I think collectively we've slept about three hours." He rubbed his eyes. "We staked out one that sounded real good, but the tipster was anonymous."

"Where was it?"

"Over on the west side." He handed her a copy of the information taken from the caller, and she skimmed it while he talked. "Guy calls in and gives us this great description of a girl wearing what he calls 'doctor clothes.' Says she's a neighbor of his and she wasn't pregnant—in fact, he thinks she's too young to be a mother, but she came home yesterday with a baby. We watched the place for a couple of hours, and . . . well, nothing. I'm still having black-and-whites run by there from time to time. But this girl, if she really existed, seems to have disappeared."

"I can see why you were hopeful; that sounded good."

"It did. But now I'm thinking it was just someone yanking our chain. I think legit people will give their names."

They sat in silence, munching on their pizza. The phones in the room rang sporadically.

After lunch, Carly—though frustrated at the lack of progress—felt energized to stay awhile longer. It was tedious work at times, especially when a known crazy named Morris called. She knew the voice immediately because he used to call in to juvenile all the time. Sometimes he'd stay on the line for several minutes talking nonsense, and other times he'd hang up abruptly.

"Schultz—is Schultz there?" Morris always asked for Schultz, a long-retired narcotics detective who apparently knew Morris before he went crazy. Morris usually called to complain that he was being followed or bugged by the FBI and he wanted Schultz to make them stop.

"Morris, is that you?" Carly rolled her eyes, knowing if she hung up, he'd call right back. "Why are you calling this line?" *This won't help find A.J.*

"Where's Schultz? Gotta talk to Schultz."

"He retired, Morris."

"Oh. Okay, bye."

Carly replaced the receiver and stifled a yawn.

"Rough job?"

Carly looked up to see Nick standing in front of her, leaning on his cane. Straightening in her chair, she smiled. "Only when Morris calls."

Nick chuckled, and the sound soothed Carly's soul. "Morris, good old Morris. He calls report review from time to time." He leaned against the counter in front of her. "I don't mind talking to the guy—you know, humoring him. But I have this fear one day he'll start calling and saying 'Anderson' instead of 'Schultz.'"

"Don't think it would have the same ring to it."

"Hope not. In any event, Morris is harmless."

"Maybe so, but every wasted minute means A.J. is farther away."

"I understand the urgency to find him, but half the department is looking, along with every major news outlet. Think you can take a little bit of a break? You up for some coffee or something to eat?"

The question made Carly's spirits soar. She glanced around the room and decided she could afford to leave. "Pete brought in pizza a little earlier, but coffee sounds great. Kelly's?" Kelly's Coffeehouse was at the marina, not far from Walt's.

"Yeah, I haven't been there in a while."

It was two in the afternoon and still hot, but not as searing as the last few days. At the coffee shop, Nick opened the door for Carly. Kelly's planned to be part of the new marina, and pasted on a back wall was a rendering of what the renovated Kelly's would look like. The fan-cooled coffeehouse was a little stuffy. But any place where she and Nick were together and on the same page was a comfortable place. Heart light, at least as far as her relationship with Nick was concerned, Carly did something she never did—ordered iced coffee.

"Hey, what's up with that? I've never seen you drink coffee that wasn't steaming hot," Nick said, watching her with a half smile playing on his lips as she took a sip through the straw.

Carly swallowed, enjoying the iced, slushy liquid. "I just felt like something cold. I'm surprised; this is refreshing."

On their way to sit outside, they stopped to look at the rendering.

"It will look nice," Carly said.

"Yeah, but I'll miss the old charm of the crumbling marina. And one of our first dates was down here; remember that?"

Carly smiled as a kind of giddy warmth slid through her with the happy nostalgia the memory of the date nurtured. "Yeah, I remember it well." They were still in the academy then but nearing graduation. The date was filled with talk about their training officers, learning beats and radio codes, and hopes for their new careers.

They found shady seats, and Carly was reminded of her dinner the day before with Trejo. Guilt flowed through her, chilling her like the ice in her drink, at the thought of Trejo. She tried to stem the flow. After all, she and Alex had only talked, nothing more.

"We haven't really sat and talked in a while." Nick studied his coffee mug. "I guess it's been my fault, and I wanted to apologize."

"No need," Carly said quickly—and just as quickly admonished herself to calm down. *I know Nick too well; we've been together too long for me to act like a love-starved teenager.*

"I know you've been having a hard time in therapy and all," she said. "I've tried not to take it personal." Carly smiled and felt more of the knot that had taken up residence in her stomach for weeks start to dissolve. "I only want to help you; you know that."

"I know; I know. Which makes what I have to say even harder." He sat back in his chair and looked at her, meeting her eyes somewhat reluctantly. Carly couldn't read the emotion there. Immediately the knot re-formed, rising from her stomach and sticking in her throat.

"What? Bad news from the therapists?"

"No, they keep insisting I'll get past this. That it will just take time." He paused, frustration and impatience reflected in his eyes. "I just think that maybe we moved too quickly. Maybe we talked about reconciling too soon. I—we—need to step back for a little bit . . . you know, to reevaluate things."

A sledgehammer hit the knot in Carly's throat, sending it straight to her head. Her temples pounded; she felt her face grow hot. She'd just heard what she'd feared most, and her heart screamed, *How could he?* Looking away, she fought back angry tears and tried to think, tried to know what to say.

"Why? Four months ago, things were perfect. We were happy; the past was behind us. What's happened to change your mind so drastically?" *I hope I'm not whining.*

"It's not drastic. I didn't say it was over. I just said we need to slow down, step back. That's all."

"It's the same thing. I love you. And I miss you. You've been holding me at arm's length, and I hate it. Now you're saying I'm supposed to forget how I feel?"

"Time won't change feelings if they are real."

"What's that supposed to mean? That you don't believe I feel the way I do, or that you don't love me?"

"I do love you. That's why I'm giving you this break. You'll have time to think."

"Think about what? Right now I'm thinking I want to slap some sense into you! What's so different now as opposed to four months ago?"

"For heaven's sake, I'm not the man I was four months ago!" He slammed his hand down on the table and spilled his coffee. Heads turned their way.

He continued in a lower voice, and Carly could see the months of pain etched into his face. "I need help putting my own shoes on. I have to use those aids they give to old people with bad hips. No one can tell me when, or if, I'll ever be normal again. Last night, talking with those agents and officers, I realized how lame I am—and I may stay this way.

I'm not going to have you hanging in there because you feel sorry for me."

So that was it? His hip maybe being a permanent handicap was the problem? Carly felt her mouth gape. Jack and Joe had pegged it correctly, and Carly didn't know whether to laugh or cry.

Swallowing and willing her voice to stay level, she said, "The only one with a pity problem is sitting across from me. I don't care about your hip. And swimming with you to encourage and push you during therapy is something I look forward to. It's a temporary condition, and I can't believe you would accuse me of being so petty." She wanted to add, "And where is your faith?" but thought better of it.

"I know you're not petty, but I'm being practical. I may never be a cop again, and I want to give you the chance to think about that long and hard before we commit to anything."

"So now I only love you because you're a cop?"

"That's not what I said. Come on, don't make this harder than it is."

"Harder than it is? How much harder can it be?" Carly's hurt meshed with anger, suffocating her. She needed to get away and get some air, clear her head. "If you want to wall yourself in, I guess that's your prerogative. If you think you don't need anybody and nobody needs you, go for it. But I love you, hip or no, cop or no. I don't want to be on a roller coaster with you, sure you care one minute and tossed away the next. But the problem is with you. So once you get it straight, call me." She stood.

Glaring at him, she stayed silent for a moment, not trusting herself to speak. But the stinging hurt she felt would not let her stay silent. "You know, we were married for eight years, for better or worse, and you threw it away for a waitress. But I believed you'd changed. I believed you were now a man I could trust again, a man who would go the distance. But you can't or you won't, and you're just choosing a different out this time."

Nick recoiled as if slapped. Reacting in slow motion, he tried to stop her as she moved to leave. "Wait."

She jerked away from his hand.

"I drove. How are you getting back to the station?"

"Right now I don't care if I have to walk." Carly stormed away from Kelly's and made a beeline for the jetty, hoping the sight and sound of the water and seagulls would drown out the pounding in her head. It had taken her so long to overcome the hurt from their divorce and forgive Nick. Falling in love with him all over again, walking out on a limb, trusting again—only to have him, in one instant, saw the limb off. Long, irritated strides carried her to the end of the jetty, a place called Seaside Point. She stopped because there was simply nowhere else to go. Carly was sweating, and her eyes stung with tears.

Lord, I don't know much, but the Bible says you give believers the desires of their heart. Nick is the desire of my heart. He's been my example, my strength for four months. How can he do this now?

It was a struggle for Carly not to give in to old feelings of anger and resentment toward God. *Trust—that's all I hear: trust God. I'm trying, so help me, I'm trying, but this is hard. It feels like I've trusted the wrong jury to return the right verdict.* Standing on the jetty in the afternoon heat, Carly wanted the verdict to be her and Nick, remarried and together forever.

But what if all the people who doubted her decision to forgive Nick were right? They'd both changed; she was certain her commitment to God had changed her. Yes, she'd found God, and that was something she'd never regret. But had she somehow tied God and Nick together so getting one meant getting the other? What if Nick wasn't her future?

11

CARLY LOST TRACK OF TIME while standing out on the jetty, but her tears eventually quit. She ignored the sun beating down on her head and stood for a very long while staring at the water, vaguely aware of some fishermen to her right. Their laughter and conversation, mingled with the sound of waves slapping the jetty wall and the occasional cast and splash of a weight in the water, kept her connected. The smell of the ocean air was stale and salty and far from refreshing. But Carly could breathe now, and her mind cleared. Part of her regretted storming out. *Maybe I shouldn't have thrown a tantrum, but I don't want to let you go, Nick; I don't.*

Everything boomeranged back to trust. *I have to trust God for Nick. And I have to trust that if Nick isn't for me, God will give me peace and ease the hurt.* Carly shivered in spite of the heat and fought down the internal rebellion. *I don't want to trust. I want to scream and yell and make Nick know what a jerk he's being! But I won't. As hard as it is, I'll wait, trust, and pray. This Christian stuff is hard, God.*

Footsteps approached from behind, too even and quick to be Nick's. Carly turned.

"Hey, I hope I didn't scare you."

She shielded her eyes and took in the form of Alex Trejo. "You didn't scare me, but I'm surprised to see you here."

"Were you expecting Nick?"

"I don't think so. Why do you ask?"

Trejo smiled. "I'm not psychic or anything. I ran into him over there by Kelly's. He was watching you, and he kind of explained you were a little upset with him. Anyway, I told him maybe you needed some time to yourself and that I would give you a ride back to the station." He reached into his pocket and pulled out a handkerchief. "Here, you might want this."

Carly self-consciously touched her cheek with one hand, taking the offered handkerchief with the other. There was dried tear residue to be wiped off, and she was suddenly embarrassed about what Nick might have told Alex.

"Thank you. What, uh . . . what was it Nick told you?"

"Don't worry, Edwards. No dark secrets were revealed. He just said he'd made you mad and he didn't think you wanted to get back in the same car with him." Alex kept smiling, shoved his hands into his pockets.

"He's right about that, and . . . well, it's a long story." Carly finished wiping her face, then looked up at Alex. "Look better?"

"You always look great to me."

"Thank you for the hankie and the ride." His scrutiny made Carly uncomfortable, and she turned to walk back toward the marina. Trejo fell into step next to her.

"So, you want to tell me the long story?"

"Not really. Right now I don't want to talk about Nick. I want to find A.J."

"Okay. But if you change your mind, I'm a good listener."

For a couple of minutes only the sound of the waves and the crunching of their feet on the jetty sand filled the walk. Alex broke the silence. "How's Joe? I haven't heard anything new on that front."

"I haven't talked to him today. I'll check in with Harris when I get back to the station." Carly was glad for the subject change and tried to overrun her thoughts of Nick with thoughts about Joe and A.J. She glanced at Trejo, surprised she could feel so normal in his company. At the moment it was good to call him a friend. *I can't believe I think of him as a friend. He's a reporter. Can I really trust him?*

Alex caught her looking, and she turned away. "Why did you look at me that way?" He smiled a dazzling smile.

"Sorry, a thought just crossed my mind. It wasn't pretty." She hoped he couldn't see the blush on her cheeks.

"About me?"

"Yeah." When they stopped at his car, Carly faced him

with a question. "All this sudden interest—is it me, or are you just after a story?"

Alex was silent for several long seconds. She wondered if the question hurt his feelings.

Suddenly he laughed. "That's one of the things I love about you. You don't play games or indulge in subterfuge. I don't meet many women who tell it like it is." He took her hand in his and held it to his chest. "Edwards, I'll return the favor; I'll be boldly honest. Four months ago, you burst into my life and turned things upside down. I've always hated cops; I looked at them as racist storm troopers. They covered for one another." At her raised eyebrows, he laughed again. "Sorry, I did. But you were different. When Mayor Burke was murdered, it was truth you were after even if it meant a cop would go to jail. On top of that, you saved my life, no matter that I printed stuff that hurt you."

"Alex . . ." Emotions still churning, she tried to pull her hand away. He held it tighter.

"No, let me finish. I want this out in the open. I've been bonkers for you for months. The only reason I looked forward to court was the chance to cross paths with you there. All I think about is you, but I had no idea how to get close. How do you get close in the hallway of the court building?" He paused and threw his hands up before continuing.

"This tragedy happened, and I asked to cover it because I really want to help Joe—and in doing that, I knew I could see you as well. Now you ask me if it's a story I'm after, and yeah, I guess I am. It's my job, after all. But I want you first, and to help Joe any way I can. I'm trying to be here for you and prove I care. Anything you tell me in confidence stays in confidence, okay?" He pinned her with a steady gaze. One hand held hers to his chest while the other stroked her forearm.

He wants to give me everything Nick just took away. She took a deep breath and firmly pulled her hand away.

"Thanks for being honest. And thanks for being a friend, but that's as far as we can go. I don't know what's going on with Nick, but I still love him. That wouldn't be fair to you, would it?"

He shrugged. "I guess I'm not thinking fair right now. Just don't close the door on me, and remember, I'm a good listener." He smiled and shoved his hands in his pockets again. For a minute he just looked at her with a goofy expression on his face.

"Okay, thanks, Alex. You think we can head back to the station now?"

Trejo rolled his eyes and laughed sheepishly, quickly unlocking the car.

• • •

Fortifying herself with some station coffee that had been cooking all day, Carly stayed at the phone lines until she felt herself dozing. Fatigue was closing her eyes, and she knew she was useless. Nick had not come back to work the phones, and she didn't want to ask if he was helping somewhere else. It was disappointing that none of the calls were promising. But tomorrow was the beginning of a new week. All the local morning news shows planned to air A.J.'s information first thing in the morning and throughout the day. Anticipating a blitz of new information, she'd decided to go home when her phone buzzed. It was Pete.

"Carly, can you come up to the homicide office? Agent Wiley, our FBI liaison, is going to share a profile of the kidnapper."

"I'll be right up." Though tired, Carly was glad the FBI was helping as much as it was and prayed she'd hear something encouraging in the profile. Carly had read a lot about FBI profilers and profiles, and she believed they were useful tools for most investigations.

Nelson waved her into the office when she reached the door. "Have a seat. This is Agent Wiley, and he's got a possible profile worked up of our kidnapper."

Carly sat and gave the agent her attention. He looked so much like an agent in his dark suit and tie, Carly felt that his picture could appear in the dictionary under the definition of *FBI agent.*

Wiley dove right in. "I'll start with a little history. Between 1983 and 2010, there were 271 cases of infant abductions reported to the authorities. Of these, 47 percent occurred in hospitals—with almost 60 percent of those babies being taken from the mother's hospital room—compared to 40 percent taken once the baby reached home; the remaining cases occurred in various other places. This may sound like a lot and it may scare you, but statistics also show that 95 percent of the children abducted were rescued safely.

"In infant kidnappings, the suspect is usually a woman—

many times an overweight woman. This allows for a fake pregnancy. The suspect may have impersonated a nurse or some other health care employee, and she may have visited Memorial on a prior occasion."

Pete groaned. "That means reviewing more hospital security recordings."

Wiley went on. "We find that the motives for an infant kidnap can be divided into two main camps. The most common is to replace a baby the woman recently lost. The second is the need in the woman's life to validate a lie. By that I mean there are women who will lie about being pregnant to keep a hold on a significant other. When their nine months are up, they need to produce a child and often seek to take a child from a hospital or private setting to prove they were pregnant."

"I have a problem with that one," Nelson said. "A.J. is an older child; it would be impossible to pass him off as a newborn."

"Yes, I've noted that. We don't have enough information to say with certainty the motive behind this abduction. A profile is a guide, not a hard-and-fast rule. We've not received a ransom request or any indication there will be one, so it's safe to consider other motives.

"Add more neighborhood canvasses to your to-do list," Wiley continued. "The suspect is likely from the area and plans to raise the child as her own. And while she may have planned the kidnapping carefully, it's rare that such an individual targets a specific infant."

"You mean A.J. was just the lucky one?" Carly said, unable to hide the bitterness she felt.

"Correct. But the odds are that the suspect will care for the child as if he were her own. The parents can take solace in that statistic at least."

• • •

"Do you feel any better now?" Pete asked Carly as they walked out of the station.

"You mean because of the profile?" She shrugged. "In a way, but we already know our suspect is not overweight. That being said, I guess chances are good A.J. is being taken care of, but the longer he's gone the colder the trail gets."

"I know we'll find the kid."

"I hope you're right. And I'll let Joe in on the profile."

After they said good-bye, Carly hopped in her car and headed for the hospital. *Lord, I'm the one who's supposed to have hope and stay positive. I know you're in control. But everything seems to be going nowhere. Please keep the baby safe and give us a break somewhere.*

Before heading for Christy's room, Carly stopped to check on Andrea, see how she was doing. But her roommate was nowhere to be seen; her name wasn't even on the duty board. Granted, Carly hadn't checked her schedule on the fridge that morning—maybe this was one of Andi's days off—but the uneasy feeling in her gut returned. She continued on to visit with Joe.

Carly poked her head into the room and caught Joe finishing a burger. "Hey, partner." He was alone with his wife, and she guessed his parents had gone to get some rest.

"Hi, it's good to see you today." As he hugged her, she noticed he'd finally shaved and looked as though he'd gotten some sleep. She was also happy to see that Christy was in a private room away from critical care. The monitors were beeping with normal vital readings, and she appeared to simply be resting. "She's better." Joe seemed to read Carly's thoughts. "All the doctors agree the worst is over and she'll wake up soon."

"What was the matter?"

"They think it was an allergic reaction to something. They're still doing tests. But she was home with just A.J. before she called 911. I've been home and can't figure out what she could have eaten or been exposed to. Man, I can't help feeling like I'm in an episode of *Mystery Diagnosis*." He squeezed his wife's hand and turned to Carly. "Anything new about A.J. and the investigation?"

"The tip lines are manned by plenty of volunteers, and a lot of people have called." She sighed, holding Joe's tired eyes in a steady gaze. "Nothing great so far, but Harris is confident we'll get a break soon, so I am too."

"Have you been officially loaned to homicide?"

"Yeah, but saying okay looked about as painful to Garrison as a root canal."

"He'll never forgive you for showing him up and exposing all the dirt in the department he should have caught," Joe said. He turned his focus to his wife and was silent for a moment.

Carly felt the need to talk and told him about walking neighborhoods with Harris and about how the people they visited were interested in doing what they could to help.

Joe listened, nodding occasionally. "This woman really planned this, didn't she?" he asked, looking at Carly.

"It looks that way. I'll bet any baby would have done. Somehow A.J. just became available." She told him about Agent Wiley's theory that most female abductors plan to raise the child as their own.

"What do you think?" he asked.

"I agree. Look at all the trouble she went to. I refuse to believe she did all that to hurt A.J. in any way."

"Thanks. I hope that helps when I tell Christy."

12

THE ALARM JOLTED Carly back to the real world at 6 a.m. She checked her BlackBerry, and there were no messages or texts waiting. A quick call to dispatch and she learned that nothing had changed: A.J. was still missing.

Groaning, she got out of bed and dressed quickly in a bathing suit. A swim would help clear her mind for work. In order to beat the summer beach traffic, she needed to hit the sand early. And a swim would not only fit into her training schedule; it would energize her mind. The Maui Channel Swim, at 9.5 miles, would be the longest swim she'd ever competed in. She had managed to swim to safety after jumping from a speeding yacht to avoid being shot somewhere in the middle of the channel between Catalina and the Las

Playas harbor, but she estimated that was only two or three miles. There was no way to be certain how far she had traveled that night.

With Nick's encouragement and his promise to be in a support boat while she swam ringing in her ears, she'd mailed off an entry. It was meant to be a relay race, but there were twenty slots available to those who wanted to swim solo. She'd made it just in time to be number twenty. Her training had been going great until Nick's therapy went south. Every time she was in the water, she swam with the intention of competing in the race, but now pain pierced her as she realized this was something else Nick was backing out of. Now that he wanted a break, would she do the swim without him?

I still want to, she thought, *but will it be the same without Nick there? Will anything be the same without Nick there?*

"Enough," she muttered. *Life goes on.* Covering herself with a big T-shirt, she gathered Maddie, and together they jogged to the beach. Maddie would wait patiently on a towel while Carly completed her swim.

Carly's mood improved immensely as she reached the sand. She loved the water and often found that the ocean soothed whatever ailed her. Today it was worry about A.J. and stinging memories of Nick's wanting a break that caused her pain, but she vowed to think of the race and only the race once she hit the water.

She stripped off the T-shirt and ran into the waves, trying to leave the emotional pain on the sand. *I got over him once. If I have to, I'll get over him again.*

There were only a few surfers in the water this time of the morning, and they were on the other side of the pier. Carly had the ocean to herself. She pounded out a three-mile swim that took her out to a buoy and back. The ache over Nick was still there when she finished, but now she knew she could deal with it. *I have too much to do, too much to concentrate on to be distracted. I'll hope Nick changes his mind, but I can't change it for him.*

Carly left the waves and walked up the beach to where Maddie's tail thumped rhythmically on the sand. Her thoughts shifted to her roommate, and she decided she was ready to face her now and hopefully find out what was really bothering her.

"Ready to go home, sweet face?" She flicked water at the hound, and Maddie jumped and barked excitedly. Carly threw on her shirt and pushed wet hair away from her face, standing still for a moment, drying in the sun and appreciating the heat for the first time in a long while. *Four months ago, Lord, I swam for my life. I prayed to you, and you answered. So many people told me to trust you, but it took that swim and the fear of death to make me cry out. Now I know you are with me and that whatever happens, I will stand. I can't do anything but leave everything to you, and ask that you help me make the right decisions—about Nick, about the tips I follow, about life, about everything.*

Carly turned and jogged across the beach toward home, Maddie on her heels. This time she was successful in leaving painful feelings in the sand.

Andrea was gone when she got home. *Probably best, because I'm late.* Carly showered, ate a bowl of cereal, and beat feet for work. In the locker room, she changed into what was known as a soft uniform. Tennis shoes, jeans, Sam Browne gun belt, white T-shirt under her Kevlar vest, and over her vest, a white polo shirt with an embroidered badge on the front and *POLICE* emblazoned on the back. She'd be moving around—following a lot of clues and leads, she hoped—and planned to be comfortable and prepared.

When she arrived at community relations, her mood got an immediate positive injection when she was told Nelson wanted her up in the homicide office this morning. She hurried up the stairs, ready to do more than field phone calls from Morris.

As she walked into the office, Nelson, who was on his way out, hailed her. "Morning." He held out a stack of papers. "Here are some tips I want you to follow up on. Call or head out to investigate, your choice. Harris will be up in a while. He's monitoring the news broadcasts. Use his desk. I'll be in the field, 1-Sam 9."

"Gotcha. Thanks." Feeling significantly better than when she'd gotten up that morning, she took the offered stack and leafed through it.

Before she sat at the desk, she checked the progress board set up for A.J. It was a large whiteboard where the main players in the investigation recorded their activities and actions. She learned everything that had gone on while she'd been asleep. Once she'd soaked it all in, she sat down at the desk and turned her attention to the tips Nelson had given her. The first page in the stack was a list of tipsters who gave their names and numbers; people who were willing to be contacted again were always more credible than those who remained anonymous. There was also a list of citizens who lived near the hospital that she could talk to. The second page was a bunch of anonymous tips. Nothing looked really special, but Carly sat and began dialing. She'd only been calling for about half an hour when Weaver, the burglary detective, walked into the office and took a chair next to the desk, tell-tale bulge in his right cheek.

"I'm glad I found you. We've got a problem."

"We? What's up?"

"The burglar, Stanley Harper—he's up in jail refusing to leave his cell and walk across to court and be arraigned."

Carly sat back in her chair and rubbed eyes still red from her morning swim. "Why? And what does it have to do with me?"

"He says he has information, but he'll only talk to the 'lady cop' who arrested him." Weaver shrugged and spit tobacco into a Styrofoam cup. "If it was up to me, I wouldn't bother you. But the SOs in jail don't want a use of force if they can avoid it. Harper took off his pants and tied himself to the toilet. The supervisor asked me to talk to you."

Carly bit back an irritated whine and tried to erase the image that popped into her mind of Harper tied to a jail toilet with his trousers. She knew why the security officers wanted to avoid a use of force. Three weeks ago, they'd had an in-custody death following a use of force. Since the investigation was ongoing, she guessed they were being overly cautious. "I don't have time for this. He screamed for his dirtbag lawyer the other night. Where's Caswell now?"

"Seems to have abandoned the poor soul. Maybe give him five minutes?"

"I guess." She sighed and pushed back from the desk. "I hope this isn't a total waste of time. Maybe he'll give up the guy who got away." She unhooked her gun belt—guns weren't allowed in the jail—placed it in a bottom desk drawer, left a message for Harris, and headed upstairs.

• • •

"Thanks, Officer Edwards." Stevens, the jail supervisor, looked relieved as Carly stepped off the elevator. "I really don't want my guys to pry him from the cell. The skinny ones always seem to have the most fight. Besides the paperwork involved in a use of force, there's always the chance that someone will get hurt."

"No problem. Can you tell him I'm here? Maybe he'll put his pants on and walk to an interview room. I don't really want to talk to him while he's tied to the toilet half-naked."

Stevens laughed. "I don't blame you. Have a seat in room A, and I'll see if I can persuade him."

While the security officer walked down the hallway to the felony holding tanks, Carly sat down in the interview room. Several minutes passed before she heard people walking her way. The skinny burglar she remembered from a few nights ago appeared at the door, handcuffed and flanked by Stevens.

The jailer sat the man down in a chair across from Carly and asked her, "You want me to hang out?"

Carly shook her head. "No, that's okay. He's not going anywhere."

Stevens shrugged and left the room, closing the door behind him. Carly tried not to breathe too deeply. Harper smelled like a man who hadn't showered for days, and he probably hadn't.

"What's up, Mr. Harper? A few nights ago, you didn't have anything to say to me. Why the sudden change of heart?"

"I was thinking we could work a deal." He leaned forward, a posture forced by the handcuffs behind his back.

Carly clicked her tongue and stood. "Look, I'm not a burglary detective, and I'm not a DA. If you want a deal, you should have called for one of them. I don't work deals."

"No, wait! Don't leave!" the burglar begged.

At the door, Carly turned to face him. He was sweating and nervous. Probably coming down off of speed.

"I have something for you. It's just that . . . well . . ." He tried to rub his chin on his shoulder. "It's just that once I say what I gotta say, my life won't be worth much up at county jail. You have to promise to protect me."

"Talk. Depending on what I hear, I'll tell you what I can do. I'm not making any promises." She stood at the door, one hand on the doorknob, the other on her hip.

He leaned back as far as the cuffs would allow. "I ain't a

snitch, but I'm scared for my girlfriend. Her name's Mary Ellen. I've been trying to call her, and she don't answer. I'm afraid they done something to her." He looked away.

Carly checked her watch. "This is touching, but what does it have to do with the burglary?"

"It ain't about the burglary, at least not directly. It's about that kid, the one that got snatched from the hospital."

13

CARLY STARED AT HARPER for a minute before she sat back down. "What do you mean?" On the edge of her seat now, her entire body tingled with anticipation; she didn't notice the smell anymore, and she leaned close to hear what he had to say.

He swallowed. "I saw you on TV next to the dad when he was asking for his kid back, and . . . well, I think my girlfriend took the baby, and I think she's in trouble." He swore. "I think they're both in trouble."

Carly pulled a small notepad and pen out of her back pocket. "Talk, Mr. Harper. If you are on the level, I'll help you. But if you're yanking my chain, I'll personally drag you across the street for your arraignment."

"Will you take the cuffs off?" he asked hopefully, trying to raise his shackled hands above the tabletop. At Carly's glare he dropped his hands and leaned forward. "I'll tell you the truth. I got nothing to lose. It's like this: I work for a guy who finds things—all kinds of things—and he even finds people if that's what the buyer needs. He's good at moving everything under the radar so the cops don't find out."

Carly studied Harper and digested this information. "What do you do for this guy?"

"Odd jobs, mostly grunt work. Sometimes I steal for him." He looked away, and Carly struggled to keep her expression neutral.

Harper licked his lips and continued. "He pays good. Anyway, I was shredding paperwork they asked me to shred, and I read some stuff I wasn't supposed to. Some people wanted a baby and they were willing to pay big money for one. But my boss didn't think they were willing to pay enough, so he told them to pound sand. I figured if I did the job, I'd get the cash. It was a lot of money to me. That's why I was at the hospital when you arrested me. I asked my employer if I could do the job and pocket the cash."

"Whoa! You were going to steal a baby to sell it?"

Harper looked indignant. "It's what I do. I steal things to make money. But I only earn a few hundred here and there. And I got a big gambling debt to pay. So I figure there's no big difference between a baby and a TV or stereo. Anyway, I ain't saying I'm proud of it, but how else would a guy like me earn twenty-five grand?"

Carly swallowed her disgust and nodded for Harper to go on.

"My employer laughed, said there were things I didn't understand about the deal, but he gave me the go-ahead and told me to see what I could do, but be sure not to get caught." He shook his head and stared at the table.

"Who's your employer?"

"I can't tell you that."

"Can't or won't?"

"Can you get me a deal?"

"For what? You'll have to tell me a lot more than you have so far for me to even consider still talking to you." Carly scowled and leaned back. "Who wanted the baby? Who were you going to sell the baby to?"

"That I don't know. I figured once I got the kid, my boss would connect me with the buyer."

"Do you know where the buyer is? Here in Las Playas?"

He scrunched his face as if trying to remember. "I don't think so. I think they may be in another state."

"Why does this buyer want a baby?" Carly pressed a fist into her vest, working hard to control her anger.

"I don't ask why people want things; I just get them. All I can say is, I was promised twenty-five large to deliver a baby." He looked up at Carly, and she felt her stomach turn.

He talks about selling a baby as if it were a puppy. A.J.'s life has a price tag: a paltry $25,000.

"I told you I need the money to pay some big debts. I owe a guy who has people hurt you if you don't pay him.

Trouble is, you pinched me. When you got me, I was taking the security schedule so I could figure out the best time to snatch a baby. I been burglaring since I was twelve. You seen my record. I thought it'd be easy."

"I still don't see why you think your girlfriend took the baby. You're in jail, and the security schedules are locked up where they belong. Besides which I'm certain hospital security has changed things. Why are you so sure she has this kid?"

"She never liked the idea of taking a kid in the first place, but she feels responsible for me getting caught. I talked to her after I got here. The guy I owe threatened her. He sent some muscle to tell her he was counting on me giving them what I owe. I'm way overdue. They told her she better find a way to get me out of jail or to get them the money. They threatened to kill us both."

He stopped talking and studied his shoes. Carly sat back in her chair to prevent herself from reaching across the table and slapping him. When he looked up, his eyes were watering. "I thought I would be bailed out and maybe still be able to do the job. But Detective Weaver raised my bail. I talked to Mr. Caswell, and he wasn't going to pay that much money. That's when it all went sideways. Mary Ellen was driving the car that night—"

"She was parked by the trash enclosure?"

He nodded. "She's smart. Smarter than me. It don't surprise me she lost the cops. That's why she thinks me getting caught was her fault. Last thing she said to me was that the guy I owe money to smacked her around and told her

I would pay what I owed either with money or blood. He scared her bad. She said the only way she could pay him back would be to take the baby. I told her it was crazy to try and snatch a kid now, and by herself, but she thought she could do it, being a girl and all. I didn't think she would, but I seen the news and I know it was her that took the baby. She's going to try and get the twenty-five grand and pay my debt."

Carly said nothing as her mind tried to wrap itself around this scenario. She knew there was no shortage of desperate couples wanting babies, couples who would spend thousands if need be. But A.J. was way too hot. What Harper was saying made no sense, yet he seemed completely sincere and completely terrified. What was going on?

She studied the man in front of her. Finally she said, "With all the publicity surrounding this abduction, what makes you so sure these people will want to buy this baby?"

"I ain't sure. I'm just telling you what I think Mary Ellen did." He held Carly's eyes. "She's smart, but she's just a kid. She don't know the guy I work for or the guy I owe like I do. They're both mean, and they'll make good on their threats. If I go to county jail, I'm as good as dead. No telling what will happen to Mary Ellen."

Carly stood and paced a small bit of the interview room. "If this is true, why are you telling me? Why not let your girlfriend sell the kid, settle your debt, and save your worthless life?"

"I would've, but she's gone and I'm still here. Maybe like you say, no one will want the baby now, but I just know

something bad has happened. I've been calling and calling."
He started to cry. "Please, I'll tell you where we stay. The
address I gave you the other night was old because I didn't
want you to find her. But now—please—I do want you to
find her, see if she's okay. I swear if you find her, you'll find
the kid," he pleaded while tears streamed down his face.

Carly wrote down an address for the girlfriend, Mary
Ellen Barber. Her system was given a jolt when she recognized the address on the west side as the one Harris told her
that he and Nelson had staked out yesterday.

"Is there anyplace else she'd be? You two steal for a living.
There must be other places you hide, people you trust. She
got clean away the other night. Where else might she go?"

Harper thought for a minute. "She might go back to
where I met her. She was down in Las Playas South, you
know, in the flood control under Sixth Street?"

Carly nodded. She knew the area well; it was a nuisance,
and it didn't surprise her that a runaway like Mary Ellen had
been there. The homeless called the place Las Playas South,
while officers simply referred to it as the catch basin—the last
stop before the sewer met the sea. Located under the Sixth
Street Bridge, a freeway off-ramp that brought traffic into the
city over the flood control channel, the area was a well-known
homeless encampment that usually saw peak residency in the
summer months when the foliage grew tall and thick.

The flood control channel, a concrete man-made river,
funneled water from as far as San Gabriel, thirty miles away,
into the ocean. In the summer months barely a trickle flowed

down to the surf, less than a mile from the bridge. But in the winter the amount of water grew exponentially and became a raging river. To prevent backup, debris and fast-growing shrubs were cut back in the fall, and that usually coincided with the breakdown of any homeless village that had developed during the dry months. It was dangerous for people to be under the bridge anytime, but particularly in the rainy months. So when public service was ready to clean the channel, they would request police assistance in breaking up the homeless village.

Normally the catch basin was the first place she would look for a runaway, but Carly knew that this year, way before the channel was scheduled to be cleaned out, the homeless village was already gone. There'd been a stabbing down there that ended in a murder, and the chief had ordered the place cleared a few days ago. It was unlikely the girl would be down there now.

"I was down there looking for an old pal a few months ago, and I saw her being hassled by a couple of guys. I got her away from them, and we been together ever since."

"What about other friends she might be with?"

He shook his head. "She don't trust none of my friends, and she don't have any of her own. It's just me and her, you know? And she ain't a thief like me; she's just a kid." Tears began to fall again.

A kid who may have kidnapped an infant—wonderful. "I'll do what I can."

She couldn't slow down the arraignment, but she could

ask Stevens to keep Harper back as long as he could until she had a chance to check out his information.

"Just get back to me as soon as you can," Stevens admonished Carly as she climbed on the elevator. "He has to be arraigned within forty-eight hours, so the clock is ticking."

"Will do." In the elevator Carly pounded her forehead with her palm. *I hope this isn't a drug withdrawal–induced game he's playing.* But the story was just crazy enough to ring true.

The homicide office was empty. Carly sat down at a computer and logged on. She shot Weaver an e-mail about the interview, asking him to use any clout he had to delay Harper's arraignment till the last minute. Homicide would need time to check out his story.

Finished with the computer, she picked up the phone to check in with the tip line and was told Harris was meeting with the press information office, working on a new press release. She grabbed her gun belt and put it on while she wondered how to handle this tip in the quickest way possible.

I want to get this done. She drummed her fingers on the desk for a minute and made a decision. She could probably free someone up to take with her, but she didn't want to take the time. Quickly she penned a note for Nelson, saying she'd call him from the apartment if anything came of this new lead, and jogged out of the office.

• • •

The address Harper had given Carly for Mary Ellen Barber was located in an area of Las Playas known as "tweakers alley" because of the prevalence of drugs like speed and metham-phetamine and an overabundance of users. Carly parked one house down from Mary Ellen's apartment building and did a double take at a black Lincoln Town Car parked on the other side of the street, two doors down. It looked like the kind of car you hired to take you to the airport. The windows were tinted too dark for her to see if the vehicle was occupied.

Carly radioed dispatch with her location and told them to put her code 6 and out of the car for investigation. She hur-ried down the walkway and up the four stairs to the entry of the apartment building. Pausing on the top stair, she turned to study the expensive vehicle one more time, all manner of alarms going off in her head. *That car is out of place here. Are they dope dealers or dope buyers?* But the clock was ticking on Harper. She didn't have time to check the car out now. She couldn't see the Town Car's license plate from where she was but vowed to check it before she left.

Carly turned and continued into the apartment building to find number seven. From the layout she could see that the apartment was in the corner on the second floor.

The enclosed hallway and stairway to the second floor smelled of a familiar mixture of garbage, unwashed bodies, and urine. It was a dope house mixture. Carly didn't look too close because she knew she'd see cockroaches, and the thought made her itch. *I pray, as much as I want to find him, that baby A.J. is not in a place like this.*

When she reached number seven, the first room on the second floor, the door was ajar.

"Hello? Mary Ellen?" She pulled her big flashlight from her belt and whacked the doorjamb hard.

There was no response. Slowly she pushed the door open with the flashlight. The small room in front of her was dirty and sparsely furnished, and it looked like a tornado had landed hard. Clothes were strewn about and the couch was upended, the cushions slashed and the stuffing torn out. She remembered Harper saying that Mary Ellen had been slapped around.

Am I going to find a body in this mess?

But there was no one in sight in the living room or kitchen, though it was obvious that someone had been here looking for something. But what? Or whom? Was Harper's employer responsible for this, or was this the work of the people he owed money to?

Carly stepped in farther, boots crunching on glass from a shattered coffee table, and called for Mary Ellen again. She was familiar with the floor plan; most of the older apartments in this part of the city were cookie-cutter. The kitchen was to the left and a single bedroom to the right.

All the blinds were drawn, and the apartment was cast in semidarkness. She clicked her light on, not wanting to miss anything, and dragged the beam across the small space. Dreaded roaches skittered across the kitchen floor and caused Carly to shiver. The air in the room was stale and smelled like a combination of cigarettes and spoiled food. Carly started for the bedroom and froze.

An edge of blue fabric caught her eye. She had to push

JANICE CANTORE || 131

the sofa to see more, and her heart caught in her throat. It was A.J.'s sleeper, the one he'd been wearing the night he was brought to the hospital. Blue with little badges. She'd noticed it when Joe was feeding his son.

She stepped forward and picked up the small blue outfit. It was in one piece but dirty with what looked like food and smudges of grime. Her gaze went to the upended sofa, and she nudged aside the debris around the couch with the toe of her boot, looking for anything else that would prove A.J. had been there.

Suddenly there was a crash of glass breaking and wood splintering from the bedroom. Carly clicked off her light, dropped the sleeper, and drew her handgun.

"Who is it? Who's there?" She pointed her weapon toward the bedroom and stuffed the flashlight in her back pocket. "This is the police! Who's there?"

She stepped quickly but cautiously to the bedroom and caught a glimpse of the back and bald head of a white man as he disappeared out the window. There was a loud thud.

Carly hurried to the window in time to see the man straighten up after landing on the roof of an adjacent laundry room and then jump to a side walkway. When he glanced up, their eyes met briefly. Carly saw a man with several days' growth of dark beard on his face before he turned and sprinted away. Quickly she holstered her gun and followed.

Carly hit the top of the laundry room as the bald man rounded the corner of the building, running toward the street. Her leap to the ground wasn't as graceful as his was.

Though she absorbed the shock by bending her knees, she still fell off-balance. When she gained her feet, she heard a motor rev. She lurched toward the street, feeling every ounce of her gear holding her back.

The Town Car sped past, burning rubber and weaving down the street.

It seemed to take forever to reach her car. She could hear the sound of the Lincoln's tires screeching in the distance as she jammed her key in the ignition and slammed her foot down on the gas pedal.

All of Carly's focus was on catching the vehicle. She headed in the direction where she last saw the car, rolling over black tire tracks in the street.

"Thank you!" she yelled when she spotted the Lincoln's taillights in the distance ahead of her. He was stopped behind traffic.

Carly reached for the radio mike to call for backup. Simultaneously, a car appeared on her left. Even as she was slowing because her prey was within her grasp, the car on the left sped past and cut right.

Carly slammed on her brakes and tried to avoid the collision. But metal hit metal, and she was jerked forward and then slammed back by the force of the deployed air bag.

14

"ARE YOU OKAY?"

Carly heard the voice and wanted to answer, but the wind in her lungs had fled on impact and her face stung from the air bag. She sucked in a breath and brought a hand to her face, which was wet and sticky. When she looked at her hand, she saw blood.

"Don't move," the voice ordered. "We called for paramedics."

Carly breathed in and tried to focus on who was talking to her. It was a man in a suit, standing at her window. She remembered the chase, the car cutting her off.

"What . . . ?" Carly tried to speak and shifted in her seat to get a better look at the man. Her face hurt.

"Don't talk. Here." He handed her a handkerchief. "I'm awfully sorry about this."

Carly took the piece of cloth and gingerly wiped her nose. As her eyes watered, she wondered if her nose was broken. She moved around, testing her body parts—arms, hands, legs, feet—but didn't seem to be injured anywhere else. Sirens were fast approaching, and she was embarrassed to realize they were coming for her.

Embarrassment quickly gave way to anger, and she turned on the man in the suit. "You—you cut me off! It was deliberate—why?" She glared at him through the open window even as she sniffed back blood.

"Look, I said I was sorry." He straightened up and moved away from the car.

Carly looked at the front of her black-and-white. It was embedded in the side of a nondescript car, but the damage didn't seem to be too bad. She'd been wasted by the air bag. There was something familiar about the man and the car, but she was having trouble focusing.

The sirens stopped as a black-and-white and a fire truck rolled up to the scene.

Mike, a beat cop, walked up a second later. "Hey, Carly, are you okay?" Right behind him was a paramedic.

"Yeah, I am. Mike, do me a favor: get ahold of Detective Harris and get him out here. I have some info for him, okay?"

"Sure thing, but you let the medic take a look at you." He stepped back and got on the radio.

The paramedic occupied Carly with questions to assess her level of consciousness. It took more than a few minutes to convince him she was okay, but eventually he let her get out of the car and walk to his rig, where he had her sit on the bumper with an ice pack on her nose. From there she brooded and watched Mike work the accident scene. The Town Car was long gone.

Harris pulled up a short time later. "What happened to you?" he asked.

Nick was beside him, and Carly felt her heart rate quicken. *Oh, Lord,* she prayed, *I don't want to deal with him right now.*

"This guy cut me off." She pointed to the man in the suit. "But that's not important. I know who took A.J." Carly stood and ignored the headache that started, the sharp pain causing her eyes to water. She told Pete about Harper, Mary Ellen, and the elusive black Town Car. He jerked his phone off his belt and called Nelson with the information.

"Nelson is sending a team over there," he said as he ended the call. "I'll join them after I'm finished here."

"I want to go back there and check the place out carefully. I would've caught the limo if this jerk hadn't cut me off."

"And I want to talk to this clown. Excuse me." Pete strode toward the other driver, leaving Carly to face Nick.

"You're not going anywhere." He leaned on his cane and looked at her with an expression she couldn't read. "Except maybe to the hospital."

"I'm fine. I've just got a bloody nose from the air bag."

"It might be broken."

"It's not broken. I'm going to help find A.J." She moved to go around Nick, but he grabbed her arm.

"No, you're going to the hospital and getting x-rayed. Do I have to make it an order?"

"You wouldn't." She jerked her arm away and glared. He was a sergeant, so he could order her, but never in their relationship had he chosen such a course.

"In a heartbeat I would. You're bleeding. Go get yourself taken care of. I'll have Nelson call you with what he finds." His firm tone assured Carly he meant business.

She was almost angry and hurt enough to force his hand; part of her wanted to dare him. In the end, she relented and let the paramedics help her into the ambulance.

• • •

The blood from her nose soaked through her polo shirt to the cover of her ballistic vest but didn't make it to the undershirt beneath. Carly stripped the sodden items off and submitted to an exam followed by countless questions posed by the day patrol sergeant who stopped in to complete the injury-on-duty paperwork and talk to her about why she crashed. Crashing a police car ate up about as much paperwork as a shooting. The sergeant made sure Carly understood he wasn't very happy with the added workload. He finished up about the time the doctor was ready to have her x-rayed. She was given instructions to report to Nelson as soon as the doctor released her.

Carly gratefully turned herself over to the care of the physician, the pain in her nose paralleling the pain in her heart. The thought of her ex-husband pulling rank hurt almost as much as losing the limousine. *Nick was going to order me. I can't think about this now. I'll choke up, and it hurts to sniffle.* After the X-ray, she was handed another ice bag. She closed her eyes, lay back in the exam room with the ice covering her face, and tried to focus on anything other than Sergeant Nick Anderson.

"Hey, if it isn't my favorite police officer."

Carly pulled the ice away from her nose and opened her eyes to see Trejo in the doorway.

"Where did you come from?" Her voice now possessed a nasal quality, as if she were suffering from a bad head cold.

"I heard the commotion on my scanner." He walked to her bedside. "You gave me a scare. My heart dropped to my feet when I heard you were hurt." Alex reached out and touched her chin with a forefinger. "I've never said this to a woman I wanted to date, but you look horrible. You're going to have two nice shiners."

Carly turned away from his touch. "I'm not gonna die. The crash wasn't even that bad. It was the stupid air bag that did this."

"Do you want to tell me what happened?"

"I wish I knew."

"Officer Edwards?"

Alex and Carly turned to face the doctor.

"The films are negative; there's no break. You're going to be black and blue for a couple of days. A nurse will be in to give you some instructions, and then you'll be released."

"Thank you very much." Carly moved to sit up and didn't

protest when Alex took her arm to help her. The ice had helped her face; it wasn't throbbing as much as when she'd come in. But she'd left her kit with her phone in the black-and-white. "I've got to find a phone."

"Whoa. Your friendly neighborhood reporter to the rescue." Trejo produced a phone from his back pocket and smiled.

Carly regarded him warily. "Suppose what I have to say is off limits to the press?"

Trejo laughed. "Always the cop. I don't know what I have to do to convince you that the majority of my interest is personal. But if you want, I'll stand in the hall." He pointed with his thumb to the hallway and raised his eyebrows expectantly.

Carly managed a smile in spite of the soreness in her face. "Always the reporter. I notice you said 'majority.' What's the minority interest percent?"

He held up a thumb and forefinger and grinned. "Minuscule, minuscule. If you don't want it in print, it won't be in print. Scout's honor." The grin faded, and the expression on his face was appropriately solemn.

"Okay, okay." Carly took the phone. Alex went out to the hall as she dialed Sergeant Nelson, who answered immediately.

"I'm glad you called. How are you doing?"

"I'm fine. Nothing's broken. Did you find anything else in the apartment? And were you able to get a line on the Town Car?" Carly was careful not to look down. When she looked down, her nose throbbed.

"I'll get to the apartment search in a minute, but first I have to tell you that you stumbled into the middle of an FBI surveillance."

"FBI?" She gaped, realizing Nelson was saying a government car had cut her off. Deliberately. "I was in hot pursuit of a suspect in the kidnapping of a cop's kid and an FBI agent stopped me?" The headache lurking in the background slithered forward and seized Carly's temples in a vise grip.

"The guy that caused your crash is an FBI agent, albeit not a very good one. He was a tail on the Lincoln. The good news is, Agent Wiley has been a big help, and he connected some dots we might never have connected. The guy you chased is a mug named Isaac Grant. He works for the suspect the FBI is watching, and the kicker is, so does Stanley Harper."

"What!" Carly slid off the bed and began to pace. She needed to move, walk, run—anything to digest this news. "But Harper's boss is the one who wanted the baby! The FBI is supposed to be helping us with A.J. Did they just help the kidnappers get away?"

"Calm down. They say that neither their suspect nor Grant has the baby. Because of their surveillance they were able to clarify some things. Grant was sent to the apartment for some keys."

"Keys? What kind of keys?"

"Well, apparently Harper had some in his possession that belong to their employer. When Wiley saw what we had and compared it to the surveillance he was able to review, it was clear that the keys were what Caswell wanted as well, since he also works for the same man. The feds have pages of transcribed surveillance and assure me that their suspect does not want a kidnapped baby."

Carly thought back to the night she arrested Harper. "Harper didn't have any keys on him when I booked him. But if he did have keys, they are likely in the car that Mary Ellen drove away."

"Already on it. You had the license plate in your report of Harper's car. It's been entered in the system now as a wanted vehicle." Nelson paused, and Carly heard papers shuffling in the background. He added, "Also, to be on the safe side, we are releasing Mary Ellen Barber's information to the media since she's a runaway from county custody and now a person of interest in our investigation."

"That's great—the more information we have out there, the better. But it bugs me that Harper said nothing about keys." She chewed on a thumbnail. "Who is under surveillance? Who is Harper's boss?"

"Here the feds clam up. According to Wiley, the main subject of their investigation and the location where they've set up surveillance are not in Las Playas and have nothing to do with Las Playas, so we have no need to know."

"But why did their agent make me crash?"

"If it's any consolation, they apologize. The agent who hit you is green, and he'll probably be suspended. You surprised him; he didn't expect you would catch the car. The only thing he could think to do was cut you off."

Oh, they're sorry. That makes everything better, Carly

thought bitterly. "What about Mary Ellen? Do the feds have anything on her?"

"Wiley admits that they know nothing about Mary Ellen. She's a wild card and someone they've never had reason to suspect was involved in any illegal activity. Wiley is on his way to talk to Harper now, trying to clarify this crazy story about selling a baby. The feds insist that A.J.'s disappearance is not in any way connected to the guy they're after."

Carly huffed. "If the baby's disappearance is not connected to what they're after, then it wouldn't hurt to tell us who they are investigating."

"They don't want that investigation compromised. I've got to go. Harris and I are going to sit in on the Harper interview. You go home and take care of yourself. Check in tomorrow morning."

"I don't want to go home. I feel like we're close." Carly clenched her free hand and pounded her hip. *Don't cut me out now!*

"You did a great job today. But you are officially IOD now," Nelson said, using shorthand for "injured on duty." "You can't get back in it until the occupational health people clear you. Thanks for being on the ball. Bye."

The phone disconnected, and Carly groaned in frustration. She looked at her watch. Occupational health closed at five and it was close to six. *The stupid crash took up my entire day.*

"Just let me know if you're going to throw the phone so I can duck." A voice from the hallway crashed her pity party.

Carly turned in surprise; she'd forgotten about Alex. "I'm sorry. Here." She handed him his phone back.

"No problem. Boy, you look like your Super Bowl team just lost the game in the final three seconds. What gives?"

"It's a long story."

Carly was spared from explaining further when the nurse came in with the release paperwork. Her instructions for Carly were rest, ice for her nose, and pain reliever if it hurt too much. Mike, the beat cop who was taking the accident report, stuck his head in the door as Carly was gathering her things.

"Need a ride back to the station?" he asked as he handed over her kit. "I took this out of your car before it was towed."

"Yeah, I do need a ride. Thank you very much."

"Hey, I can take you," Trejo offered.

"That's okay, Alex. It's out of your way." Carly stuffed her bloody clothes into a plastic bag.

"No, it's not. I bet this officer has other work to do." He nodded toward Mike and reached to take the plastic bag from Carly. "Besides, I have some information I need to give you."

"What information?" Carly frowned at the reporter. "I'm too cranky right now for games."

"No games, honest." He held up his hands, her bag dangling from one, and the look on his face resembled that of an innocent schoolboy.

"Make up your mind, please," Mike chimed in from the doorway.

"Thanks, Mike. I guess I'll go with Trejo." Carly waved at

the beat cop, who smiled and left. She turned her attention back to the reporter. "You better be on the level."

"I am. Let's go." He directed Carly out the door and followed behind.

On the way out she checked her phone for messages and saw none, not even one from Nick checking up on her.

15

"SO WHAT'S YOUR INFORMATION?" Carly asked as they climbed into Trejo's car.

"How about dinner? I bet you haven't eaten all day." Alex started the car and looked at Carly.

"You promised, no games." Carly's protest was weak because he'd hit the nail on the head: she was starving. The cereal she'd eaten that morning was a distant memory. "Besides, I look like a prizefighter who lost. Are you sure you want to be seen in public with me?"

Trejo chuckled. "This too shall pass. We can go to a nice dark restaurant so no one will notice."

Carly threw her hands up in resignation. "I'm too tired

to fight you." She leaned back and closed her eyes. "But take me back to the station first so I can put my vest and gun belt away and change my clothes."

"Roger." He reached over and squeezed her hand.

As Trejo drove, Carly thought back to Nick at the accident scene. *He was right, procedurally, to order me to the hospital. Why did it tweak me so bad? Was there anything he could have said today that I wouldn't have taken offense at? I hate this! I can't believe we came this far together to go our separate ways now.*

Once at the station Carly changed quickly and avoided the mirror. The only encouragement was that the throbbing in her face had ceased and hope was strong she'd be released back to full duty tomorrow. She paused to call Joe and see how he was doing. She didn't tell him about her fiasco and crash, wanting to leave that to Nelson. Trejo could wait, she thought. Joe sounded good, upbeat, and she promised to stop by on her way home.

But even as she locked her gun belt away in her locker, her thoughts turned to Mary Ellen, the wild card. *Harper said she was a runaway—from where? I've got to find out more about her,* she thought, *but I can't think straight right now. As soon as I eat, and before I visit Joe, I'll have to dig in and learn everything I can about that girl.*

"Where are you taking me, reporter?" she asked when she climbed back in the car.

"Pizza, Officer. BJ's, to be exact. Pizza heals all wounds." She wondered how Alex had managed to hit on her favorite food, something she would never turn down. "That is a statement I won't disagree with."

"Glad to hear it." In a few minutes he parked the car in front of her favorite pizza place. To Carly's surprise, despite the condition of her nose, she could smell. The heavenly odor of baking pizza and tomato sauce came through loud and clear as soon as they stepped into the restaurant. The aroma did a lot to soothe her mood.

"I have to admit, this was a great choice," she conceded. "I'm starved. All I had today was cereal for breakfast."

"I'm glad." Trejo grinned. "I sure could get used to this, having dinner with you on a regular basis."

Carly let his comment pass as they slid into a booth near the back and the waitress handed them menus. The place was dark, mood lighting for the dinner hour. Thankfully, he was quiet until after they'd ordered and she'd downed one glass of iced tea and half a green salad.

"That's much better," Carly said after a healthy swallow of tea. "My headache is even fading."

Trejo smiled and toasted her with a glass of water. "Are you going to fill me in on what happened today? I heard the words *FBI*, *surveillance*, and *A.J.* in your conversation with the sergeant. My interest is piqued."

"Well . . ." She looked at him over the rim of her iced tea glass and then set it down on the table. Choosing her words carefully, Carly fiddled with her fork while she spoke. "The public information officer will be putting together a press release about a person of interest in A.J.'s kidnapping. But this is off the record. I don't have any authority to be making statements to the press. Please don't get me in trouble."

"You pierce me through and through." Alex put both hands over his heart and looked hurt. "This is just me and you, not the PD and the *Las Playas Messenger*."

Carly smiled and told him about Harper, his girlfriend Mary Ellen, and her own literal run-in with an FBI agent. She paused only when the pizza was set before them, and then she ingested half a slice before continuing. Trejo listened without interrupting.

"So that's how I came to receive an air bag–induced bloody nose. Now I have to cool my jets and get a health department clearance before I can go back to work."

"They wouldn't tell you what they were investigating?"

"Not yet. Nelson said he'd keep trying to get more information."

"It's too much of a coincidence to me. Girl kidnaps baby; then her apartment gets tossed."

Carly went to work on her pizza again. "The apartment was Harper's," she said between bites. "If Grant was looking for keys Harper had, then the place being tossed might really have had nothing to do with Mary Ellen."

Alex sprinkled peppers on his pizza. "Unless she has the keys."

Carly nodded. "I would bet she does. She has Harper's car. And missing keys could explain why Caswell was in such a hurry to get Harper out of jail. I mean, it makes more sense to me that he wanted keys rather than Harper."

Alex laughed. "Sounds like Harper didn't impress you."

"He's a two-bit thief. It never made sense to me that he'd have the money for a high-priced lawyer. You said it yourself—Caswell defends money. But if Harper was in possession of something that belonged to a paying customer . . ." She shrugged.

"You could be right. And I have a guess about that paying customer. I've been studying up on Caswell since we last met. About three years ago, even though I only wrote a few paragraphs about him and his clients, I did a lot of research. I'd forgotten, but when I retrieved the file, it brought back memories. Do you remember Conrad Sperry?"

"How could I forget? The guy was creepy. He's one of Caswell's clients?" She arched an eyebrow. Sperry was an infamous ex-reserve police officer for Las Playas. A man with a diverse business empire, he'd started out as a rock star as far as the reserve corps was concerned. The department didn't want the reserves to be a stop for people who couldn't get hired to be full-time police officers; they wanted it to be a corps of volunteers, people successful in other walks of life who only wanted to help when they could and not be full-time cops.

But Sperry had crossed the line while wearing his reserve uniform and very nearly found himself behind bars.

Alex nodded, his mouth full of pizza. He swallowed. "It was Caswell who got him off."

"That figures, but what does that have to do with Harper?"

She sat back and put her fork down. "Wait, you think Sperry is Harper's employer and the one the feds are investigating?"

"Let me finish. I can do an Internet search as well as the next guy. Sperry left Las Playas for Riverside, but his legal troubles didn't end. He's been Caswell's number one client of late, and he keeps the lawyer busy. Sperry is a businessman who has his fingers in a lot of different money pies. Some of them are shady and have been investigated by various law enforcement agencies. In one case Sperry was under suspicion for some stolen artwork. It's not a leap to consider Harper his employee and Sperry under investigation, is it?"

Carly sipped her tea and digested this new information. "Maybe not that Harper works for Sperry. But the leap from stolen artwork to stolen babies is huge."

Alex held up his index finger. "A thief is a thief."

Carly hiked a shoulder and said, "Harper working for Sperry would explain a lot. I could see Caswell getting out of bed and heading to the station for Sperry. He definitely could have been doing Sperry's business. Since Harper didn't have the keys—Caswell would know that from the property inventory on the booking sheet—that would explain him sending Grant to toss the apartment."

She frowned. "But that still doesn't explain Mary Ellen taking A.J. The FBI doesn't buy Harper's story about selling a baby. If Mary Ellen took the baby and there's no one for her to sell him to, what will she do with him?"

"Maybe the whole baby thing was Harper's deal and

not his employer's. He's just trying to shift blame by saying it came from his employer. For all we know, Mary Ellen could have already sold the baby, gotten the money, and kept it."

Carly shook her head but stopped quickly as the movement irritated her nose. "If so, who bought the baby? A.J. is a hot property; his face is everywhere. Anyone taking that child now would be risking a lot. Something has been bothering me about this stealing-a-baby-to-sell thing. It can't be that profitable, not as profitable as fencing stolen goods. As an officer of the court, if Caswell knew something like that was going on, why would he risk a career on it?"

"Maybe there's more to it than the money. Maybe Caswell was working another angle with them and the baby was a side deal," Trejo offered.

Carly pressed her fingers into her temples. "I don't know, and frankly I don't care about motives right now. First and foremost, I want A.J. back. The rest can wait. Do you mind if I give Harris a call? He probably already knows all this, but I want to make sure."

Trejo nodded. Carly made the call and got Harris's voice mail. She left a message. When she disconnected, she found the reporter watching her with an odd expression.

"What?"

"Nothing. Just like watching you work." He cleared his throat. "So aren't you anxious to hear about the other information I learned?" Trejo asked after the waitress removed the remains of the pizza and they'd both ordered coffee.

"Ah, brave man, you ask me now because you know I won't storm out. I'm calmed down, satisfied, and waiting to savor a cup of my favorite hot beverage."

"At least I'm reasonably sure you won't shoot me. Remember, I'm only the messenger. I wish this news were good, but . . . Anyway, you deserve to hear it."

Carly closed her eyes and swallowed. "Bad news is my middle name right now. You go right ahead."

"Discipline is coming down at the hospital. Apparently, someone who should have been supervising was doing something else."

Carly looked at Trejo with eyebrows raised. The coffee was set between them, and she took a scalding yet fortifying sip. "Who?"

"I'm sorry, but they busted your roommate, Andrea. They say that when she should have been on the floor, she was, well . . . elsewhere." He wouldn't meet Carly's eyes.

"What do they say she was doing? Tell me, Alex. I know you know."

He took a deep breath and expelled it forcefully. "Okay, you don't pull punches. I guess I won't either. Gossip is, she was in a supply closet, making out with someone. She won't reveal his name. But whispers in the air say it was a cop—a patrol sergeant."

Carly looked at Alex and found an amazing mix of sorrow, compassion, and worry in his eyes. She put the coffee down and sat back in her seat. "Gossip," she muttered. The word left a bad taste in her mouth. "Now I have to wonder what patrol sergeant. At that time of the morning, it would most likely be a graveyard sergeant. I knew there was more going on with her the other day, but I haven't had a chance to talk to her. What's going to happen?"

"The hospital looks bad; a kid is gone. I'm afraid Andrea is expendable. They can't say her lapse is the only reason the kidnapper got away with the baby, but they'll say it contributed. My sources say she'll be suspended pending an internal investigation."

Carly brought a hand to her mouth and stifled the first word that came to mind. "Alex, how accurate is your information?"

He shrugged. "Gossip is gossip. Bottom line, she was doing something she shouldn't have been doing. I'm sorry— you know as well as I do how politics work."

Carly was about to lash out at Alex and defend her roommate, but a sudden thought struck her. "You're right." She shook her head. "I hate to say it. It wasn't the first time she's had a lapse at work, but it's never been anything to put her duties or patients at risk. She was reprimanded when she was assigned to the emergency room. I think that's why she was moved upstairs. Andi is a flirt."

"I've heard that. People say she flirted too much in the ER."

"Yeah, firefighters and police officers." Carly sighed. "Andi loves to live on the edge. At one time I envied her free spirit. I never used to look at it as a dangerous thing. It may sound strange, but it was an odd quirk in my friend I just accepted." *I knew it was wrong. I knew I should have reached out to her, tried to talk sense into her. For four months I've been going to church and hearing a positive message that would have helped, and I never shared it.*

"It doesn't sound strange. You're a good friend. Good friends overlook things."

"I don't know about that. I think I should have said something, maybe issued a gentle warning." Carly leaned back because her nose started to hurt again, mirroring the hurt forming in her heart. "Thank you for the pizza. Can we go now? Suddenly I feel a hundred years old."

She started to reach for her wallet, but Alex waved her off.

"You're welcome, and it's on me. I'm sorry to be the bearer of bad news."

He threw down some money, and they walked in silence to his car. Alex took her hand when they reached the passenger door. "Hey, is there anything I can do? You look like I hit you with a bat—and I don't just mean your nose."

"I'm not mad at you; I'm sad for Andrea. And thanks for telling me. Now I need time to think about everything."

She didn't take her hand from his, and suddenly Alex pulled her close into a tight hug.

"I hate to see you in pain," he whispered into her ear, his breath warm on her neck. The hug didn't surprise Carly as much as the fact that she didn't resist. She returned the hug and rested her head on his shoulder for a long while, enjoying the support Alex offered. But in rhythm with the thud of her heart, Carly's mind heard one word repeated over and over again: *Nick, Nick, Nick, Nick* . . .

• • •

Alex dropped her off at the station, but instead of going to the hospital right away, Carly went to work. First things first, she went to homicide to see if they'd gotten a verified name and age on Mary Ellen. They had—it was on the board. Mary Ellen Barber was a 301, a dependent minor. Her prints had been recovered off the equipment at Memorial. So she had taken the baby.

She'd never been arrested for a criminal offense; she was a ward of the court because of neglect or abuse. Carly studied the girl's picture. She had light-brown hair, brown eyes, pale, washed-out features, and the thousand-yard stare you often saw on kids in county custody. She'd run away from placement the day after her seventeenth birthday and hooked up with career criminal Stanley Harper.

Carly had to work not to pity the girl. As an officer, she'd been to enough foster homes and placement facilities to know they could be bleak and in rare occasions more dangerous than the home the dependent minor was removed from. Was that Mary Ellen's story? Did the county take her out of the frying pan into the fire?

Sitting at an empty desk, Carly admitted she was running on fumes. She turned on a computer and logged in. Pulling up all the files she could find on Mary Ellen, she started reading. Mary Ellen had to have a relative somewhere, someone she would go to. Carly had to believe Nelson and Harris had already exhausted all of those avenues, but what if they hadn't? She made a mental note to ask them if they'd sent someone to the catch basin. If they hadn't, she would make a run down there.

The girl had first been entered into the system after she was found wandering the streets in the early-morning hours alone at the age of six. The case disposition said she was returned to her father late in the afternoon of the next day. According to neighbors, Mary Ellen's mother had died suddenly and her father was having difficulty caring for the child.

Six months later there was another incident, but things had changed as far as how long the police department could keep the child. By that time the law required that the child be sent either to probation if the offense was criminal or to the Department of Children and Family Services if the child was a dependent. Carly noted that there was a report indicating Mary Ellen did well in school when she applied herself, but she was described as "emotionally immature." Which could explain why she hooked up with Harper.

Carly saw scanned paperwork familiar to her from her time in juvenile. The juvenile detective who had logged Mary Ellen in made note of an interested party, a relative willing to take the child in the event the father couldn't.

Juvenile detectives often took down names of relatives and then left the ball in the DCFS court to determine if the home was acceptable for placement until the court decided custody or disposition. This was what she wanted—relatives who weren't mentioned elsewhere, people she could contact who would hopefully help her find Mary Ellen. She clicked the mouse to get to the next page and jerked her hand away in shock when she read the scanned, grainy name of the relative.

It was Jonah Rawlings, her pastor.

16

HOW LONG SHE HAD STARED at the name and address she wasn't sure. The shock settled into her bones, and she wanted to call Nick. She even went as far as picking up her phone but in the end decided against it. There was nothing she could do right now—it was close to midnight. Tomorrow was Tuesday, and she knew Jonah would be at the church early, so she'd deal with it then.

With fatigue and questions weighing her down as if she carried a hundred-pound rucksack, Carly closed the file. She sent a text to Joe and asked him how he was. He responded that he was tired, too tired for visits. Carly said she understood and that she was praying. Wearily, she headed home.

Andi's door was closed when Carly got home. Only her

puffy nose kept her from knocking and finally talking with her roommate, though she was glad to think about a different problem for a few minutes. She let Maddie out and leaned against the sliding door, praying she'd get the chance to talk to both Andi and Pastor Rawlings and that A.J. would be found unhurt and this nightmare would end. After the dog came in, she spent a few minutes with an ice pack on her nose, undressed quickly, and just as quickly fell asleep, completely exhausted.

Four hours later the alarm jolted her out of bed, though she swore she'd only just lain down. She needed an early start; she had three stops to make before she went to work.

Her roommate's door was still closed tight, and Carly wasn't certain Andi would be up this early. Groggy, Carly started coffee, then jumped in the shower. *If she does get up, I want to be wide awake when I talk to her.*

After the shower she studied her face. It was sore, but not as bad as she'd feared. The two shiners Alex predicted were there, but not terribly dark.

Carly felt better clean and in fresh clothing. She couldn't imagine occupational health keeping her out of action because of a couple of bruises. She dried her hair halfway, trusting the heat of the day to do the rest, then took Maddie out for a quick walk.

When Carly returned, she found Andi in the living room drinking coffee. Carly poured a cup and joined her.

"Morning," she said, not wanting her voice to reveal the turmoil in her soul.

"You're up early. . . . Well, don't you look special." Andrea raised her eyebrows, regarding her roommate over the rim of her coffee cup. She was on the couch, sitting with her feet drawn up under her, still in pajamas.

"I had quite a day yesterday." Carly settled into her recliner and told Andrea about the vehicle fiasco. Stories like that usually got her roommate animated. Not today. All Carly got was polite attention.

"Sorry to hear it. I was really hoping you'd find the kid by now," she said flatly as she sipped her coffee, then looked away.

There was silence, and Carly struggled to find words. *When did this become so hard? She's always been my friend; we've always talked about everything.*

"Is there anything new from the hospital?" She winced at the lame-sounding question.

"Yeah, you know I've been suspended." Andi studied her coffee, and Carly didn't miss the strange defiance in her friend's voice.

"I heard they might. What are you going to do?" *That was lame too! Why can't I say what I want to say?*

"Don't have any choice but to face the music. My interview with the disciplinary board is later today." She stood and strode to the window. "They just want to blame someone, so they picked me." She jerked the blinds open in spite of the fact that it was still dark outside.

"Were you . . . Well, is what they're saying true?"

"Was I with a man in the supply closet?" Andrea finally

turned to face Carly, her eyes blazing with anger. "No, I wasn't. I don't know who started that rumor. I did let my break go long, and I was with a man. But I was just having a little harmless fun! Don't go giving me your uptight Christian nonsense right now. I don't need to hear it and I don't want to hear it."

Carly's head snapped back, slapped by the tone and the words thrown at her. "Andi, I just want to help. We are friends, aren't we? Can you at least tell me why you react to the word *Christian* like it's a swearword?"

"We are friends, but I can see the judgment in your eyes. That's the Christian in you, looking for fault, something to judge. Don't worry; I won't be around to taint you. Just as soon as I can find another place to live, I'm gone." She stormed past Carly and into her room, slamming the door.

"I'm not judging you. I'm worried about you!" Carly spoke to the closed door. Even though she knew Andrea heard her, there was no response. All Carly could do was stare down the hall and wonder, *What did I say?*

I will pray for you, Andi, while you're at that interview.

Numb, Carly finished her coffee, eyes roaming around the empty living room. She and Andrea had been like sisters for years. When Carly's marriage ended, Andrea was there to help pick up the pieces. How could all those years mean nothing right now? She could hear Andrea banging things around in her room but hadn't a clue how to deal with the tension between them.

•••

The Coastal Christian Fellowship was located in an old industrial complex. The main sanctuary was a large, square building flanked on either side by long, low buildings that used to be warehouses. All in all, the church owned five buildings of varying sizes. It was the perfect location for a church—plenty of parking and no neighbors to offend when the area was packed with worshipers. The back of the property bordered land that at one time had been an active and producing oil field. Long-unused oil pumps still dotted the field.

Carly knew Pastor Rawlings hoped to buy the land from the oil company in the hopes of turning a large part of it into a park. He had a lot of vision for the area, and there was always a project going on. Even now construction was under way on a new fellowship hall, to be located in a building to the west of the main sanctuary.

Normally Carly loved coming to church. The place had become a second home in the few months she'd been attending. Jonah was a bear of a man, a lumberjack kind of guy; he always reminded Carly of the representations she'd seen of Paul Bunyan. With his calm, gentle demeanor, he instilled trust and confidence in people. He'd won Carly over in short order, once she realized he was not an adversary but an ally. To Carly, he was now a father figure. Someone she could go to with questions and problems.

But as she pulled into the parking lot with dawn's light spreading, she felt as though she were in unfamiliar territory.

Uncertainty colored her thoughts. She pulled in next to Pastor Rawlings's car, the only one in the lot. For a second she sat in her car, motor running, debating putting this off. While she sat, the paper delivery person drove up and tossed a newspaper out onto the walkway. Carly watched the car in her rearview mirror until it left the lot. Turning her attention back to the church, she sighed.

No, she decided, *I need to see what Jonah knows about Mary Ellen, and I want to find out before I arrive at work.* Shutting down the motor, she was getting out of her car when the sound of another car approaching startled her. She was more unnerved when she recognized the truck that parked next to her. It was Nick's.

What is he doing here? He couldn't know about Mary Ellen's connection to Jonah. She'd purposely come early—the construction workers hadn't even arrived yet—because she wanted to talk to Jonah uninterrupted. Now Nick's presence threw a wrench in that plan. He turned her way, and she saw the perplexed look on his face. He was just as surprised to see her as she was to see him. Carly fought to keep her face neutral, not wanting personal issues to cloud the bigger picture.

She stood on the walkway in front of her car and waited as he got out and limped her way, leaning on his cane.

"Wow. Does that hurt?" he said as he reached her.

For a second she didn't know what he was talking about, and then she remembered her black eyes. "No, not now. Nothing's broken. I'll be at occupational health when it opens. I'm sure I'll be cleared."

He nodded. "Good. I'm glad nothing was broken. What brings you here this early?"

"I was going to ask you the same thing."

"I needed to talk to Jonah." He shrugged.

"So do I," she said before bending down to pick up the newspaper on the walkway. She was a little surprised to see Alex's story on the front page—about how the police had named Mary Ellen a person of interest in the kidnapping—but he probably filed the story right after they parted. He had a way of making things happen. Next to the text was a picture of the girl.

"I'm here because of this." She showed it to Nick. He took the paper, studied the headline and the photo caption, frowning.

"We have a suspect, but what does this have to do with Jonah or the church? Did you come for prayer?"

"The girl—our suspect—is Jonah's niece."

Nick stared at her. "I didn't know Jonah had a niece. You're sure?"

Nodding, Carly took the paper back and turned for the door. "I just want to ask him if he has any idea where she might be."

Nick followed. "I have an appointment, so I know the combination to open the door. Jonah told me to just come in, that I'd find him in the prayer room."

She stopped her progress at the door, dying to ask what the appointment was for but biting her tongue. Standing to the side while Nick punched in the combination, Carly

realized that until now, no one knew who had taken A.J.
Mary Ellen's possible involvement was just discovered yesterday, so Jonah couldn't know. It would be a shock, and suddenly she was grateful she wouldn't be doing this by herself.
Nick was another cop as well as Jonah's friend. Putting aside
their personal issues, Carly realized that it was probably best
he'd be here when she broke the news.

They entered the quiet church, and Nick made certain
the door locked behind them. The prayer room was at the
other end of the sanctuary, so Carly started that way, noticing
Nick was keeping up with her. Was he moving better, or was
that her imagination?

They walked the long hallway in silence, and when they
reached the prayer room, Nick knocked.

"Come on in, Nick," Jonah called out.

Nick opened the door and motioned for Carly to go in first.

"Hey, Carly, what a surprise! But it's good to see you."
Jonah stood and stepped toward Carly to give her a hug.
"What made you decide to join Nick today?"

"I'm not here to join him. It's a coincidence we arrived
here at the same time. I wanted to ask you something."
Sucking in a breath to brace herself because she was not sure
what his reaction would be, she said, "I just wondered if you
knew where she might be." She opened the paper and showed
him the picture.

As he looked at the picture and read the text, all color
drained from Jonah's face.

He reached out and took the paper from her. "I can't believe it."

Carly let Jonah read. Nick pulled up a chair and sat, but Carly didn't sit until Jonah did. By then he held the paper down between his knees. He sighed, and it didn't escape Carly's notice how tired and defeated he looked. Normally larger than life, the pastor seemed smaller somehow, and she realized this news was heart wrenching.

"I'm sorry to spring it on you this way. I was really hoping you might have heard something from her."

He met her gaze with watery eyes. "I haven't seen Mary Ellen for ten years. Seeing her name connected with the kidnapping just now shocked me more than I thought possible." His sad expression touched Carly. "She was a little girl the last time I saw her, and there is no reason to think she'd even remember me."

"What happened, Jonah?" Nick asked in a quiet voice. "How did she end up involved in something like this?"

He dropped the paper and rubbed his face with both hands. Leaning back in the chair, he said, "Anita, my first wife, was killed in a car accident. I've shared that in church before."

Carly nodded. She remembered hearing the story. Anita and her sister were on their way home from a women's retreat in the mountains. The car hit some ice and left the road, crashing into a ravine, killing both women instantly.

Jonah continued. "When Anita and Lorna were killed, John, Lorna's husband, blamed God. Seeing as how he couldn't confront God, he turned all of his hurt and anger toward me. I had just been appointed head pastor here, and the church was growing. We'd just bought this property."

He paused, looked up, and stared past Carly. "John descended right away into the bottle. I heard he was neglecting Mary Ellen, but I could do nothing. John wouldn't let me near her. When news reached me that the county was going to remove her from his custody, I stepped up and said I would adopt her. We had been a close family before the accident. She used to call me Uncle JoJo, and I called her Little Bit." His voice broke, and it took a minute for him to regain composure.

"John went ballistic. We physically came to blows. He told me if I kept trying to take his daughter, I'd be sorry, said that she'd be better off with the county than with a deluded Bible-thumper like me. He swore he'd convince everyone who'd listen that I had molested her and couldn't be trusted. He said that he would convince her of the most vile and sick things, and he would make her believe that I had done those things to her."

Rawlings covered his face with his hands, then let them drop to his lap. "God help me, but he scared me. Even though I knew he planned to spread pure lies, all I could think about was what the allegations would do to me, true or not. I could say I was worried about what a fight like that would do to her, but that wouldn't be true. I was afraid for me."

"So you stepped back," Carly said.

He nodded. "I stepped back, withdrew my petition,

and left that little girl in the custody of the county." Tears flowed freely. "I didn't trust God to defeat the lies, and look what my weak faith has wrought. She kidnapped that baby. Is that what the county system did to the sweet little bit of a girl?"

Carly swallowed her own emotions. Her pastor's devastation moved her. "If it's any consolation, I don't think she's completely responsible. I think there's more going on here than we can see right now."

He wiped his eyes with the back of his hand. "What are you saying?"

Carly glanced at Nick, wondering if she should go into Harper's fears for Mary Ellen and tell Jonah about the trashed apartment. She decided that she wouldn't. "Just that we need to find her, not only to clear up the kidnapping, but because we think her life is in danger."

"Jonah, are there other relatives, anywhere else she might go?" Nick asked.

Rawlings shook his head. "Grandparents are all gone. John was an only child. I have, over the years, prayed for him and for Mary Ellen. I was never able to reconcile with John, and I'm sorry to say he's dead as well. Two years ago he died of lung cancer." He sucked in a breath. "Maybe I should have tried to find her then. Maybe this could have been avoided."

Carly digested this for a minute. "If you hear from her, you'll call?"

"Of course. And I'll pray she comes to me. I want to help her. I should have helped her ten years ago."

Carly thanked him and turned to leave.

"Wait," Nick said. "I'll walk you out. We can talk later if you want, Jonah."

"I don't mind keeping your appointment. I'd like you to stay for a bit, if that's okay."

"Of course. I'll be right back." He limped toward Carly, and they headed back the way they came. She glanced at the clock; she just had time to make it to OH when it opened.

"Where are you headed now?"

"Occupational health."

"I knew you wouldn't settle down and take it easy. I stopped by the hospital last night, but you'd already left. Mike told me your nose wasn't broken."

Did Mike tell you I left with Alex? "I didn't crash that hard, just hard enough to activate the air bag. I feel like I was smashed in the nose with a volleyball."

"I'm glad you feel better today. And about the order—I'm sorry, but you really were a sight with that bloody nose. You needed to see the doctor."

They'd reached the front door. As she turned to face him, Carly felt the pressure in her chest ease. *At least he's sorry.* "Thanks. I'll admit you were right," she conceded to herself as well. "I was just so pumped up. I felt like I was on the right trail and then a roadblock was thrown up in my face, literally and figuratively."

"You did a good job, the best possible under the circumstances. Now, don't strong-arm the doctor at occupational health. If he wants you to rest, rest, okay?"

Fat chance. "It's not so bad today. I don't think I'll have a problem."

"Well, maybe I'll see you later. After therapy I'll stop by the homicide office. I might be helping out on this, more than just working the tip line. Bye, Carly." He pushed the door open for her, and she returned his smile before heading to her car.

17

THE DOCTOR AT OCCUPATIONAL HEALTH spent five minutes with Carly, checking her nose, eyes, and reflexes. Concentrating on the doctor's words helped her keep from dwelling on Nick. He'd almost seemed normal today at church, and this changeling personality of his was maddening. What was he going to talk to Jonah about? Jonah used the word *appointment*—was Nick there for counseling? *Why should it matter to me?* She should leave it at that.

The doctor patted her shoulder to get her attention, and she shoved thoughts of Nick away to concentrate on getting this doctor's signature on her clearance letter.

He spoke broken English and was difficult to understand, but he signed her release, and for Carly that was all that mattered. As she left OH, she felt rejuvenated. She could still be a part of the investigation, and now they had more information to work with. Most importantly, they had a named suspect. What happened the day before had injected new life into the search for A.J.

Carly prayed that Mary Ellen was taking good care of Joe's son. It didn't escape her that Mary Ellen not only did not fit the FBI profile, but her motive for the kidnap wasn't even in the ballpark. *We don't even know her true motive, just Harper's speculation. Maybe if she saw that the police knew who she was, she'd give up and bring the baby back.*

The last stop on Carly's to-do list before the station was the hospital. As she made her way to Christy's room, she ran into Soto, the public information officer, on his way out. Carly knew he'd been tasked with developing a flyer, along with the job of keeping all the news agencies apprised of the investigation's progress. Judging from the thick file folder he had under his arm, he must have the flyer, she decided.

He studied her with raised eyebrows. "Should I ask?"

"I wish you wouldn't. You can use your imagination."

"Don't say that to someone who writes press releases for a living."

Carly smiled and pointed to the folder under his arm.

"I just ran them by Joe, and he approves." He pulled a couple out and gave them to Carly. "Leave these wherever you think they'll do the most good."

"Will do. Thanks." Carly stepped onto the elevator while Soto headed for the hospital exit. The flyer had a picture of

Mary Ellen Barber and an admonition that she was wanted for questioning in connection with the kidnapping. Carly knew they needed to be distributed, and normally the first place she'd drop something would be the church. But she didn't know if she wanted to bring them there now, not when she remembered the stricken look on Jonah's face.

At Christy's room, Carly tapped on the door, and Joe waved her in, motioning for her to be quiet. "Wow! What happened to you?" he exclaimed in a whisper.

Taken aback because Nelson obviously hadn't told him about her escapade the day before, she said, "I didn't see the truck. And I do have some news for you. Why don't we talk in the waiting area?"

He nodded and stepped out of the room. Once seated in the sedate waiting area, Carly told him all about her day and how and why she had crashed. When she finished, he was quiet for a minute. The only thing she'd left out was Andrea. She wondered if Joe knew that Andrea was taking some heat for A.J.'s kidnapping.

Finally Joe looked at her, eyes moist. "I knew there was more going on when Soto showed me the flyer. There's a lot more information there. But my brain isn't thinking clearly right now. You think this girl has my little boy, this runaway?"

"Yeah." Carly told Joe everything Harper had told her and about the connection to FBI surveillance.

He blew out a breath, fists clenched. "Sell my baby for twenty-five thousand dollars? Do you think the FBI is jerking us around? Maybe the guy they're watching is the buyer?"

"No, I don't think that. At first I was mad because they caused my crash, but I can't believe they wouldn't act if they knew who had A.J. or who made an offer like that for the baby."

He rubbed his face with both hands.

"How's Christy doing today?" Carly asked.

"She woke up and she's lucid. I can't say she's better, because as soon as she came around, I told her about A.J." He stood, shoved his hands in his pockets, and looked away, and it broke Carly's heart to see how hard it was for him to hold it together.

"Did they ever figure out what was wrong in the first place?"

He shook his head, then started to pace the waiting room. "They think it was a spider bite."

"A spider bite?"

"That's what the tests show she's most allergic to." His shoulders gave a tired shrug. "One of the doctors said her case will be a journal article. Frankly, I'm just glad she's okay, that she's getting better physically at least. I was so happy to see her open her eyes."

His voice was thick with emotion, and now Carly could feel her own tears forming.

"It broke my heart to tell her about our son. . . ." He trailed off and closed his eyes. "I've hurt so much the last couple of days that now I'm numb. This girl who has my little boy . . . do you think he's okay?" The last question was a whisper as tears rolled silently down Joe's cheeks.

Nodding, Carly stood next to him and took his hand in

hers, unable to speak. *Lord, please help us find this baby, and please keep him safe until we do* was all she could pray, over and over.

• • •

"Good morning, Officer Raccoon." Harris smiled at Carly from his desk. Leaning on the corner of his desk was Parker from vice. He returned Carly's hello. "You've been cleared?" Harris asked.

Carly waved the pink occupational health clearance before handing it to Sergeant Nelson. "Here's the proof."

"Thanks." Nelson took the form while Carly sat down next to Pete's desk.

"By the way, I just talked to Jonah Rawlings, Mary Ellen's uncle and the only family member I could find in the paperwork. He hasn't heard from her but will call if she contacts him."

"Good work," Nelson said. "I was going to head over there. File a follow-up about your talk."

"Will do." She wondered if Parker had something to do with the case, but she directed her question to Pete. "Any more information from the feds? Did Wiley get anything more out of Harper?" Carly asked, noticing that he looked like he'd slept in his clothes. He'd likely been working into the wee hours of the morning.

"A little. Harper says he didn't mention that he had keys belonging to his employer because they were still on his key ring—the key ring with his car keys, which were in the car and not on his person when you arrested him. He claims to be so worried about Mary Ellen, he can't think straight."

"Did he say why they are so important to his employer?"

"No, he didn't. But even without that information, Wiley was a big help. You know, when the feds set up surveillance, they are meticulous and thorough; they want to be certain they do things by the book and collect enough evidence to support a conviction. That's why they're so territorial. Wiley got a little bit out of the ASAC about the nature of the investigation, that it has something to do with smuggling, but there's no reason to believe A.J.'s kidnapping is in any way related."

Nelson shrugged. "They did reassure us they are watching Grant's employer."

"Gee, that makes me feel better." Carly clicked her teeth and sat back in the chair. "But I think I can put two and two together." She looked at Harris. "Did you get my message about Caswell and Sperry?"

Harris smiled and glanced at Nelson, who seemed to struggle to hide a grin. "You think their target is Sperry?"

Carly gave an exaggerated nod. "Yeah, and so do you guys. I always thought that guy was slimy. I think he wanted to be a reserve so he would learn how cops work in order to fool them."

Sperry's poster child status for the reserve officer corps had ended when Sperry's teenage son was arrested as one of the suspects in a brutal gang rape. Sperry was caught in reserve uniform trying to access and alter evidence in the case.

"Uh-huh." Harris gestured toward Parker. "That's why

we let this grungy-looking guy in the office. He was part of the team that investigated Sperry when he got into trouble here in Las Playas."

Parker snorted. But he was grungy. His wispy blond hair was longer than Carly's, hitting almost between his shoulder blades. His beat-up tennis shoes were filthy, and his jeans and T-shirt were holey. Undercover vice.

"I'm a working stiff just like you guys," Parker said. "And I know Harper; he used to be a snitch of mine. He couldn't help me with that case back then, but I happen to know he does work for Conrad Sperry from time to time. He also likes to gamble at a card club over on the west side. It doesn't surprise me that he racked up big debts."

"Would he mastermind the theft of a baby on his own?" Carly asked.

Parker hiked a shoulder. "He's not the sharpest knife in the drawer, but he's an opportunist. If he thought he could get away with something like that and it would make him money, he'd go for it. But someone would have to put the idea in his head."

"Is it possible the people he owes put it in his head, and he was misdirecting us by implicating his employer?"

"That's too complicated a plot for him. But just to be sure, early this morning, vice raided the card club and talked to the manager who holds Harper's tab. When he found out we were asking about the kidnapping, he was happy to talk to us. He admitted sending some guys to rough up the girl, but he swears he never told Harper to snatch anyone. I believe him. That kind of crime is way over his head. But he could have Harper hurt in county jail if he wanted to."

"That leaves us with Sperry wanting the baby," Carly said.

"Why would Sperry want a baby?" Harris asked. Parker gave Carly an inquiring look.

"It just wouldn't surprise me that he'd set up the sale of a baby. I never understood why so many people thought Sperry was a noble soul. He struck me as the worst kind of used-car salesman." Carly saw the coffeepot was full and poured herself a cup. "According to Trejo, Caswell got him acquitted."

Parker nodded. "Yeah, coincidence that—Sperry being Caswell's star client. Actually, Caswell worked a deal. The city had Sperry cold for tampering with evidence, but Sperry filed a countersuit alleging harassment. City attorneys wanted it all to go away, and they came to an agreement. Conrad quit the reserves and dropped the suit, so no harm, no foul. But while Caswell saved Daddy, the kid went down for rape. He's still in prison."

"I remember, but I thought Sperry left Las Playas after that."

"He did. Sold most of his businesses here—a couple of car washes and some commercial property—and moved to Temecula, I think. But he still owns some property here. The building Harper told you he and Mary Ellen live in is Sperry's."

"That's interesting." Carly sipped her coffee. "The feds say Mary Ellen wasn't even on their radar. Maybe it's possible that Mary Ellen is not involved with Sperry and the search was only related to Harper."

Parker cocked his head. "I didn't even know Harper had a girlfriend. If the feds don't know anything about her, I doubt she works for Sperry."

"But Sperry being the subject of the federal investigation is a no-brainer," Pete said. "He went right rudder after his kid went down. He's had a lot more legal trouble since he left. I live in Temecula, and he's in the paper every other week for something or other. He still owns a lot of commercial property in Riverside County. I think high-dollar real estate is how he makes his money now. Caswell covers him like a blanket."

"Word on the street is that Sperry always flirted with the dark side. It was a pretense that he was solid gold when he was a reserve. But after his kid's arrest, he seems to have dropped all the masks. He's working on becoming a crime lord," Parker said. "He really nurses a grudge over his son being arrested. He thinks the whole case was trumped up by people jealous of the kid because his dad was wealthy."

"Wait," Pete said. "His moron son taped the whole crime."

"Don't confuse him with facts. Anyway, ever since then, he tells people how much he hates cops, thinks they're all stupid. He's thought to be involved in smuggling drugs and people up here from Mexico, but other than rumors about him loan-sharking in Las Playas—" the vice cop held his hands out, palms up—"we've got nada solid on the guy in our jurisdiction."

Carly blew out a breath. "At least we have a picture and a name for the baby snatcher. She won't be able to hide. But I admit, I don't get how taking a baby fits in with all this. And for only twenty-five thousand dollars?"

"I talked to Harper, hoped maybe he'd give me some more info since he used to be a snitch, but he didn't say anything different to me than he said to you," Parker said. "He's convinced Mary Ellen took the baby to sell it, but I agree with you. Twenty-five K for such a risk would be chump change to Sperry or Caswell."

Pete leaned back and rubbed his stubbled chin. "Something else is working here. We have to find out what it is. Mary Ellen is our best lead. We've got a warrant in the system and a BOLO has been broadcast all over Southern California."

"Is Harper still here?" Carly asked.

"Yeah, we arraigned him and then made arrangements for him to stay here rather than be sent to county. We couldn't get a no-bail hold on him, and the arraignment judge thought the million-dollar tab set by bail deviation was excessive, but I doubt anyone will post the lower hundred-thousand-dollar tab. Just in case, I asked the jail to notify us if anyone does post bail."

"Do you mind if I go talk to him again?"

Pete shrugged. "No, why?"

"I want to clarify the issue of the keys. Why they're so important to Sperry and what they open. Thanks for your help, Parker."

"No problem." He gestured with a chin-up motion to Nelson. "If you need grungy for anything, you know who to call."

JANICE CANTORE || 183

Carly smiled as Parker left and Nelson rolled his eyes. She left her gun with Pete and took the elevator up to the jail, fielding questions about her black eyes from everyone she passed.

"Hey, Johnston," she greeted the jail supervisor on duty. "Can you bring Harper to an interview room for me?"

"Harper?" Johnston scrunched his brows in confusion.

"Yeah. Stanley Harper, the burglar? He was supposed to be in isolation."

Johnston pulled his status clipboard and flipped through some papers. "Here he is." He pulled a paper off the board and handed it to Carly. "Someone posted bail half an hour ago."

"Bailed out? By who?"

"You have to ask the front desk," Johnston said to Carly's back—she was busy pounding the elevator call button.

18

"GARY!" CARLY JOGGED, breathless, into the business desk area. "Who posted bail for Stanley Harper?"

Gary looked up from the report he was filing. "Hey, I'm glad to see you. Wow, nice eye makeup. I wanted to tell you Harper got out, and it wasn't that jerk from the other day." He got up from his chair and walked over to the bail log. "It was Ace Bail Bonds." He showed Carly the log. "I asked him if the money came from that attorney and he wouldn't say. He left the bond and told me to send Harper to his office; a ride would be waiting there for him."

"Thanks. Is that the place over on Elm?"

"Yep. It just happened; I doubt he's walked all the way to the bond office yet."

Carly left the business desk and took the stairs back to homicide. "Sergeant Nelson, someone bailed Harper. He's gone."

Nelson stood. "What? Who?"

Carly explained what she knew, and the sergeant muttered a curse before picking up the phone.

Carly jogged back to Pete's desk and gathered her gun belt.

"The jail was supposed to notify us if anyone showed interest in bailing him out." Pete shook his head in disgust. "How long ago did he leave?"

"About thirty minutes, I guess," Carly said as she hooked her gun belt on. She and Pete turned in surprise as Nelson read the jail the riot act and then slammed down the phone.

He looked at Carly. "They say there was no communication at shift change, so they didn't know they were supposed to tell us. Carly, go see if you can find him—or at least find out if it was Caswell who posted the money for the bond."

"On my way." Carly took the stairs down and almost ran into Nick at the back door.

"Whoa, where's the fire?" He smiled warmly, and like always, her heart did a flip-flop. "I guess OH cleared you," he observed before Carly could collect herself and say hello.

"Yeah, they said I'm fine."

"Good. What do you have going?"

"Someone bailed Harper out. I'm going to try and find him."

"The guy who sent you over to the west side yesterday? Want some company?"

Carly knew her face registered surprise. "Are you cleared to work the field?"

"I'm cleared to assist in this investigation. I won't slow you down." He jerked away from her and scanned the lot, shoulders stiff while he leaned on his cane. Carly rolled her eyes behind his back and slapped her thigh with her palm. *What did I say?*

"I didn't mean it that way." She stepped even with him. "You're wearing plainclothes. I just . . . well, I thought they wanted you to stay at a desk."

"I'm cleared for some fieldwork and I'm armed." He moved his coat to show his shoulder holster. "They don't think I'm totally disabled." He started down the back steps.

"I don't think so either!" She raised her voice and immediately regretted it.

Two officers coming in from the field looked at the pair curiously.

Nick faced her. The warmth in his eyes faded, replaced by anger. "Look, we have a job to do. Let's get a car and go to work and forget all this other nonsense."

"Fine." Carly bit her lip and stepped past him. She saw a car marked for homicide and moved across the parking lot quickly. She was in the driver's seat with the key in the ignition before Nick opened the passenger door. It took him a minute to slide into the seat and get comfortable.

Carly started the car and headed for Ace Bail Bonds. Her knuckles were white on the steering wheel. The silence in the car grated on her nerves like fingernails on a blackboard.

A couple of hours ago they were allies with Jonah, and now they were frenemies. *This has to be resolved, but—God, help me—I don't know how to resolve it.*

Ace Bail Bonds occupied a dingy office in an old section of downtown Las Playas untouched by redevelopment. The previous mayor of the city had worked hard to redevelop all of the downtown area with remarkable success. Only isolated pockets of old, unrestored buildings still existed.

Carly parked in front, in the red, and got out of the car. It took resolve not to slam the door and storm into the office, leaving Nick in the wake of her anger and frustration. Instead she took a deep breath, hitched up her gun belt, and walked around the rear of the car to the sidewalk. Nick was out and starting for the door. Carly fell into step beside him, careful to match his pace.

The bondsman was a big, thickly built man with long hair tied neatly into a ponytail. Carly never liked dealing with bondsmen. They were a necessary evil, but in her mind they were cowboys, one step removed from being on the other side of the bail bond. She let Nick do the talking.

"I understand you posted bond for Stanley Harper." Nick flipped out his badge and ID.

"Yeah, I did. It was a big bond, nice payoff for a day's work. What can I do for you?" The man spoke with his mouth full. A large, sloppy hamburger in his hand dripped grease onto his desk.

"Who put up the money?"

The bondsman put his hamburger down, wiped his

hands on his jeans, and turned to grab a file. "That would be Unique Imports Incorporated." He set the file down and returned to his dinner. "Is there a problem?"

"A business posted bail?" Carly asked.

"Yep. Apparently it was Harper's employer, and they wanted him back at work. This was all arranged by our office in Riverside." He stood with his hands on his hips. "Anyway, on the phone they told me to have Harper wait here and someone would be here to give him a ride. Harper showed up, but the driver never did. This Harper's not going to skip on me, is he?"

"No telling." Nick shrugged and looked at Carly as if to ask if she had any more questions.

"How long ago did Harper leave here?" she asked.

"'Bout ten or fifteen minutes. He said he had to be somewhere and couldn't wait for a ride. The bond was valid. I had no cause to hold him." He sat back down and took a huge bite of the burger, grease running down his chin.

Carly and Nick thanked him and left.

Once in the car, if the frigid atmosphere still existed, Carly was oblivious. Her mind was running in a thousand different directions.

"You were expecting Caswell to have posted bail?" Nick asked.

"Yeah, I was kind of working on a theory. This info blows it. At least I think it does. We'll have to find out how Unique Imports fits into things. When I asked Harper his employer in booking, he said unemployed. Later, when he was spilling his guts, he said he didn't want to tell me who his employer was." She started the car.

Nick put a hand on her wrist. "What's your theory, and where are we going?"

"We're going to the apartment Harper shared with Mary Ellen because I think that's where he'll go. As far as my theory goes—" she took a deep breath—"let me work on it a little more. It's foggy."

"Okay. Let's go, then." He slid back into the old Nick.

Carly started to say something about his mood swings but thought better of it. *I can't trust myself to say something that won't start a fight.*

"If Harper's on foot," Carly thought out loud, "unless he's jogging, it will probably take him twenty or thirty minutes. Keep an eye out. He's thin, looks like a tweaker." She drove the car along the most direct route to the apartment and prayed her hunch was right.

The streets were teeming with busy workday traffic. Carly chafed at the delay, reminded of one of the many good reasons she liked working graveyard. *At least it's not hot today. It's actually beautiful outside. I hope that's something that will work in our favor.*

"There are a lot of people out." Nick scanned his side of the street. "He might be able to blend in."

Carly's eyes continually roamed the landscape on her side.

They were westbound on Fifth Street, close to Mary Ellen's, when their vigilance was rewarded.

"I see him." Carly pointed to Nick's side of the street, in front of them.

Harper had just come out of a corner liquor store. Carly saw a bag in his right hand. They were still half a block behind him. He was also traveling westbound and waiting at the corner for the light to change so he could cross the street.

"I won't be able to get over to him until after the light changes."

"I'll keep an eye on him."

Carly was stuck in the middle lane of a one-way street. She activated the rear ambers on the light bar, hoping it would clue motorists in to the fact that she needed to get over. She didn't want to spook Harper. The last thing she wanted was a foot pursuit.

The signal turned green for westbound traffic and cars moved forward, but the lane to Carly's right, the lane she wanted to move to, stopped for Harper to cross Magnolia. Several things happened in front of them so quickly Carly wasn't sure she could remember the sequence exactly.

Harper reached the middle of Magnolia, and the lane Carly was trying to change to inched forward. She was looking over her right shoulder when Nick yelled.

"No!"

Tires screeched, and Carly jerked forward in time to see a southbound pickup truck career into the crosswalk and slam into Harper.

The burglar flew into the air. The truck never slowed as it turned right, onto Fifth Street, accelerating away into westbound traffic. The sound of cracking glass, blaring horns, and scraping steel split the air as the truck sideswiped two cars while it fled.

The final thud of Harper hitting the hood of another car reverberated down the street before he rolled off onto the pavement.

19

CARLY HIT THE SIREN, and a path cleared to the body. She started
to grab the radio mike, but Nick beat her to it.

"I've got it. Check him out!"

"You saw the driver?" Carly knew the profile she'd seen
of the pickup's driver would be branded in her memory. She
also knew she'd seen him before. He was Grant, the bald man
who had run from Mary Ellen's apartment.

"Enough to describe him," Nick said. "Go."

She leaped from the car. Harper's broken body lay in the
middle of the intersection. The pickup truck had disappeared
onto the freeway. Several people got out of their cars to try to
help the injured man, but Carly waved them back. The last
thing she needed was for someone else to get hurt.

Kneeling down, Carly knew it was too late. Harper had

landed awkwardly, and his head lolled at an unnatural angle. The bag of goods he'd just purchased lay flattened on the street a few feet away.

She could hear Nick's voice on her handheld radio explaining the situation, describing the driver of the pickup—a male white, bald with sparse facial hair—and asking for help. Unfortunately, nothing would help Stanley Harper. She did her best to direct traffic and people away from him until more units arrived. The woman whose hood the body had bounced off of was distraught. It took Carly several minutes to convince her to pull off to the side and stay inside her car to wait for paramedics.

"He dead?" Nick asked, limping around to help.

Carly nodded. "He didn't have a chance."

Nick moved away to lay down flares. Once he'd shut down several lanes of traffic, he walked back to Carly. "That wasn't an accident."

"Nope, I didn't think so either."

Screaming sirens stifled the conversation. Fire trucks and assisting police units crowded the scene. Paramedics double-checked Harper and then covered him with a yellow tarp. Carly and Nick talked to the beat units who would handle the crash, gave them all the information they could. Once the scene was in capable hands, they returned to their police car. The beat unit would file the report. Carly wanted to talk to Trejo.

"Do you mind if we make a stop before we go back to the station?" Carly asked.

"Where?"

"The *Messenger*. I want to ask Alex Trejo about Unique Imports."

"You think a reporter can help us with this case?"

"I know he wrote an article on Thomas Caswell a couple of years ago. He might know if there is a connection to this business."

"Go ahead," Nick said and then was quiet as Carly extricated the vehicle from the tangle of police cars and flares. "You and Trejo are getting pretty tight, aren't you?" he asked after a few minutes.

Carly turned to find him watching her, a blank expression on his face. "I like Alex. He's been a good friend." *Especially now, since you and Andrea have shut me out.*

"Is he a Christian?"

"No, why?" Bewildered, Carly found herself slowing, concentrating more on Nick than her driving.

"You shouldn't be getting involved with someone who's not a Christian. I mean, not romantically. He could pull you away from the church, weaken your relationship—"

"What?" Carly cut him off, jerking the car to a stop in front of the *Las Playas Messenger* building. She slammed the car into park and turned to face Nick. All the anger and frustration she'd kept on the back burner whooshed out like water from an unkinked hose. "You have the nerve to lecture me about what might pull me away from the church? I think you need to look in the mirror. I love you, but for the last month you've treated me like an unwanted groupie. You won't give me the benefit of the doubt that I honestly don't care if you're a cop or not, if you walk right or not. All you toss me is some self-serving drivel about how you don't want to be a burden. You aren't being honest with yourself or me. And Alex, heathen that he is, has been honest and he's been supportive. Why don't you practice what you preach before you tell me what I should or shouldn't do!"

Carly was breathless when she finished and astonished at the words and emotion that came out of her. But not sorry. No, not sorry.

They stared at one another as her heart rate slowly returned to normal. Nick looked away first.

"I don't know what to say. I—"

A rap on the roof of the car interrupted him. They both looked up guiltily. Alex smiled at them from the sidewalk. Carly welcomed the interruption. She turned the car off and got out, sweat on her brow in spite of the fact that she'd been sitting in air-conditioning.

"What's up? I was just heading over to the scene of a fatal traffic accident—do you guys know anything about it?" Alex asked.

As Nick also climbed out of the car, Carly didn't miss the glance Alex shot the two of them.

"Yeah, we were witnesses. Can we trade you information for information?" she asked.

He raised his eyebrows and tilted his head inquiringly. "I'm intrigued. What happened at the accident?" The reporter folded his arms across his chest, and Nick leaned against the passenger door.

Carly stood on the sidewalk next to Alex while she explained what had happened to Harper. Working to control her tone, she related clearly and concisely what she'd seen. The act helped to calm her. The blood slowly stopped pounding in her ears, and she felt drained and empty. Empty, that was, but for the ache in her heart. But the words needed to be said, and she wouldn't take them back. Now she hoped for strength to deal with the consequences.

"Purposely ran him down?" Alex asked when she finished. His eyes glowed at the prospect of front-page headlines.

"Yeah, but don't print that until we get some confirmation," Nick cautioned.

Trejo rubbed his chin and looked at Carly. She prayed her face was neutral. He shrugged with reluctant concession. "So what can I do for you, then?"

"What can you tell us about Unique Imports Incorporated?" she said.

"Off the top of my head, not much. The name rings a bell. . . . I think it belongs to Conrad Sperry."

"Is it located in Riverside?"

"I'd have to check my notes. Do you need me to make sure?"

"No, that's okay," Nick said. "We have to go back to the station now; we'll be able to find out there."

"We'll send you a release about the accident," Carly added.

Alex nodded but didn't turn to leave. "Is everything okay?" he asked as he continued to study Carly.

Carly felt Nick's attention on her also, and she didn't want to look at him. "Yeah," she said, walking around to the driver's side car door. "As okay as it can be, considering another day has gone by and A.J. is still missing."

She heard Nick thank Alex before he shut the car door. And she noticed Alex in the rearview mirror watching them as they drove away. Silence dominated the ride back to the station.

20

"HIGHWAY PATROL FOUND A TRUCK matching the description of the one you say hit Harper." Harris hung up the phone as Carly and Nick walked into the office. It had been a little over two hours since the crash.

"That was quick. Where?" Nick asked. He sat next to Pete's desk while Carly walked to the coffeemaker and poured herself a cup. She took a deep gulp, wishing it were hot enough to scald her mouth and give her something different to think about, but it wasn't.

"Abandoned off the 91 freeway in Corona. It was still hot and smoking, obviously recently left. It was stolen from that same area sometime last night. They're trying to pick up the trail of the driver now."

"There's no doubt in my mind that the truck accelerated into Harper. And Carly is certain it was the same man who was in Mary Ellen's apartment, right?" Nick looked to Carly, who nodded in agreement. She didn't trust herself to speak.

"Just our luck the feds weren't tailing him today," Harris said with a curse.

The two men began talking about the case. Harris called Nelson because the sergeant would have to contact the FBI. And since the FBI had been following Grant, they should know where to find him.

She found an empty desk at the other side of the office and called Joe. "How are you holding up?" she asked, happy her voice sounded normal.

"Okay, I guess. Christy is stronger. The toxin that caused her reaction has been neutralized and is out of her system. She was up and walking today. The doctor says he'll release her tomorrow." He paused, and Carly heard him take a deep breath. "I don't look forward to taking her home to face an empty nursery."

Carly tried to encourage him, telling him about Harper being bailed out and the connection to Conrad Sperry. But as she hung up, she knew her words rang hollow. They were even further away from finding A.J. because their only lead was dead. Her phone buzzed and she saw she had a text from Alex. She called his number.

"What's up?" she asked.

"I'll tell you everything I know about Unique Imports, but first you tell me something: are you really okay?"

"Alex . . ." Carly drew in a deep breath and pushed on her vest. With raw emotions ready to burst forth, she found the restrictive Kevlar a comfort. "Please, I don't want to talk about me right now. What's the story on the business?"

"All right." He paused. "It is owned by Conrad Sperry."

"What do they import?"

"Says here they specialize in importing unique and difficult-to-find items. Guess that could be just about anything."

"Where is the business?"

"Mailing address is in Riverside, but I don't have a physical address."

"That's why the bond was posted at the Riverside office of Ace Bail Bonds."

"Shouldn't be difficult for an awesome police officer to find a physical address and an excuse to visit the business." She could hear the smile in his voice, and it made her feel somewhat better.

"Thanks. I appreciate the information."

"No problem. And if you ever need to talk, you know where to find me."

"Thanks."

"I'm always here for you; remember that."

"I know, and thanks again." Carly put the phone down and looked up to see Nick standing by the desk.

"Who was that?"

"Alex, confirming that Unique Imports belongs to Sperry."

Nick nodded. "My bet is that the feds have a lot more information about this, and we need to get it out of them."

"Nelson will get back to me as soon as he talks to the feds," Pete said. "He told me to get started on the probable cause for an arrest warrant and a search warrant."

"I can help with that." Nick turned back to Harris. "I've written my share. Then Carly and I can head out to Riverside."

"Carly and I." The words branded Carly. She excused herself to go to the restroom. Instead of using the one on the third floor, Carly bounded up the stairs and escaped to the quieter locker room. The tears began to fall as soon as the door closed. She wiped them away and opened her locker. Taking off her gun belt, she hung it up and took down a small pocket Bible from the top shelf. Sniffling, she grabbed some paper towels and went to the small sleeping room at the end of the locker area. It was empty, so she turned the light on, closed the door, and sat down.

The tears flowed freely at first, and she let them. This ache was different from the ache she'd felt when she'd learned about Nick's infidelity. Then, the burn was raw and open but diluted somewhat with anger. This was more like what she'd felt on the jetty—agonizing hurt and profound loss. *I was so certain it was right to be back with Nick. I believed we were both changed for the better and that our life together would be blessed. What went so wrong?*

When the tears stopped, Carly wiped her face, blew her nose, and opened the small book. Relatively new to the faith, she stumbled around at first. But after a bit, she settled down to read her favorite psalms. The verses she often referred to were Psalm 27:14, 52:8-9, and 91:2. She read all three passages, then focused on the verse from Psalm 91: "I will say of the Lord, 'He is my refuge and my fortress; My God, in Him I will trust.'"

She read and prayed a lot, closing the book after half an hour, feeling better, calmer, and somewhat stronger. She could hear her phone beeping from her locker and knew it was probably Nick wondering what happened to her. *Well, I can deal with him now,* she thought as she stood and stretched. After washing her face, she hooked her belt back on and took the elevator down to homicide.

"Everything okay?" Nick asked when she entered the office.

"Fine. I just needed to do some thinking. Sorry to leave you to do all the work alone. What have you got?"

For a second Nick studied her, and she wondered if he'd press the issue. He didn't.

Nick held up the information he'd written on a yellow legal pad. "Learned a lot about Unique Imports from Agent Wiley. It's not a working business right now, but it used to be owned and operated by Sperry's son."

"The rapist?"

"Yeah. Apparently he ran it out of his home. But it's been idle since the kid went to prison and hasn't been part of the federal investigation. Grant is using the house as his place of residence, says he rents. We have their blessing to go and arrest him. I notified the Riverside County sheriff that we're coming out there, and someone will meet us. Pete is working

on getting a warrant to search the place, which the feds have
made easy. They're fine with us taking down Grant since they
don't believe it will affect their case on the big boss. When it's
ready, Pete will fax the warrant to Riverside."

"You've been busy." Carly was impressed.

Nick smiled. "A lot is at stake. I hope this is the right track
and we find A.J. . . . or at the very least a clue that will lead
us to him. Ready to go?"

"Sure." *As ready as I'll ever be.*

21

CARLY WAS VAGUELY FAMILIAR with Riverside County. The area was largely rural, but portions had exploded with new housing developments in recent years. Cops like Harris moved out there to buy large, new, relatively inexpensive homes. In the past, she'd been out there many times for parties at different officers' houses, often with Nick.

"I never understood how people could move so far away from work and then spend hours commuting on this freeway every day," she said as she headed east on Highway 91. She was simply making conversation. By the time she and Nick hit the freeway, it was after noon. The drive would take an hour and a half at the very least. She wished something would make it go faster.

"We're in agreement there," Nick said. "I hate this stretch of road. Luckily, the address for Unique Imports is in the Wildomar/Menifee area. That's a little closer than going all the way to Temecula. I'll call as we get closer, but the deputy said someone would meet us on Bundy Canyon Road, which is off the 15 freeway. They'll accompany us to the Unique Imports address."

Carly nodded but said nothing. She was driving at Nick's request. His hip tended to cramp if he had to sit for long periods of time and couldn't move freely, so he'd chosen shotgun. Carly didn't care for the 91 freeway any more than Nick and couldn't help but remember the times they'd driven it in happy circumstances. They were almost to the transition for the 15 before Nick spoke up again.

"So do you want to tell me what you were thinking about when you left the homicide office?" he asked as traffic slowed to a crawl before they could take the ramp for the 15.

"I needed to get some things straight in my mind, that's all. This hasn't been a very good week."

"Partly because of me, huh?"

She glanced sideways. "Well, Christy and A.J. are a big part of it, but yeah, you've caused a huge knot of angst. I'm not going to apologize for what I said earlier, either."

"I'm not asking you to. You were right. I've been doing a lot of thinking myself." He shifted in his seat. "I visited Jonah this morning hoping he could help me with my thinking."

"Did he?"

"He pointed me to Scripture. What you said earlier, I wish

you'd said it a month ago. For someone who tried to convince you to reconcile because I'm a Christian now, I haven't been acting very Christian. I've been stupid and drowning in self-pity. What you said at coffee the other day also hit the mark."

Carly quickly looked over at Nick. He was leaning against the door, turned her direction, watching her.

"Sounds as though your talk with Jonah was all about us."

"Not 100 percent, but we did take up a huge chunk, in spite of the issue with his niece. He was able to offer me some good advice. At least I hope you'll think it's good advice."

She swallowed and hit the brakes as the car in front of her came to a stop. "What kind of advice?" Traffic inched along.

"First, I do want to reconcile, even though I haven't acted that way lately. I don't have to tell you how very difficult it's been, struggling with this hip. That's no excuse to snap at you all the time, but it's the best I can do." He stopped and looked away. "I know it won't be easy getting back together and putting the past behind us, and I didn't want my immobility tossed into the mix. Would you agree to set up some counseling with Jonah? Something like premarital counseling?"

Carly nearly choked when Nick said *premarital*. She watched the slowing traffic ahead of her and chewed on her bottom lip, emotions churning. Was he moving toward remarriage? The question he asked said a lot without saying a lot. Was Nick being sincere, or was this a way to let her down gently and end with "Let's be friends"? She couldn't ask, not now, because what if he said they were over?

Again the fear was there that this was the end for her and

Nick. But she had to trust God that whatever this was, God's best would be in the outcome. "I don't mind counseling, but I'm tired of this roller coaster." She glanced his way. "I want things resolved, one way or the other. Do you think that's possible with counseling?"

Nick nodded. "Yeah, Carly. I think we can resolve things once and for all."

Traffic opened up as they sailed down the transition and onto the southbound 15. The Bundy Canyon Road exit was several miles down the road.

"Okay then, as soon as this case is over, let's call Jonah." She warmed to the idea of counseling, knowing they both needed to get a lot of baggage out into the open.

"Agreed, and thanks," Nick said as he pulled out his cell phone. "Thanks for sticking by me."

"There's no place else I'd rather be," she said, and she meant it. The pain and ache of earlier was gone, and as Carly looked out at the freeway stretching ahead, it was somehow brighter.

Nick made the call to the Riverside County sheriff's office, who said they were to turn right off the freeway and a patrol car would be waiting for them with hard copies of a search warrant for the business and an arrest warrant for Grant.

The area where they exited was tired and dirty. The gas station looked like one you'd see out in the middle of farm country on Interstate 5, worn and dusty from all the passing-through traffic. Past the station, on the other side of a vacant corner, there were some ramshackle houses on a street with no sidewalks. Carly saw the deputies' car waiting in the station parking lot on the right as soon as she made the turn from the freeway off-ramp. She pulled into the lot, and she and Nick got out to talk to the deputies, an older deputy with corporal stripes and a younger man with a shaved head whom Carly took to be a rookie.

"Hello." The older man identified himself as Deputy Gordon Rivers. He introduced his partner as Deputy Timothy Quan, and they shook hands all the way around. Rivers pointed to Quan. "He's got the warrants, so we're good to go."

Nick explained why they were there and what they were looking for. Carly knew he'd probably done this over the phone to the person who sent the deputies here, but most cops she knew always wanted to hear the information firsthand.

"I'm familiar with the area. I've worked it for about six years now." Deputy Rivers pointed up the road. "That area is still very rural, lots of manufactured homes on big lots and areas that used to be ranches. We used to have a problem with meth labs, but not so much since that law passed restricting the amount of cold medicine a person can buy."

Carly knew what he meant. A main component of meth was obtained by cooking down cold medication. But the cooker needed a large quantity of cold pills to make enough product. Severe limits on the sale of cold medication had slowed the home meth lab problem—at least temporarily.

Crooks usually needed a little bit of time to discover how to circumvent new laws.

"What problems do you see most up here now?" Carly asked.

"Some pot farms, maybe meth coming up from Mexico, and illegal immigrant smuggling. An hour from the border, we see a lot of that."

"Are you familiar with this particular property? Do you know Conrad Sperry?" Nick asked.

Rivers made a face. "Everyone out here knows that name, but I've never met the guy. I've had words with his attorney, Caswell. He handles anything that has to do with complaints against Sperry, cleans up all his messes. Sperry taunts us in subtle ways, makes sure we get the message that he's the biggest and baddest who does what he pleases because we're not smart enough to stop him. Please tell me you're onto something that will put him out of commission."

"Maybe. Does the name Isaac Grant mean anything to you?" Carly asked.

Rivers shook his head but hiked a thumb toward Quan.

The rook spoke up. "I know the name. I stopped him for speeding, wrote him a ticket. He told me five times he worked for Sperry. Said I'd lose my job because I wrote him a ticket."

Rivers grinned. "He wrote the ticket anyway and got an excellent on that training day. Now you want Grant for a homicide?"

"Yeah. If he's at Unique Imports, he goes to jail. But first and foremost we need to find out what he knows about a missing baby."

"Fair enough." Rivers nodded. "Follow us up. We'll be there in about twenty minutes."

They followed Rivers and Quan down a residential road lined with manufactured homes—some with thin, sagging fences, some with no fences. No more traffic lights, only stop signs now and again at intersections. They crossed an intersection, and on the right, like a mirage, a brand-new housing development sprang up, houses shiny and clean. On the other side of the street, the small, older houses just looked that much shabbier.

The housing development ended as abruptly as it had started, and they began to pass bigger properties, some with horses. The houses stayed small and modest, but the lots got bigger and more spread out as they journeyed up a winding canyon road. Soon, the area could no longer be called semi-rural. It was definitely rural, and civilization was behind them. The blunt hills showed evidence of past wildfires. Carly knew from the news that the area had its share. She always thought of most of Riverside County as desert because temps in the hundreds were not uncommon here in the summer. The combination of dry brush and high temps spelled fires out here. Summer in this part of Southern California was often called the season of shake and bake—earthquakes and hot weather.

Shortly, it seemed as if they were the only two vehicles on the road. No traffic followed, and none passed traveling the other way.

"This place is out in the boonies," Nick observed.

"Reminds me of terrain from an old spaghetti western. Did the feds say anything about how Grant might behave? Is he violent, cooperative?"

The deputies turned right onto a hard-packed dirt road, and Carly followed. Along the way they passed mounds of huge boulders.

"His rap sheet is full of nonviolent offenses—fraud, embezzlement, falsifying prescriptions, possession charges. They didn't think Grant would give us any trouble. But we just saw him run down Harper, so expect anything."

They bounced along the road for a few more minutes and passed a couple of places before they went through an area with nothing. Then they drove up a rise, and off to the right, Carly could see a structure.

"You know, the longer we drive out to the middle of nowhere, the more I'm thinking not only would this be a great place to hide just about anything; it would be the perfect place to hide a baby. No neighbors around to notice a new addition." Carly tapped the steering wheel and shook her head.

"That must be the place, but it doesn't look much like a business." Nick pointed to a small, faded blue home. As they got closer, it looked to Carly like a double-wide trailer.

"You said Sperry's son ran the business out of his house before his arrest."

"Yeah, and they can see anyone approaching for a mile." He looked at Carly and cocked an eyebrow. "Gives them plenty of time to hide or destroy evidence and prepare."

The rise leveled out, and the patrol car turned onto a road that led to the trailer. In contrast to the shabby house, the property was fenced and gated with a shiny new and sturdy-looking chain-link fence. A hefty chain and lock hung from the gate, but it stood open. She didn't miss the cameras mounted just inside the fence, apparently focused on who or what came up the drive. But still she thought it odd that nothing was locked. If they were hiding A.J., or anything for that matter, wouldn't they want to be securely locked in and possibly guarded?

She followed the deputies up the road without slowing. They again ascended a slight grade that leveled out as they reached the front of the house. Three vehicles were parked around the front: a panel van, a sedan up on blocks, and a small pickup.

The deputy parked behind the van, and Carly pulled up next to him. She, Nick, and Rivers stepped out and met behind the van. Quan was on the car radio, and Carly guessed he was informing dispatch of their status.

"This is the place," Rivers said.

"I wish we weren't so exposed." Carly pointed to the cars. "Counting the vehicles present, the chances are good Grant isn't alone. And don't you find it odd that the gate was wide open?"

Rivers arched a brow. "That looked like state-of-the-art video surveillance on those poles. Maybe the gate wasn't locked because they can see who's coming and prepare if need be. I'm more concerned about who's here, waiting for us.

Deputy Quan is running the vehicle plates. I want to know who they belong to before we go in."

"How long has he been on?" Nick asked.

Rivers smiled. "Six months. You know you're getting old when your trainee looks to you to be twelve. He's sharp; I trust him. How do you want to work this?"

Nick looked at Carly.

"I'd like to take the front," she said. "How about two in front, two to the back?"

Nick and Rivers both nodded.

Quan stepped out of the car. "No want or warrant on any of the vehicles. The van is registered to Unique Imports, the little pickup to Isaac Grant, and the one on blocks is application in process."

Rivers said, "Be nice if the big man himself were here." He pointed at Nick. "How about you and I take the back. Tim, you and Officer Edwards make contact."

Carly would have rather been with Nick, but she knew what Rivers was doing. He wanted the rook to get some experience without taking things over himself. And each team would need a radio.

She nodded. "We'll give you a few minutes to get back there before we actually knock."

Carly and Quan started for the front door while Nick and Rivers went right to go around to the back. Carly noted with a wince that Nick had left his cane in the car. He limped but kept up with Rivers. Biting her tongue, she concentrated on Quan and their mission.

They approached the porch cautiously. Carly watched the windows, which were all shaded. She saw no movement, no one pulling a shade open to look out at their approach.

They walked up the four steps to the front door. Deputy Quan took up a position on the right side while Carly stood to the left of the door. She counted to ten and was certain Nick and Rivers were in position, then nodded to Quan. He took his nightstick from his belt and rapped the door firmly.

Carly leaned close to the house, and after a minute, just as Quan was about to knock again, she heard shuffling.

"Who is it?"

"Police, Mr. Grant. Open the door."

There was movement as the blinds were pulled back on Quan's side of the door. Carly couldn't tell if someone looked out, but if they did, they'd see Quan, and there was no mistaking the uniform. She waited a beat, but the door didn't open.

"Open up—now," Quan ordered.

Carly heard footsteps as if Grant was running away from the door.

"Get on the radio. Tell your partner—"

Boom! A loud blast from a shotgun cut her off mid-sentence. The shotgun round blew a hole in the front door. Carly was peppered with bits of wood. Instinctively she ducked and drew her weapon, while Quan hit the floor.

"I'm not going back to prison!" she heard a voice scream.

Boom! A second blast blew out the window where Quan had been standing a second ago and sent glass everywhere.

"You okay?" Carly yelled to Quan.

He held up a hand as he brushed glass away from his face. "I'm not hit." He rolled to his side and drew his weapon.

Carly heard more footsteps and yelling, and she realized the man with the shotgun was heading toward the back of the house, toward Nick. She stood up quickly and peeked into the hole in the front door, gun up on target. She saw the flash of a man's back, heard the crash of glass and Rivers's voice yell something and then the sounds of a struggle.

She grabbed the doorknob, but in spite of the shotgun blast, the lock still held. She kicked at the door and made the hole big enough to charge through. As she went through, she heard cursing. All she thought about was Nick in the back-yard facing a panicked man armed with a shotgun.

She sprinted toward the back, Quan on her heels. Through the living room, then the kitchen. The back door was in shreds. Rivers was on the floor, bleeding from the head, and the shotgun was next to him.

Carly looked out the back door, and there was Nick. He had his knee on Grant's back. One hand had firm control of Grant's hands, and the other was removing the handcuffs from his shoulder holster as he prepared to apply them. The relief that flooded through her cleared her head. But she knew they needed to be certain no one else was in the house before they could relax.

"You got him under control?" she called out to Nick, and he nodded, holding up four fingers for code 4. Turning back, she saw that Quan was checking on Rivers, who was conscious.

"I'm okay," Rivers said. "Sucker smacked me with the butt of the gun. Clear the house; don't worry about me."

Carly nodded. She and Quan went through the place carefully, room by room. It was a sparsely furnished house. The only thing of interest Carly found was a box of shotgun shells and a wall safe that was open and empty. She found herself wondering what had been in it. In the back bedroom Quan got her attention.

"Look." He held up a half-used package of diapers.

Carly tore through every room again, but there was nothing else.

There was no A.J.

22

BY THE TIME Carly and Quan finished searching the house, Nick had brought Grant to the back porch and sat him down on the top stair. Rivers was holding a towel to his forehead. He told Carly he'd called for another unit to assist since he was pretty much out of commission.

"I heard the gunshots, and I was going to get the drop on him from behind," Rivers explained, "but he ran back through here like a tornado and caught me by surprise."

"Almost blew by me as well," Nick said, "but I caught him." He looked at Carly, and the light she saw in his eyes, confident fire she hadn't seen in a long time, made her fight back a smile. "Nothing in the house?"

"Just these." She held up the diapers and stepped to where Grant sat. He wore dirty jeans and smelled as if he had a transient relationship with the shower. "You're under arrest for murder. Do we add kidnapping to the charges?"

He looked away. "Talk to my lawyer."

Frustrated, she knelt down to speak at his level. "Look, you will be going to prison for running down Stanley Harper and shooting at us no matter what. I can ask for leniency, but not if you stonewall me with your lawyer." She got no reaction. "The baby. All I care about is the baby. Was he here?"

Grant ignored her.

A wave of fatigue washed over Carly. They were close—she knew it. But she couldn't shake the information out of him. She stood and paced the back porch. Then she noticed Nick in the backyard staring at something.

"What are you looking at?"

Hands on his hips, Nick turned, forehead wrinkled with a frown. "These vents." He pointed, and Carly followed his index finger to where he indicated. She saw blunt poles and took Nick's word that they were vents.

"There's something underground," Rivers said, taking the towel off his head, which had stopped bleeding. "An underground room, I'll bet." He motioned to Quan. "You see anything that might have been a trapdoor in the house?"

Quan shook his head. "We can tear up carpet if you want."

"I'll keep an eye on him." Rivers pointed to Grant. "You guys search the grounds. I'll bet dollars to donuts there's an underground room out here."

With renewed energy, Carly hopped off the porch. "What am I looking for? A trapdoor in the ground?"

"Or a room . . ." Nick stopped, and Carly followed his gaze off to the right, where two four-wheel ATVs were parked next to a shed.

They hurried over. The shed was padlocked.

"To do this by the book," Nick said, "we should get another warrant."

"What about the one we already have?" Quan asked. "Wouldn't this fall under that search warrant?"

"No, it's not specific enough. We didn't include outbuildings. Search conditions apply to Grant and what falls under his care and control." He pointed at the sullen prisoner. "I doubt he even has authority to give us consent to search."

"We can call—"

Carly cut the rookie off. "Exigency. A.J. could be underground, dying as we stand here talking. I'm willing to stand up in court and defend this search on those grounds." She held Nick's gaze and knew what he was thinking. If they found something incriminating and the search was thrown out as illegal, Grant, and probably Sperry, would skate. But she knew she had to take that chance. They'd found diapers. A.J. had been here.

Nick nodded. "I'll testify right next to you. Let's find a way in."

In a couple of minutes Quan came up with a crowbar. He and Nick destroyed the door and opened the shed. Inside they found a trapdoor and another lock.

"In for a penny, in for a pound," Nick muttered as he applied the crowbar to the second lock and it shrilly squeaked open. Carly jerked the door up and peered down a flight of stairs. She jumped when she saw a bruised and bloody face looking back at her.

Alex Trejo.

It wasn't until he spoke that Carly realized she'd been holding her breath.

"Edwards, I nominate you the patron saint of police beat reporters."

Carly looked at Nick and imagined the shock on his face mirrored her own. She took a step toward Alex. "There better be a good story behind what you're doing down here, Alex."

"Yeah, yeah, there is. I'm not alone. But first, you need to know—I saw the baby. I saw A.J."

23

CARLY ALMOST FROZE in shock when she stepped down to where Alex sat. The room was huge, and there were faces everywhere, peering at her in the low light emanating from recessed lights in the ceiling. Alex turned to the faces. *"No tengan miedo. Quiere ayudarlos."*

He looked back at Carly. "I told them not to be afraid of you, that you will help them."

"How did they get here?" Carly asked as she bent to untie Alex. His hands and feet were bound with thick rope.

"They were promised work and smuggled over the border in a truck. They're waiting for someone to come and take them to work."

In spite of the bruises, Carly could see the pity on Alex's face.

"I've read stories about Mexicans dying because they're packed into trailers and hauled up here. I think that's how they got here. Transported like cattle."

"We'll see they're treated well, given medical attention if they need it. But right now I need to get you out of here. I want to hear about A.J."

Alex nodded and rubbed his wrists when they were free. *"Esperen con calma,"* he said to the group. *"Pronto vendrán a ayudarlos."* Wait. Help will be here soon.

He and Carly went back up the stairs. As they climbed out of the hole and stepped into the backyard, two Riverside County patrol cars pulled around the house and came to a stop. Quan waved the deputies over.

Carly took Alex to the house, past Rivers still watching Grant on the back porch, while Nick and Quan explained to the assisting deputies what was going on and about the occupants of the cellar. Carly didn't miss the shock on a couple of the new faces, and she knew there'd be a huddle to determine how to handle the can of worms that had just opened. Her focus now was on what Alex had said.

"Tell me about A.J."

"He was here with the girl, Mary Ellen." The urgency in Alex's voice had Carly on edge. "She stole my car and left. You need to get my license plate out there. You need to start looking for my car and you'll find the baby."

Carly took down the plate number and gave it to Rivers

to put out over the air. She then called Nelson and told him what Alex had told her. When she finished making all the notifications she could make, she returned to Alex, who sat at the kitchen table holding ice to the side of his face.

A glance into the backyard made Carly happy that this was not her jurisdiction. More deputies had arrived, but they were reluctant to bring the people up from the hole because they didn't know what to do with them once they were out. She'd heard some chatter on Rivers's radio and knew that two Spanish-speaking deputies had gone down to determine the health and attitude of the people, but for the most part the deputies were unsure how to proceed. It just wasn't a situation any of them had handled before. She'd also heard that agents from border patrol and Immigration and Customs Enforcement were on the way.

"How many of them are down there?" she asked Alex.

"Thirty-five men, women, and children. They told me they came up from Mexico sometime night before last and they've been down in that hole ever since. There's one toilet down there, and all they've had to eat is trail mix and bottled water. Good thing I speak Spanish." He set the ice down and regarded her. "You better let me start from the beginning or none of this will make sense."

Carly nodded and joined him at the table. "You'll start with what you're doing here, I hope."

"Yeah. I found the address through a web search—I was driving out here when I talked to you on the phone. I decided there was a story here and I wanted it. Anyway, when I got to the gate and found it locked tight, I wasn't sure what would get me in. I was going to try and pick it when that bald guy came tooling down to the gate on an ATV, holding a shotgun."

"Yeah, I'm familiar with his shotgun."

"Anyway, I thought on my feet. I told him I'd been sent by Thomas Caswell to pick up the girl and the baby."

"What?"

Trejo smiled sheepishly. "Well, I figured that one statement would let me know right away if he had the baby. I thought he bought it, since he opened the gate and told me to follow him up."

"Is that when you saw Mary Ellen and A.J.?"

"He took me right to them. They were locked in a bedroom in the house, and the baby looked fine—happy and healthy."

Carly sat back and digested this information, feeling relief and frustration at the same time. If only they'd gotten here sooner.

"Like I said, I thought he bought my story. I was talking to the girl, telling her to leave with me, when *wham*, something hit me on the back of the head."

He put a hand on the spot and winced. "I've got a knot there. Next thing I know, I'm tied up and he's dragging me down to the cellar. He smacked me around for a bit, wanted to know what I was up to. I told him the truth: I was a reporter and the police were on the way. He freaked out and left me down there with the illegals. It must have been about ten minutes later he came back down with the shotgun and I thought I was dead. He was hysterical, said the girl had left—she'd raided the safe, taken my car, and left—and he was beside himself. He had the gun in my face; he was crying and screaming that Sperry would kill him for letting her leave with his stuff." Alex swallowed and held his head in his hands for a minute.

Carly put a hand on his shoulder. "It's okay, Alex. You're okay."

"Yeah, you saved me. There's a TV monitor down in the cellar; they monitor the drive. He glanced at it and saw you guys coming up the drive. He hit me one more time and then took off to deal with you."

Carly told him what had happened at the door.

Alex blew out a breath and leaned back. His right eye was going to be a lot blacker than either of hers, but she decided now was not the time to point it out.

"I really thought I was dead. He had the barrel of that shotgun pressed into my cheek. I've been to enough shootings to know what that can do to a person." He ran a hand down his bruised face. "This is hard for me, but you remember when you told me about your swim—when Galen Burke tried to kill you, taking you out on that yacht? He was going to make you fish food but you jumped, and for at least part of that swim you thought you were going to die?"

Carly nodded, and Alex continued.

"Well, I've been in a lot of hairy situations. It comes with being an investigative reporter. But—" he paused and wiped his brow—"today I really thought I was dead. Out here in the middle of nowhere would be the perfect place to dump the body of a nosy reporter."

Carly arched an eyebrow and folded her arms. "I could inject something about trying to play policeman, but I'll give you a break for the moment."

"Ha. Anyway, when I thought he was going to pull the trigger, I remembered what you'd said about praying to God, and . . . well, I did. I haven't been to church since I was a little kid, so I hope I did it right. I did feel a peace. It was weird—here I was tied up in a hole with a bunch of strangers, being poked and prodded by a shotgun held by a madman, but I felt calm and the fear was gone." His bloodshot eyes got wide, and he shook his head in disbelief. "Then he saw the monitor and he was gone. The next face I saw was yours. Did God answer my prayer, or was it just a coincidence?"

Carly smiled. "I've heard it said that there's no such thing as coincidences, only God-incidences. If I'd been in your position, I would have done the same thing."

Alex shook his head again. "It's just all so unbelievable. I mean, if you're right, this could change my whole life. I'm supposed to be the skeptical reporter, remember?"

"Yeah, I remember. And what I say is, go ahead and investigate. A guy with your talent, if you set your mind to finding out if God is real and if he answers prayer, you'll get an answer."

"Thanks." He held out a grimy hand, and Carly shook it. "Looks like I owe you my life twice."

"You don't owe me anything. I did my job. Now you can keep doing yours. There's got to be a huge story here."

Nick came into the kitchen. He looked at Carly and jammed a thumb toward Trejo. "I take it he told you what he's doing here?"

"Yeah. I'll write a report that will sound like a novel."

He nodded, his expression unreadable. "Alex, you need to get checked out by the medics. They just got here, and they're going to be busy with all those people in the hole in a few minutes. Why don't you go talk to them now. Plus, ICE will definitely want to talk to you. They're also on the way. And Carly is right—this will be a huge story. This place looks to be a hub of human trafficking. Those people down there are not the first group to be held here."

Alex shrugged and pushed himself up from the table. "Yeah, I'll go out there and talk to the paramedics. Strangely enough, I'm not thinking about the story. I'm just glad I'm alive." He left them in the kitchen.

As soon as he was gone, Nick took her hand.

"What?" she asked.

"Just a little delayed stress reaction," he said as he gathered her in a hug and squeezed tight. "Carly, when I heard that shotgun blast, I—" His voice broke, and he pressed his cheek to her head.

Surprised and moved, Carly brought her arms around his back. "Hey, I'm okay. I know not to stand in front of a door. And you caught the bad guy."

They stood like that for a few minutes before he sighed

and released her. "I know. Like I said, it was a delayed reaction, something I needed to do."

He looked at her with such warmth in his eyes she felt it down to her toes. "Thanks, Nick," she said, giving his hands a squeeze. "I guess I needed it too."

• • •

Their private moment didn't last long. The Riverside deputies were joined by ICE agents, and they began bringing the Mexican nationals up from the cellar. Soon, the scene outside the cellar could only be described as organized chaos as the minutes ticked by. The thirty-five illegal aliens were seated on the ground all around the backyard. A mixture of Riverside County deputies and ICE officers mingled throughout taking down names. The media had gotten wind of the situation, and at least three news choppers circled above.

"Wow," Carly said as they stepped out the back door and she looked up. "This is a circus."

"Wait until you walk around to the front."

She saw what Nick meant. There was a paramedic rig, a couple of fire trucks, several large SUVs she guessed belonged to ICE, and numerous sheriff's vehicles. Down the road, behind a barricade, were the news vans. Light was fading, and as much as she wanted to get involved in the search for A.J., she knew they'd be stuck on scene giving statements for a while.

ICE officers met them on the porch, and Carly and Nick told them everything that had happened when they got there.

When the agents were satisfied with their statements and had all of their contact information, they told Carly and Nick to stand by while they searched the house in case there was anything else they needed to know. The agents then began a thorough and destructive search.

Carly and Nick made their way to the paramedic rig, where Alex, Rivers, and Quan were conversing with the EMTs. Rivers had a bandage on his head, but his eyes were bright with something Carly recognized. This was a big case that was going to involve a lot of big arrests before it was all over, something cops loved to be a part of.

"Hey, the DA is talking about an arrest warrant for Sperry," he said as they approached.

"Really? They think they can tie this to Sperry?" Carly had her doubts. She could see Sperry claiming it was all Grant, the renter, and had nothing to do with him.

"Grant decided to talk. Once we found the illegals, he saw everything falling on him. He's with one of the ICE guys, spilling his guts."

"Did you hear anything about the girl and the baby?"

Rivers nodded, expression grim. "Another of Sperry's goons, moniker Boxer, brought them out here last night. Grant claims he was told to lock the girl up and wait until Sperry got here to deal with her. ICE asked who the buyer for the baby was. Grant called Harper a moron and said no one wanted to buy a baby."

"Then why did this Boxer bring them out here?"

"For some keys, which Grant says Mary Ellen told him

she didn't have. Then Grant got incoherent. He said she must have had the keys because she got the safe open. He began to curse her and stopped being helpful. ICE was badgering him about what was in the safe when I left."

"We don't really know any more now, do we? Except that Alex saw her with the baby." Carly felt a weight of despair as surely as if it sat on her shoulders.

"There's an Amber Alert out for the girl and the baby," Quan said. "Since we know what she's driving, the description and license plate are being flashed all over."

"Thanks for that," Carly said with a sigh. "I pray we find that baby."

"If it's any consolation," Alex said, "from what I saw, that kid was being well taken care of."

Carly only nodded. They still had no idea what Mary Ellen planned to do with A.J.

24

IT WAS ABOUT 10:30 P.M. before Carly, Nick, and Alex were finished and released from the scene. ICE and the Riverside County agencies would be busy for a lot longer. Carly and Alex headed for the car while Nick went to ask a couple of deputies to move black-and-whites that blocked their exit.

"Those guys are storm troopers," Alex said, nodding toward a group of ICE agents in the front yard.

"Why? Did they give you a bad time?"

"No, it's just the air about them."

Carly gave him a dismissive wave. "Sounds like you got hit too hard in the head."

"Nope, I know storm troopers when I see them," Alex said as they reached the car. "Can I ask you something?"

"As long as it's not about storm troopers, shoot."

He gestured toward Nick. "I see something different between the two of you. Is it good news or bad?"

"I guess that depends on your perspective." She sighed. "We're talking about counseling, and Nick has said some things that make me very happy."

"You had to put it that way, didn't you?" He slapped his thigh and sighed. "I can't say I'm not disappointed. But I do want you to be happy. I just wish it were with me. . . . We can still be friends, right?"

"Sure, Alex." Carly climbed in the driver's seat and started the car while Alex got into the back.

With an exaggerated yawn, he said, "I never thought I'd see the day when I looked forward to the back of a police car, but I could sleep for a month."

"Just don't snore."

• • •

"Thanks for the ride." A very tired Alex Trejo waved good-bye as he ascended the steps to his house.

"He's a lucky guy," Nick said as Carly drove back to the station. "Grant could just as easily have shot him. I hope the paper pays to replace his car if for some reason it's not recovered."

She yawned. It was after eleven thirty now. "Knowing Alex, he'll talk them into a brand-new car, way better than the first." Carly smiled, but her mind was elsewhere. She'd called Andrea—half-scared that her roommate was already no longer her roommate—to tell her what was happening and ask her to walk the dog. Andi was mildly interested in the information about A.J., and her agreeing to walk the dog seemed grudging. When Carly asked how the disciplinary hearing had gone, Andi said she wouldn't know the decision for a couple of days. All in all, the vibes had been very chilly.

After a few minutes, Nick broke into her thoughts. "By the way, what's up with you and Andrea?"

"You could tell from my side of the conversation that things were kind of strained, huh?"

"Yep. You guys are usually as close as the pages in a book. You speak in this kind of BFF language, and that wasn't there tonight. What's the matter?"

Carly considered hedging, but then she was always honest with Nick and saw no reason to sugarcoat the truth now. "I asked her not to bring guys home. That's part of what she's upset about. And she doesn't like it that we're friends, that I forgave you. She doesn't trust you."

He sighed, and she continued. "She's not happy with me either, thinks I've changed too drastically. And to top it off, did you know she's been suspended?"

"Suspended? I'd heard someone at the hospital was in trouble for the kidnapping and was going to take a fall, but I didn't know it was her." Nick looked at Carly, a clear question in his expression. "She was the one in the supply closet?"

Carly shook her head. "Andi says that didn't happen. She just let her break go too long, though she was with a guy." She cleared her throat.

Nick's eyes went wide. "Wow." He shook his head. "I hate to say it, but maybe she'll learn her lesson."

They pulled into the lot behind the station, and Carly parked the car.

"Maybe she did step over the line and deserves discipline, but she seems to think it's all my fault. She's moving out and barely speaking to me. I'm at a loss—she's been my best friend for years."

"Moving?"

"Yeah. She's been so hostile about Christians and Christianity, and I've been trying to figure out why."

"Give her time. My bet is she's scared about losing her job and taking it out on you. I know a little about misdirected anger."

"Yeah, I guess you do." Carly reached over and punched him in the shoulder.

"Ow." Nick made a face and rubbed his arm.

"Yeah, like that hurt."

He laughed and then took her hand. "You know, when we were separated and waiting on the divorce, you wouldn't even look at me, much less talk to me. After I became a Christian, I asked your mom what I could do to get you to speak to me. Do you know what she said?"

Carly shook her head, and Nick continued. "She told me to pray and leave it all up to God. I really didn't believe that was enough, but I didn't have a choice. I mean, there was a real fear you'd shoot me just as well as look at me."

Carly laughed ruefully. "True enough. I was hurt and

angry, and I'm armed." Her good mood faded a bit as she remembered her roommate. "You think prayer will work with Andrea, the wild woman?"

"I think prayer works with everything and everyone. Just look at us. Give her time."

They locked up the car and stood staring at one another in the quiet parking lot.

Carly felt slaphappy with fatigue and giggled. "We must be a sight. You're filthy from your tussle with Grant, and I'm just as filthy with two black eyes." *But we're happy with each other for the first time in a long while.*

The fatigue faded from Nick's face when he grinned and moved closer to her. "I'll see you tomorrow. But now, if you don't mind, let's make a little bit more of a spectacle."

When he leaned forward, Carly thought he was going to kiss her. Instead, he pulled her into a tight hug. She felt his lips brush her ear as he whispered, "I hope your raccoon eyes aren't too painful."

Carly buried her face in his shoulder. "They'll fade. I'll be back to normal soon."

"I hope that will go for both of us." He pushed back and grasped both her hands in his, brought them to his lips, kissed them, and then turned to walk to his truck. Carly watched him and wondered if suddenly he wasn't walking better. She shrugged, deciding that was a topic for another day, and headed wearily to the locker room. As happy as she was about Nick, her heart was heavy when she thought about A.J. and the fact that it seemed like one more time they'd been just a little too late.

Pulling out her phone, she called Joe. He answered on the second ring.

"I've been waiting for your call." His voice was full of hope. "Tell me everything."

She filled him in and then learned that he and Christy were home. Christy had been released with a clean bill of health.

"Alex couldn't say why the girl had A.J.?"

"No, sorry. He didn't get much of a chance to talk to her. But she was taking good care of A.J. Hang on to that, Joe. And we know now what she's driving. On our way back to the city, we saw the vehicle description and license plate flashed on every freeway message board. We'll get him back—I know it."

Though he sounded dispirited when she disconnected, while she showered and changed, she prayed that hope would infuse Joe and Christy and that they would find A.J. soon. *Where can that little boy be?*

25

BOXES FILLED THE LIVING ROOM of the apartment when Carly got home. Andrea wasn't in her room, but she'd already removed all of her pictures and most of her knickknacks. Carly would have sat down and brooded, but Maddie didn't give her time. The exuberant canine wanted one last walk. Carly grabbed the leash, defeated now that it was apparent Andrea was really leaving for good.

"Sweet face, what will I do now? Your aunt Andi won't listen to me, she won't talk to me, and I can't believe she won't be my friend anymore." Carly vented to the dog while they walked. Stress drove some people to food; it drove Carly to talk to Maddie as though her dog really understood. "I've had too much emotional stuff in one day, sweetie. Between Nick, Alex, and Joe, I feel chewed up like one of your old toys."

The dog just wagged her tail, sniffed here and there, and did what dogs do.

Carly sighed as Andrea's earlier scathing rebuttal of her newfound faith rang in her ears. *Lord, I don't know what to say to her. I can't believe she's moving because I complained about the men she brought over. It's always bothered me, but now she calls me a Goody Two-shoes. Help me figure out how to reach her.*

The twosome made their way to a vacant lot just a block up from the beach. Lots of rabbits lived in the lot, and Maddie loved to chase their scent. Carly took the dog off the leash. There was no one around, and she loved to watch the dog sniff and zip around the area, looking for bunnies. She sat for an hour before Maddie wandered back, tail wagging, tongue lolling, spent. Carly clipped the leash back on, and they walked home.

As she lay down, she remembered what Nick had said about prayer. Of course it would work with Andrea. It had to. She prayed for her friend and for their relationship before closing her eyes and dropping off to sleep.

• • •

Peter Harris phoned early, waking Carly before the alarm.

"What's up, Pete?"

"You need to be at the federal building by ten for a debrief over what went on yesterday."

Carly groaned and looked at the clock. It was 8:20. "Okay. Have you already called Nick?"

"He's next. Meet us at the station's back steps at nine, and we'll all drive up together. See you there."

The apartment was quiet. Carly got up and let the dog out. The boxes were still everywhere, so Andi wasn't completely gone—yet.

When the phone rang again, this time it was Joe.

"I didn't call too early, did I?"

"No, I have to go in for a debriefing. What can I do for you?"

"I've been looking for Alex's phone number. I don't have it. Christy wants to talk to him about A.J. Do you think he'll talk to us?"

"I'm sure he will. There's nothing classified about what he saw." She read off the phone number.

"Thanks. Christy was sitting in the nursery, and . . ." He cleared his throat.

"Hang in there, Joe. We'll find him."

"Thanks. Thanks for all your hard work, Carly. We both appreciate it."

Though the thanks was sincere, Carly heard a note of defeat in her partner's voice, and it broke her heart.

• • •

Since she hadn't asked if there was a preferred dress for the meeting in the federal building, Carly was glad to see that her choice of business casual hit the mark. Pete was dressed in a suit for homicide, but Nick was wearing jeans and a blazer—very casual handsome, she thought.

"The eyes look better," Pete said when he saw her. Nick nodded in agreement.

"Thanks. They feel better."

He pointed to a car. "Nelson and Garrison have been up in LA all morning. We need to get going."

Carly took the backseat and let the guys take the front. Pete had questions for both of them about the day before, but she was content to listen, let Nick answer, and fret. Interacting with Captain Garrison always put her on edge, and she couldn't help but wonder why he was part of this meeting. Jake had been running the investigation and doing a great job.

At the federal building, Carly and Nick joined Jake, Sergeant Nelson, a couple of ICE agents, and Captain Garrison in a large conference room. Agent Wiley took the lead and started the debriefing by explaining the status of the FBI investigation.

The agent looked at some notes and then began. "First of all, I'd like to state the obvious. By now you have all figured out that the subject of our investigation is Conrad Sperry. But all of our resources—and those of immigration and customs—were concentrated on his properties in Temecula and farther south in San Diego. The operation you discovered yesterday was a surprise."

He gave them a nod of thanks, then went on. "ICE has conducted a thorough search of the Sperry property and found that it was likely used to traffic hundreds, if not thousands, of illegal aliens into the country over several years. The immigrants appear to have been ferried from that property to places all over the country. Also recovered was an abandoned truck, a few miles away. Isaac Grant claims the truck was en route to the property to pick up the illegal immigrants and transport them north. We surmise that the driver got spooked by all the police activity and split. Currently there's a search under way for Conrad Sperry. He seems to have disappeared."

"What does his attorney have to say?" Nick asked.

Wiley shrugged. "The usual—that his client is innocent and a victim of unscrupulous and devious employees. He won't name names, of course, except for Grant. But we have the names of three other individuals known to work for him who are so far unaccounted for. They have all been known to be in the company of Grant at one time or another." He slid some wanted flyers across the table. "And according to Caswell, Sperry is angry about being such a sap and hiring a criminal like Grant."

"Then why has he disappeared?" Carly asked.

"Caswell says that his client has every intention of appearing and answering the charges, but he's tied up at the moment."

Laughter rippled across the room. Wiley looked up at the ceiling and then back down before continuing. "Caswell is stalling, and we think we know why. While we suspected his client's smuggling activities included human cargo, that was not the main focus of our investigation. Five years ago, thieves pulled off a theft of rare colored diamonds in Geneva, Switzerland. They were never caught, the gems never recovered. But Swiss authorities contacted us six months ago to say there was a possibility the gems were headed our way. Conrad Sperry's name came up as a possible buyer or fence. We've been watching him since then, and we have reason to believe he does have the gems and was trying to broker them."

Carly frowned. "What about the baby? According to Grant, Sperry had Mary Ellen and A.J. brought out to the property. If he wasn't going to sell A.J., what was going on there?"

"The entire baby caper is not related to the bigger picture," Garrison said with a derisive snort. "Conrad wouldn't profit by selling a baby."

Carly stared at the captain for a second, then looked back to Wiley. "Then why bring the baby there? Has Grant told you that?"

Wiley answered, beginning with a shake of his head. "We don't know, but I can offer a hypothesis. I think it was all a misunderstanding. From listening to what we have recorded, Sperry often referred to smuggled goods as his 'babies.' I've read your reports, and I believe your burglar, Harper, misunderstood what Sperry meant by having a buyer for a baby. Why Sperry let him believe that was what he wanted, I can only speculate. All Grant will say is that according to Sperry, Harper and the girl were a problem. And there is the issue of the missing keys. Sperry insisted Grant get the keys from

Mary Ellen at all costs. He claims he searched her and didn't find the keys."

"Why did he kill Harper?" Nick asked.

"He won't answer questions about his crimes but is more than willing to drop a dime on Sperry."

"Then everything he tells you is self-serving," Carly said. "And regardless of whether it was a misunderstanding or not, A.J. is still missing."

Nelson spoke up. "We're doing all we can to find the girl and the baby, Carly. You know that. We just don't believe that crime can be laid on Sperry."

"That's not all." Wiley held up a hand to stop Garrison, who started to speak. "The girl may have more than the baby. Grant swears five ways from Sunday that it wasn't his fault, but he indicates that she removed something important from the safe at Unique Imports. It's a manila envelope. He doesn't know what was in it, but he knows it was very important to Sperry. For all we know, she could have taken the stolen diamonds. If the girl has the envelope, you can bet Sperry wants to find her. That's why Caswell is stalling. He's giving Sperry time to search. If he finds her before we do, she's dead. And we can surmise that the baby will be collateral damage."

26

A.J. AS COLLATERAL DAMAGE.

As they returned to the police station, the thought made Carly sick to her stomach. She'd only been able to listen to the rest of the debriefing and study the three wanted flyers. One of the men went by the moniker Boxer, just like Rivers had said, so Grant was telling the truth about him. Even though she was amazed that the feds detailed so much of their ongoing investigation, she couldn't offer anything. And Garrison was really beginning to get to her. It was clear why he had been there: he was trying to prove he was in control, that he was a leader. To Carly he just looked arrogant and puffed up. And he called Sperry by his first name. When he'd made that comment, Carly remembered he and Conrad had been close when Sperry was a reserve. Back then, Garrison was a lieutenant in community relations, and it was his job to recruit for the reserve program. He spoke at a lot of business meetings and neighborhood watch functions and handed out applications for the reserves. Sperry was Garrison's prize applicant at one time. More than once she'd seen the two of them together, chatting or having lunch. Did that have any bearing on the situation now?

She hated to think there were still bad apples on the force after what she had gone through with Drake and Tucker, but Garrison seemed to be a twisted advocate for Sperry. Could he be helping the dirtbag hide? The thought disturbed her, and she shifted in her seat.

"Any tips on Alex's car?" Carly asked Harris when they were halfway back to Las Playas and she was tired of brooding about Garrison.

Harris nodded. "Yeah, people are calling in from all over. Not sure which tips are good and which are bad. The car has been seen everywhere from San Diego to Santa Barbara. CHP is on it. We transferred the tip line to them, and the car is in the system as a stolen vehicle."

Nick looked over his shoulder at her. "We have the resources working. We'll find them."

Carly nodded, glad to see the old, optimistic Nick. But she had a bad feeling about the situation, and she couldn't shake a thought that kept popping into her mind: *What if Garrison is sharing our information with Sperry?*

At the station, Sergeant Nelson met them at the back

steps. "I'll see you upstairs, Pete," he said before turning to Nick and Carly. "I've got some news for you two."

Carly didn't like the look on his face and braced herself.

"What is it?" Nick asked.

"Word from Garrison—he's cutting out all extra personnel. Says the overtime well is dried up. Everyone goes back to their regular schedule, and if they're over forty hours this week, then they're off until the start of the next pay period."

"What?" Carly stared at him, fists clenched. "But A.J. is still out there."

"I know, I know, but the captain says with all the federal help, we don't need as much local help. His exact words were, 'Let the feds spend their money.' I don't like it and I know Lieutenant Jacobs tried to change his mind, but it's his decision." Nelson shrugged.

"That is so wrong." Carly felt like stomping her foot and screaming. "Joe is one of ours. This should be our invest."

Nick laid a calming hand on her shoulder. "Hey, the feds want Sperry as much as we do, maybe more."

"Right, they want Sperry and the diamonds; they don't care about A.J. Can we at least go check out the catch basin? It's possible Mary Ellen is hiding there."

Nelson considered her for a minute. "Pete and I were out there once. But you're right; we should check it again. I'll send a black-and-white out there right now and make the area a DCC—fair enough?"

Carly nodded. A district car check meant every downtown cop would make a point to check out the area a few

times during each shift and log in whether there was anything to report. She had to be satisfied with that.

"My hands are tied on this," Nelson said. "I've got your
time sheets and you are both over forty hours, so you're off as
of now. Carly, you're back to work in patrol Monday night,
and, Nick, you're back to report review." He threw his hands
up, turned, and went inside the station.

Carly looked away from Nick, hating that she felt like
crying.

He spoke softly and soothingly. "I know you want to stay
involved, but you have to trust that the investigation is in
good hands."

Trust—a simple word that often meant an impossible
action. She faced him, wanting to tell him her fears about
Garrison but hesitating. What if she was overreacting?

"We have to leave it to the feds now, Carly." He stepped
close, and his presence calmed her. "We can pray, but we can't
be part of the invest. So why don't we blow off some steam,
and then I'll buy you lunch."

Folding her arms, she sighed. "What did you have in
mind?"

"What do you say we go for a swim?"

"A swim?" She realized then that he'd been without his
cane all morning.

"Yeah, we can fight the summer traffic and get in a mile
or two in the surf."

"Well, I need a good, hard swim. Are you okay to swim
in the ocean?"

"Cleared and ready."

"I hope you're ready to eat salt water as I beat you."

"We'll see," he said as he turned to walk down the steps to the parking lot. And he was walking better. This time she was positive.

27

THE PLAN WAS FOR CARLY to go home and get ready. Nick would meet her at the apartment after he went to his house and picked up his swimsuit. He'd park near her apartment, and they'd walk to the beach for their swim. When she pulled into her space, she saw Andi's car and next to it, in the loading space, a truck she didn't recognize. But some of the boxes in the back looked like Andi's, so she figured this must be her latest boy toy helping her move.

Carly started up the path to the front door feeling as if she were walking the green mile.

"Are you leaving too?"

She turned, surprised by the voice. It was Mrs. Shane. She was relaxing in her rocker.

"Not today. Just my roommate."

"Is she getting married?"

"I don't think so—just moving."

The woman nodded, and Carly continued on to her apartment.

"That's not mine; it stays." Andrea's voice was clear through the open front door as Carly reached it.

"You should mark your stuff." The second voice, male, was familiar, but Carly couldn't place it.

She stepped inside slowly, knowing she wouldn't have picked this moment to talk to Andi, but now might be her last chance. She took a deep breath, wondering if there'd be a confrontation or any chance for her and Andrea to talk without the company of the helper.

"Hey, what's going on in here?"

"Carly!" Andrea turned, a guilty look flashing across her face for the briefest moment. "I didn't realize you'd be home so soon. I thought you were at work." Andi stood at the kitchen counter, a plate halfway wrapped with paper in her hand.

"I got sent home, busted the overtime limit. So you found a place? Where?"

"Downtown. I found a great studio loft-type deal."

"Good, glad to hear it. And you know, I would have helped you move if you'd let me know when."

"You've been working a lot." She looked away, finished wrapping the dish, and put it in a box. "Besides, I have someone helping me."

Just then her friend walked into the living room, holding a box.

"'K, Andi, there's room in here—oh, hi, Carly." It was Sergeant Barrett, Carly's supervisor.

"Hello, Sarge." Carly stiffened and fought to keep shock from showing. Boy toy? Not only was Barrett not a boy; he was married with five kids, the oldest probably close to Andi's age. Carly felt light-headed. Andi normally went for young and beautiful. While Barrett was fit, he was old enough to be her father. *He's the one Andrea took the long break with?* Carly couldn't get her mind around the situation.

"You can call me Hal; we're not at work now." He juggled the box to reach out a hand, and Carly shook it by reflex, her mouth dry.

With an ill-at-ease feeling, she remembered that Andrea would not say whom she'd been with on her long break. She was covering for Barrett? Carly saw her supervisor in a whole new light—a dingy one. *You're letting Andrea take the fall all by herself!* How could a man so calmly cheat on his wife and act as though it were nothing?

"I don't have anything else to put in that box. And there are two book boxes over there that are ready to go." Andrea pointed to a pair of boxes in the corner.

Hal grinned ruefully. "Slave driver." He was able to stack the two corner boxes on the one he already had. The two women watched him leave.

"He's helping me some with the rent also, since my job is still up in the air," Andrea said. "He's a really nice guy."

"Andrea, he's married."

"There we go with the judgment." She threw her hands

up and faced Carly. "He makes me happy! And I return the favor. What else in life is more important than being happy?"

"Happy at someone else's expense? No thank you. How about morals and common sense? Do his wife and kids know?" Bile rose in Carly's throat as she remembered being pierced through and through when she'd learned about Nick's infidelity.

"Of course not. What they don't know won't hurt them. The life Hal and I share is different—it's special in its own way. It has nothing to do with her or the children."

"He's doing the same thing to his wife that Nick did to me, remember?"

"Oh, stop; it's nothing like that. That waitress wanted Nick to leave you. I've no intention of taking Hal away from his family."

Carly struggled as Andrea turned into someone she'd never seen before. Part of her wanted to lash out at Andi and Hal, and part of her wanted to run away and pretend she hadn't found out about this relationship.

"Andi," she managed after a few deep breaths, "I can't ignore this, because you're my friend and I love you. You're lying to yourself if you really believe what you're saying." Her voice was low and even. "Do you really think you can have an affair with a married man in a vacuum? Do the two of you have any sort of future?"

Andrea's face scrunched with disdain, and she spoke in a harsh whisper. "You are such the prude now. Judging me when you think you can trust Nick. What makes you think

I want to marry Hal? I just want whatever fun he can give me. I don't have to live my life like you, waiting for marriage to a guy who is already a proven louse just so you can spout some Christian nonsense about forgiveness. You forget my mom's second husband. You know, the churchgoing deacon who was a drunk? He kept begging my mom's forgiveness for his drinking, saying he'd change. She believed him right up until the night he wrapped their car around a tree and nearly killed her!"

Carly, mouth agape, stared at Andrea. She had forgotten that. She remembered the crash, but back then she was not a Christian and she really didn't pay attention to people who were.

"I had forgotten. I'm sorry."

Andrea gave an angry wave of her hand. "My life is guys—as many as I want—parties as often as I like, and freedom. Just remember that. I don't want your Christian narrowness!" She swept up the box she'd been packing and stormed out of the apartment. She passed Hal in the doorway and left him looking sheepishly at Carly.

"I guess we'll come back for the rest later."

"Yeah, that would probably be best." Carly crossed her arms and tried unsuccessfully to keep the edge out of her voice.

Barrett turned and closed the door behind him. She stared at the door for a minute, the pain in her heart raging.

Someone knocked, and she lunged for the door ready to lash out at Barrett, only to find Nick there.

"Oh, it's you."

"Yeah, and I saw why you're all wound up." He shook his head, sadness on his face. "Never saw that coming."

She invited him in and went to let Maddie in from the patio, where Andi had likely put her. "I can't believe she's with Barrett. It's wrong on so many levels. But so is the fact that I forgot about her mother."

Maddie bounded into the room, saw Nick, and charged him, tail wagging. Carly explained about the long-ago crash. "I guess there's a reason for her anger. And it's been festering for such a long time." Carly folded her arms and leaned against the wall while Nick knelt down to play with the dog. "I so need a swim," she said. "I could swim all the way to Catalina right now."

Nick stood with his hands on his hips and faced her. He was wearing his swim trunks and a tank top Carly had given him one Christmas. "Sorry. I know it bites to have all this happen on top of Andi moving out. Doubly so that she's with Barrett." He glanced around the room.

"A proven louse," Andi had said, and a thought crossed Carly's mind that burned: *Will Nick be like Barrett years from now? Once a cheater, always a cheater? Is it a blessing he's been pulling away and a mistake to consider counseling?* Her throat tightened as she looked at him and remembered that word: *trust.* Then he did something that surprised her.

Nick stepped toward her and held out his hand. "Come on, let's sit down and pray for Andrea and A.J. We can trust God to work out everything we can't see or understand right now."

As if a light came on and burned away all the darkness

in her thoughts, Carly relaxed, thinking that maybe, at least where God was concerned, trust was not an impossible action. She took Nick's hand and gripped it tight. They sat close on the couch, hands and hearts intertwined, and bowed their heads.

28

THE BEACH WAS CROWDED, but Nick and Carly swam out beyond the recreational swimmers and body boarders and then turned parallel to the shore. In her element in the ocean, Carly kept ahead of Nick in much the same way he had kept ahead of her in the pool. She wondered about his hip, but since he didn't seem to be hampered by it, she said nothing and pushed herself hard, knowing he pushed himself to keep up.

"Wow," he said, reaching her side as she pulled up to indicate they'd finished. "Top form, babe, top form. I'm impressed."

"This felt good. I have to confess that I was worried about more than A.J. and Andi." While they treaded water, she told him about her fear of Garrison's involvement with Sperry.

"He's not dirty. He's just not a leader, never has been. Rumor is, he's losing his captain slot."

"For sure?"

Nick was a sergeant; he heard gossip from people of rank and therefore usually had reliable tidbits.

"Yeah. Jake is going to be promoted. They're not going to demote Garrison, but he'll be given the option of retiring or moving to records. All that posturing for the feds—" he made a face and splashed—"I'm not sure what that was about, but I don't believe he's helping Sperry. They were friends before, but now the guy is wanted."

"I feel better hearing that from you. . . . You know, you almost scored a hundred points today."

"I didn't realize today was a test, but since it was, where did I lose points?"

"You haven't fed me. I'm starved."

"Ha. So I have a chance at a perfect score?"

She nodded, and when he splashed her, she splashed him back before together they headed for shore.

They dried off, gathered their towels and Maddie, who'd been sitting patiently waiting for them, and started the walk back to Carly's. Nick reached out and grabbed her hand, and Carly felt blissfully content. Then she saw the police car and the fire truck. She'd heard the sirens a bit earlier but never expected them to be heading to her apartment building.

"What now?" Carly picked up the pace, pulling Nick and Maddie with her. Ugly memories surfaced of a confrontation she'd had in her parking area with a masked man not too long ago. He'd tried to smash her head in, and she'd ended up shooting him dead. *Has there been another attack, this time in broad daylight?*

"Carly! Sergeant Anderson!" One of the uniforms saw them coming and waved them over. He was an afternoon guy.

"Hey, what happened?" she and Nick asked simultaneously.

"We think it's Joe King's baby."

"What?" Carly broke into a run, Maddie jogging with her. There in the courtyard were the paramedics, kneeling next to Mrs. Shane, who was still seated. In her arms was a squirming bundle. Bobby, the medic, was checking the child's vital signs.

Carly reached them and stood speechless. It was Nick who appeared at her shoulder and asked what was going on.

"A young girl came walking in here with this sweet child right after you and your friend left." The old woman beamed down at the bundle. "She was in a rush, didn't want to wait for you. I told her I'd watch the baby until you came back."

"She wanted to give the baby to me?" Back in the recesses of her mind, she wondered how Mary Ellen knew where she lived. But that troubling question was overshadowed by her elation at A.J.'s safe return.

Mrs. Shane nodded. "She said Officer Carly Edwards."

"Who called the police and the medics?" Nick asked.

"I did. I watch the news. I know this is the child that's been missing. I couldn't stop the girl, but I could make certain the baby was okay. I guess the girl had a change of heart and wanted the baby back where he belonged."

"He's dirty, but he looks fine," Bobby reassured them as he took A.J. from Mrs. Shane and held him as if he were holding his own child. The baby had started to cry. "We'll get him to the ER and let the docs check him out. Will the parents meet us there?"

"Yeah, Lieutenant Jacobs is sending a patrol car to pick up Joe and Christy and drive them to the hospital so they don't crash in their excitement," the officer said.

Relieved but bewildered, Carly shook her head. "I don't understand it, but I'm happy." Numb and disbelieving this wonderful turn of events, she could only agree as Nick told the officer they'd follow the paramedics to the hospital.

Nick grabbed her in a hug. "Do you want to change?" he whispered in her ear. "Or you want to go to the hospital in your swimsuit?"

Laughing, she looked up at him. "Give me half a minute. I'll change." She reached a hand out to Mrs. Shane. "I can't thank you enough."

"I didn't do anything but hold a precious baby for a minute. The girl certainly didn't look like a kidnapper." Mrs. Shane pointed to the uniformed officer. "I gave him the note she gave to me. It was addressed to you."

The officer stepped forward. With gloves on, he held the note up for her to read.

Carly read the note aloud with Nick looking over her shoulder.

"'I'm sorry I took the baby. You can see he's not hurt. He may be hungry in a few hours, but he's not hurt. I thought if I took him, it would save Stanley, but now Stanley's dead. I'll be dead too if they find me, and they're after me. Right now I'm only one step ahead, but at least I know the baby will be okay. Please tell the parents I'm sorry for their pain. Mary Ellen.'"

Carly looked up at Nick, certain the astonishment she saw on his face was also evident on her own.

29

JOE GRABBED HER SHOULDERS, his face glowing. "Thanks, partner! Thanks. Only *thanks* doesn't cover it." He pulled her into a tight bear hug that took her breath away.

"I wish I could take credit, but the baby just showed up at my doorstep, so to speak," she said, gasping for breath and trying to explain.

"For some reason she thought she could leave A.J. with you, and for that I will be forever in your debt."

"Ditto that," a radiant Christy said without looking away from A.J.'s face.

Carly leaned into Nick, who put his arm around her shoulders. Everyone was smiling, and it felt so good. But something was missing. There were a couple of people who needed to know about this happy development. For one of them, Carly needed to ask permission.

"Do you guys mind if I call Alex Trejo and let him be the first reporter to document the reunion?" Carly asked.

Joe and Christy looked at the doctor, who nodded and smiled. "We're going to do a thorough exam to be certain he's all right, but from what I'm seeing so far, whoever had him kept him fed and changed. Save for the need of a bath and clean clothes, he appears fine. You can give an interview while we run tests if you want."

Joe nodded. Carly bet his grin was permanent. "Go ahead," he said. "We just talked to him, and he helped us to calm down and have hope. Turns out the hope he gave us was justified. I want to tell the whole world my son is safe." Joe hugged Christy, whose face was wet with happy tears.

Carly walked out to the waiting room to use her phone, passing Sergeant Nelson and Pete Harris as they arrived. They would need to investigate, see if the kidnapper left any clues along with the baby and the note. The report they filed would be a happy one since the doctor seemed certain the baby was healthy.

But two questions kept poking Carly like a sharp stick: *Where is Mary Ellen, and is she safe?*

She started to pull up Alex's number and then changed her mind. Andrea needed to know that the baby was safe as well. Carly wasn't sure if the news would do anything to help repair their relationship, but it might help assuage Andi's guilt. The call went to Andi's voice mail but she left a detailed message, certain the news would be welcome. She prayed briefly for her friend and then punched in the reporter's number. He answered on the first ring.

"My favorite storm trooper."

"Ha, the comedian. Don't give up your day job. Do you want to sharpen your pencil and get over to Memorial?"

"Why—?" She heard him suck in a breath. "The baby?"

"Back safe and sound, and you get the scoop."

"On my way."

Carly disconnected the call and smiled.

"You look awfully pleased with yourself." Nick had followed her out.

She laughed and reached out her hand, and he took it. "This is a great moment." She stepped up to hug him and caught her reflection in the emergency room window.

"Ahh," she groaned as she pulled away, realizing what a sight she must be. A hand flew to her hair. "Oh, I'm a mess! I changed, but I should have managed a quick shower to get the salt water out of my hair. I didn't even comb it out."

It was Nick's turn to laugh. "You look great."

Carly's smile faded. "Do you want to call Jonah, or should I?"

Nick sobered and took his phone out of his pocket. "I will. This is a good news, bad news kind of call."

Carly stepped back as he made the call. From Nick's side of the conversation, Carly could tell that Jonah was relieved and worried at the same time.

When Nick finished, he put his arm around her shoulders

and pulled her close. They walked back to the exam room where Joe and Christy were watching as the doctor examined A.J.

"By the way, I noticed earlier that you're walking better and barely limping."

"Yep. I'm going to force this leg to work. Okay if I lean on you for a bit?" His eyes were a blazing sapphire color, and Carly felt as if a shell had just cracked and fallen off her heart, letting the sunshine in.

"Fine with me, Sarge."

• • •

It was dark when Carly and Nick left the hospital. Alex was in full reporter mode, interviewing the elated parents. Exhausted and hungry, Carly sat back in Nick's truck and closed her eyes.

"I think after I eat a couple of pizzas, I could sleep for a week."

"Yeah, I am definitely up for some food. Pizzamania?"

"Great. Mind if I call my mom to join us? She's been a prayer warrior on this." She remembered her hair and winced at the thought of the auburn locks sticking out in every direction. "On second thought, why don't we get it to go and take it over to her house?"

Nick chuckled. "As long as we eat."

Carly called Kay with a sigh of relief, glad to have a happy bit of news to share.

"She left the baby with Mrs. Shane?" Kay exclaimed.

"Thank God it all worked out. I'm so happy to know the baby is back where he belongs with his mother and father. But Joe and Christy should probably stay on the church's meal ministry list. They shouldn't be bothered by routine chores yet. Maybe I'll make a welcome-home cake."

"I wish I could have contributed with a meal. But I'm glad the main reason for help is no more."

"You've been busy with so much. No idea where Mary Ellen is?"

"No. We know we have to find her, but right now, no leads."

They'd reached the pizza place, but Nick told her to keep talking; he'd go in and order.

"Jonah told me she's his niece. He's had the church open for prayer. He is so broken by the knowledge that he wasn't there for her."

It didn't surprise Carly that Jonah had confided in her mother about Mary Ellen. Kay was the head of the prayer ministry, so it made sense he'd ask for prayer and want the church involved.

"Nick and I are picking up some pizza. Do you feel like some or have you already eaten dinner?"

"That sounds great. I haven't eaten, and Jonah said he might stop by. He must have called me before he talked to you. I'm sure he'll have more questions for you and Nick."

"I wish we had more answers, but I look forward to talking with him."

Nick knocked on her door and put two pizzas in her lap.

•••

Jonah arrived at her mother's house a few minutes after Nick and Carly got there. He and Nick chatted in the living room while Carly and Kay set the table and fixed a salad to go with the pizza.

"Pray for Andrea, Mom," Carly said while they worked. "She's been suspended, and she's moved out."

"Suspended? What happened?"

She told her mother about the work lapse, Andi's disciplinary hearing, and the scene that had played out earlier in the day.

"Now she's moving out? I'm so sorry to hear that. The two of you have always been so close. I'd think she'd want your support during this difficult time."

"All she seems to want is to get away."

"I can't believe you've done anything so horrible it will end your friendship. I love Andrea too, but she has always been a wild one. I think she's hurt and scared about losing her job—she's venting. And moving out seems like she's running away, as well."

"Running from what? I'm her friend. I don't know why she's so angry with me."

"It's fear, I think, and you're a convenient target."

"I can't imagine Andi's ever been afraid of anything. She's always gone at life full speed ahead."

"Sometimes people live like Andrea out of fear, jumping into things before they have a chance to think about them."

"But I never preached to her."

"Maybe you need to preach to her."

"What?" When Carly remembered the anger in Andi's voice and body language, she couldn't imagine trying to broach the subject of God or Christianity.

"She needs to know she's loved. And job or no job, man or no man, Jesus will always love her. Pray about telling her that without judgment."

Carly sighed and set out a pitcher of iced tea and some glasses. "I don't know. It might just make her more upset."

"Maybe at first, but the truth is always best. And she needs to understand that even with Christ, people are still flawed. I'm sorry her mother found that out in such a painful way and that it has affected Andrea all this time. And I will keep praying for her. Just look what prayer did for you and Nick."

Her mother's advice made sense. Carly remembered her own life before she realized she needed God. Once she came to that realization, it was as if someone had turned on all the lights and she saw things clearly for the first time.

Carly smiled at her mother's reminder about her and Nick. "Okay, Mom, I get the picture. I'll pray for an opportunity to tell her the truth. Until then I will miss her. By the way, make your German chocolate cake for Joe and Christy. They'll love that." Her thoughts went back to A.J. as she called the guys into the kitchen for dinner. It was definitely an answer to prayer, the baby showing up like that. *But where is Mary Ellen?*

"Plenty of pizza," Nick said as he and Jonah sat. "Hope you're hungry."

"I am, but like I said, mostly I'm somewhat relieved."

They sat at Kay's kitchen table, and Jonah blessed the food.

"I'm so happy she brought the baby back and he's okay," he said as they began to eat. "What will happen to her when she's found? Won't the fact that she did bring him back help her case?"

Carly held a piece of pizza in her hand, a little disconcerted by the thought that she'd always believed the juvenile justice system was too lenient and now, in the case of Mary Ellen, she found herself hoping it would be very lenient.

"Initially, she'll be treated as a minor charged with kidnapping, which is a felony. But because she's seventeen, they can direct file and charge her as an adult."

"In your experience, what do you think will happen?" Jonah had a slice of pizza on a plate in front of him but wasn't eating.

"Usually it's when a teen like her commits a violent crime that they're tried as an adult." She chewed a bite and swallowed. Her time working juvenile had not been happy—all she could think about then was getting back to patrol—but that hadn't stopped her from paying attention. "But there are extenuating circumstances. We don't know why she ran away from placement. She has no criminal record. And Harper told me Mary Ellen had been slapped around, so you could argue she took A.J. because of fear. Once she had the baby, she kept him safe, and he was returned unhurt. That may count for something."

Jonah drank some iced tea, a thoughtful expression on his face. "When they catch her, will she be sent to jail or back to foster care while she awaits a hearing?"

"Since she's a ward of the court already, and she ran away from foster care, she'll probably be placed in a secure facility. Jail won't happen unless she's tried and convicted as an adult. Once she's in custody, she'll be evaluated by probation. The level of security will depend on whether probation sees her as violent or a danger."

"Will I be able to offer any kind of testimony, any kind of help to her?"

"I'm sure you can write a letter to probation, but the person who can most help Mary Ellen is Mary Ellen. If she's obviously contrite, understands that what she did is wrong, and is straightforward with probation, her report will be positive. A positive probation report goes a long way with juvenile judges."

Rawlings considered this for a moment, then finally nodded and picked up his pizza. "Thank you for explaining. But I can't help thinking that her soul is in great danger because of the dark world she's traveling in. I pray fervently she will be found soon."

"That's for sure," Carly agreed as she thought to herself, *And we need to find her first, because if Sperry finds her, I'm afraid her life is in danger.*

30

"WOULD YOU DO ME A FAVOR?" Carly asked Nick as he pulled to a stop in front of her apartment.

"Sure, what?"

"I know it's a DCC and Nelson takes it seriously, but I want to check out the catch basin tomorrow. Since we're both off . . ."

"You want some company? Sure. I'll come pick you up after my therapy."

They said good night, and Carly let herself into her apartment, empty but for the dog. Once alone with her thoughts, she mentally reviewed the evening. The dinner with Jonah and Kay had been bittersweet. It was awesome that the baby was safe, but Carly knew Mary Ellen was still in danger, especially if she'd taken precious gems from Sperry. After they'd eaten, Nick had called to see if there was any update, but so far there was no trace of Mary Ellen or Alex's car.

She let Maddie out for a bit, showered, and dropped off to bed, falling asleep almost instantly.

• • •

True to his word, Nick picked Carly up Thursday morning. As she buckled her seat belt, Nick told her Stanley Harper's vehicle had been discovered.

"That's great news. Please tell me Mary Ellen was in it."

"I don't have the details. I swung by the station and heard from Pete that the CHP got a tip from a passerby. The car was left in a vacant lot in LA. An officer is en route to check it out."

Carly faced Nick. "Her last foster home was on the border of Las Playas and LA. You don't think she went up that way, do you?"

Nick shrugged. "Anything is possible. But we're not on the clock, and I know that look."

Carly sat up in her seat, indignant. "What look are you referring to?"

"The look that says you want to go to her old neighborhood and nose around."

"Would it hurt?"

"We're not on duty."

"That might work in our favor. We're less threatening."

Nick smiled, picked up her hand, and kissed it. "Then let's go."

The border neighborhoods of Las Playas and Los Angeles were old and tired-looking. The foster home was one street over from the freeway, so it was noisy as well. They'd just pulled up when Carly's phone buzzed.

"It's Pete. Maybe he has news." She answered the call. "What's up?"

"False alarm."

"What?"

"It wasn't Harper's car after all—his plates, not his car. She's smart, this girl—switched plates with the same make and model vehicle. CHP didn't notice until the VIN check. Car belongs to a guy who lives in LA. We put his plate into the system as lost or stolen. But right now this is a dead end."

Carly wrote down the missing plate, speculating that the plate switch was something Mary Ellen had learned from Harper. She told Pete where she and Nick were.

"We had LAPD go out there and talk to those people. But you're right; maybe you will be less threatening."

With that, Nick and Carly got out of the car and walked up to the door of the foster home. She couldn't help but notice how depressing the place was. Clean, but sterile and devoid of any welcoming touch. The porch was empty of furniture and the number of locks on the front door staggering. She'd been to many depressing foster homes in her career, so sadly, she was not surprised. Unfortunately, a lot of foster parents saw kids in the system as paychecks only. They passed social services inspection by a thread.

Nick knocked.

After a long moment of unlocking locks, a large woman answered the door. She did not look happy. "Can I help you?"

Nick told her who they were. "We came here to talk to you about Mary Ellen Barber—"

"You got a warrant?"

"No, we just—"

"Then I got nothing to say." The door closed. She didn't slam it; she just closed it.

Nick turned to Carly. "Well, that's that."

"I guess I should have figured this might happen. Since Mary Ellen ran away and then kidnapped a baby, social services has probably been here a lot."

Nick nodded. "And we can't force her to talk to us."

They were walking back to the car when Nick's phone chimed. It was Jonah.

Carly listened to Nick's side of the conversation.

"Is there a problem?"

"He's organized a prayer meeting and wonders if we can come."

"Right now?"

"Yeah," Nick said.

"I guess there's not much we can do here." She glanced down the street and fidgeted.

Nick gripped her shoulders and whispered in her ear, "I know you want to do more, and you'd bang on every door between here and Las Playas or camp in the catch basin if you thought it would help. But Pete is still working the case, and we have to trust that the DCC will police the catch basin while we can't."

"You're right." Carly sighed. "I'm ready to pray."

• • •

With Nick's words ringing in her ear—and knowing the catch basin was being checked on a regular basis—Carly left the prayer meeting with the strongest impression that place was the key. She had learned over the years to trust her instincts. She almost made a trip there after dark but decided to leave it to the next day. As she lay down to sleep that night, she wished she were going back to work instead of to bed.

The ringing phone woke her from a light sleep at 3 a.m. Groaning and knowing that only bad news came this early in the morning, Carly answered.

"Edwards."

"Carly, it's Pete."

"Oh no. You found Mary Ellen." She sat up, wide awake with a knot of dread in her stomach.

"No, not quite, but I think you'll want to see this. Can you come over to the west side, her apartment?"

"On my way."

Carly called and woke Nick up without even thinking if she should or not. He said he'd pick her up and they'd drive over together. Her mind churned with possibilities while she splashed water on her face and dressed. She could have asked Pete more, but he wanted her to see it. What could it be?

She jogged out to the curb as Nick pulled up.

"Any more information?"

"No, I didn't call him back. He said I needed to see it."
She looked at him and arched her eyebrows. He nodded and
drove.

Carly noticed he'd worn his shoulder holster and brought
his handheld radio. Officers had the option to bring their
issued radio and charger home or leave them in their lockers
to charge. Carly usually opted for the latter. Sergeants didn't
have a choice—they were to always have their radios in case
they were called to a scene straight from home. Carly figured his sergeant's instincts had kicked in and he was treating
this like a callout. Fine with her. She had her small off-duty
weapon and liked the fact that they were both armed.

They reached Mary Ellen's street and were greeted by the
flashing ambers of several emergency vehicles—fire, police,
and an ambulance.

Nick parked in the first open space, and they negotiated
a path through vehicles and fire hoses. The air was thick
with the odor of fire, of burnt substances other than fire-
wood. Carly could smell burning plastic, charred fabric, and
unknown nasty, smoky smells. It looked as though the entire
neighborhood was up and watching the scene from behind
the police tape. As they stepped around a pumper, she saw
the source of the aroma. Mary Ellen's apartment building was
almost completely destroyed.

Carly wasn't an arson specialist, but as she looked at what
still stood, it appeared as though most of the damage was on
the second floor.

"Carly, Nick." Pete waved them over.

"What happened?"

"Possibly an arson fire that started on the second floor. Two residents didn't make it out in time: an elderly couple died."

"Did anyone see anything?"

Pete pointed to a paramedic rig where an older man was being treated. His face was blackened with soot, and he was wearing an oxygen mask while a medic bandaged his hands. "Mr. Frances heard voices. His apartment was directly below Mary Ellen's. Two men were looking for her right before the fire started."

"But he didn't see them."

"No, but he says they just missed her. He heard her moving around in the apartment about an hour before they showed up."

"He's sure it was her?" Nick asked.

"He thinks it was. He was taking the trash out when he saw her leave. But she was in a hurry and he only caught a glimpse of her running down the stairs and out the back. He called his friends who lived on that floor to check, but they hadn't seen her."

"Can we talk to them?"

"Afraid not. They're the pair who didn't make it. That's how Mr. Frances got burned. He knew the old man used a walker and that they'd never get out in time. But the fire burned hot and fast. He was overcome before he could get upstairs."

Carly felt as though the wind had just been kicked out of her.

"It gets worse," Pete said. "Come and look at this."

Carly and Nick followed Pete through puddles of brackish water and over hoses. He stopped in front of the building. There on the porch steps Carly had walked up a few days before, spray-painted in black paint, were the words *I want what is mine. Give it back or die.*

• • •

Carly and Nick stayed at the fire scene until the cleanup was almost finished. They had a minute with Mr. Frances before he was taken to the hospital. In a raspy, pained voice he told them that he'd heard two male voices calling out to Mary Ellen. Then it got quiet, and the men left in a hurry. The fire started right after that. He began crying for his friends and couldn't talk anymore.

"Arson is saying unofficially that the fire started in apartment seven and that an accelerant was used," Pete said. He'd walked over to them after talking to the arson investigator.

"Unofficially?"

"It will be official later today, after the lab confirms."

"Mr. Frances couldn't say if the men he heard sprayed the steps?" Nick asked.

Pete shook his head. "Poor guy lost his home and his friends." He took a sip of water. "This tells me that Sperry is desperate. Torching his own property, probably in an effort to smoke Mary Ellen out. And he's going in for the scorched-earth philosophy. Two innocent people were caught in his tantrum."

Carly shivered, thinking about Mary Ellen—on her own, running from a thug like Sperry. "If he finds her, he's not going to ask nice for what he wants. Nick and I were going to check out the catch basin today."

"Maybe we should head over there now." Nick pointed toward his truck.

"You know that's a DCC, right? Last time I checked the log, nothing was down there." Pete frowned. "I think it was yesterday when I looked at the log—the days are running together. Anyway, it was clean as a whistle."

"Sorry, I just have a feeling we should check again." Carly shot Nick a grateful glance.

"Don't be sorry; I trust your instincts. Can't hurt to take a look. Let's go." He grabbed Carly's hand. "See you, Pete."

Carly glanced up at the pink-tinged sky as she turned to leave with Nick. She was tired of breathing the noxious scent of the smoldering apartment building.

"Nelson will scream that he can't approve overtime," Pete called out to them.

"Doesn't matter," Carly said. "The girl needs to be found."

"We'll find her," Nick said as they climbed into his truck.

"I agree with Pete: Sperry is desperate. Burning down the apartment, killing two innocent people. Mary Ellen will have no chance if he finds her first." She fought rising anxiety as Nick drove away from the fire scene and toward the flood control channel. Streets were just starting to fill up with early-morning work traffic.

The catch basin was just past the police station and a few

blocks south of the city's southernmost limit. Hidden from view, the area was flat and sheltered. It wasn't a place a person could stumble upon. And no matter how often holes in the fence were patched after the area was cleared, like weeds, homeless camps would spring up.

The access road that led to the catch basin was an unpaved public service road. Public service needed access to the flood control in order to inspect the area and keep it clear of debris. They'd placed a heavy gate across the drive not far from the pavement turnoff. The gate was meant to keep squatters away.

Nick approached the turn a few minutes later. He started the turn as a blur of red came barreling toward them, a billowing cloud of dust behind it.

"Nick, look out!" Carly reached a hand out and gripped his arm. He swerved right to avoid a collision as the little car rocketed past them. The correction threw her into him.

"That was Alex's—"

She didn't finish her sentence as a second car came roaring their way.

A black Town Car burst through the dust cloud. Nick had started to follow the red car but stopped as the black car bore down on them. The rear window on the driver's side slid open, and Carly saw a gun barrel.

"Gun!" Nick yelled, throwing himself sideways to push Carly down.

Bam! Bam! Bam!

Three shots rang out, shattering the windshield. A shower

of safety glass rained down on both of them, and a gritty burst of dust poured in the gaping hole.

"You okay?" Nick asked.

"Fine, fine. Go after them. I'll call it in."

Brushing glass from himself, he threw the truck in gear and sped after the black car.

Carly grabbed his radio and, using his call sign, 1-Sam 20, raised the dispatcher with emergency traffic. The call was a 998—shots fired—and she knew every cop in the city who was listening would be heading their way to help if they could.

She could see the black car, but there was no sign of the red one. Traffic was getting heavy with morning commuters, and the Town Car nearly caused an accident.

"I can't read the plate yet," Carly said, leaning forward. The radio chatter told her units were coming. "What happened to the red car?"

"I don't know," Nick shouted, intent on his driving and the car they pursued. Without a windshield, street noise was loud. "I sure appreciate the way a black-and-white would handle in this type of situation."

"You're doing fine—oh no." Carly watched in horror as the Town Car clipped a school bus and sent it careening onto the sidewalk filled with pedestrians.

31

"IT'S A GOOD THING the bus hadn't picked up any children yet."
Nick handed Carly a bottle of water from the paramedics
on scene. She took the water gratefully and drank a quar-
ter of it in one swallow. They both had little cuts from the
safety glass. Nick's were on the side of his face, and Carly
had a couple on her arms. They weren't seriously hurt, and
miraculously, neither was anyone else. The bus had swerved
onto the sidewalk and smacked into a traffic signal pole but
missed hitting any of the people in the way.

The bus driver herself was shaken but didn't need medical attention. The black car and Trejo's red sports car had
disappeared.

"For two officers who are supposed to be off duty, you
sure can find chaos." Lieutenant Jacobs had stopped at the

scene on his way to work. He stood with his hands on his hips, looking at Nick's battered, steaming truck as it was pulled onto the back of a flatbed. The bullets not only destroyed the windshield, but one had hit the radiator and coolant had spilled everywhere. Even if they hadn't stopped to check on the bus, they wouldn't have gotten far. Four other vehicles had been struck or caused to crash by the black car, and there were cops everywhere taking reports. The highway patrol handled school bus crashes, so they were dealing with that, but Jacobs was right—the scene was a picture of chaos.

"Sorry, LT, it just happened," Carly said. "No one picked up either vehicle?"

"No. It's morning rush hour. If the drivers of those cars settled down and blended into traffic, they would easily avoid detection. Fox is up—" he pointed to the police helicopter— "and will continue to search, but it looks as though they got clean away. Are you both uninjured?"

"We're fine," Nick said, the tone of his voice telling Carly he was just as frustrated as she was.

"Come on, then. I'll give you a ride to the station. Nick, you can check out a plain car until you get some wheels squared away." Jake led the way to his squad car. "And by the way, Trouble, that was quite an article in the paper. First time I've ever read a Trejo article that sounded like a publicity press release."

Carly frowned. "I haven't seen the paper this morning."

"I've got a copy here." As Jacobs climbed into the driver's seat, Nick opened the front passenger door for Carly to take shotgun. The paper was on the passenger seat, and she began to read the article while Jacobs started the car.

"Huh," she huffed, feeling herself blush. The piece was way over the top, and she'd only read the first couple of paragraphs.

The lieutenant chuckled. "You have quite a cheering section there."

"I don't know." Carly skimmed the rest and then handed the paper back to Nick. "I'll have to have a talk with him."

"Enjoy it while it lasts. Soon Trejo will be back to cop bashing."

Carly settled back in the seat and shook her head. That had been Mary Ellen in Trejo's car, and she'd eluded capture again. She heard several hopeful sightings over the air, but as everything wound down, the girl was still missing.

At the station, the topic of interest was the 998. Since it had happened so close to shift change, Carly and Nick were greeted by the graveyard units who'd responded as they were coming in at end of watch. They all filed their reports in the same room, and as everyone sat, a comfortable camaraderie pervaded the room until Sergeant Nelson stuck his head in.

"CHP officially called off the chase for the Town Car. It's in the wind," he said.

Carly cocked her head. "Thanks for the update."

The sergeant left, and Carly turned back to the banter going on around her. The one positive of this whole frustrating day was that while she watched Nick, she saw the old Nick—the optimist, the man she fell in love with and married. She prayed he'd stay this way just as hard as she prayed they'd find Mary Ellen soon.

• • •

Not long after the sergeant left, there was a knock at the door. Carly looked up to see a welcome face in the doorway.

"Hey, Joe!"

He said hello, and all the other officers in the room piped up to greet him. When everyone was finished, he gave Carly a hug and then leaned against the desk where she sat.

"It's great to see you," she said. "What brings you down here?"

"I was listening to my scanner and heard some of what happened this morning. I was hoping you'd fill me in on the details."

"Of course—I was going to call you. Better to tell you in person." She started from the early-morning phone call and told him about the fire.

"Oh, I missed that part. I must have gotten out of bed after the fire. I couldn't figure out what you and Nick were doing there. Now it makes sense."

As she finished the narrative, he frowned. "I never thought I'd say this, but I feel sorry for the girl. Christy and I were talking, and . . . well, A.J. is fine—he didn't lose any weight, no diaper rash. We missed him, and we were terrified with him gone." He paused and swallowed. "We would have preferred that we hadn't lost him for a minute, but we're thankful he's home, healthy and happy."

"I'd never condone what she did, but I think there's more going on than we know. And while Mary Ellen needs to be apprehended, she doesn't deserve a death threat from Sperry."

"I agree, and I want to help. Let's go over her juvenile file again, this time with a fine-tooth comb. I know you have already, but I want to get to know this girl, maybe find a way to help her."

Carly looked over at Nick, who'd been listening. He nodded. "Can't hurt. I've got to deal with my truck and the insurance company. Not sure how they'll handle the fact that I was in pursuit. I'll meet with you two upstairs later."

Carly stood. "Okay. Come on, Joe. Let's visit homicide and go through the hard-copy file. It's easier to see everything that way."

Together they headed for the elevator.

32

CARLY AWOKE WITH A START, heart beating madly. She'd heard something. Rolling over onto her back, frowning into the darkness, she listened and waited while her heart rate slowed to normal. Had she heard something, or was it just a bad dream? She'd taken Maddie over to Nick's house earlier. Since she didn't have a roommate, she'd felt it would be best for the dog to stay where there was a dog door. So there was no four-legged alarm system to confirm whether there had been a noise.

Thump, thump, scrape.

There it was again. Someone was in her apartment. Fully awake now, Carly sat up and swung her legs from under the covers and out of bed, wincing as she bumped her knee against the corner of the nightstand. Ignoring the soreness from the car chase, she grabbed her off-duty weapon from the stand and went to the door, then placed her ear to the wall and listened.

When she heard nothing else, she wondered if she'd just imagined the noise or if it was her upstairs neighbor moving around. The clock said 4:30 a.m. She had been sound asleep for about five hours. And before that, she'd had more than a couple of full days.

Scrape, scrape.

Briefly she wondered if Mary Ellen was out there, ready to turn herself in. Carly and Joe hadn't come any closer to finding her, but they had learned a lot about her. She'd lived in a group home for a time and then started shuffling through the foster care system. At one foster home, she helped take care of several infants who were placed temporarily in the home for various reasons. That helped explain why she was so good with A.J. In her last foster home, she'd complained to a social worker about a male foster child in the home harassing her and had been waiting to be placed elsewhere. Joe guessed she got tired of waiting and ran away.

Frying pan into the fire, Carly thought, and now the girl was on the run in a big way. She had spent time with a burglar who was adept at breaking into houses, and she certainly knew where Carly lived. *I still haven't figured out how she got my address, but it would be too easy to think she'd just walk in and surrender.*

Sighing, she knew she'd have to check the apartment or she'd never get back to sleep. She quietly opened her bedroom door and crept into the hallway. Holding the gun at her side, she eased herself toward the living room. She saw a shadow and stopped. Someone was in her apartment, sitting in her recliner. Drawing in a deep breath, she moved closer, and more of the figure became visible in the light that poured through the window from the streetlamp.

Not Mary Ellen—it was Andi.

Carly relaxed, but bewilderment now creased her brow. For the first time she could remember, her normally flashy and well-put-together friend looked disheveled and unkempt. What would she be doing here at this time of morning? After a long moment, Carly cleared her throat.

"Hey, Andi." Twisting the gun in her hand, she said, "Whew, glad I didn't have to call 911 to report a dead burglar. Paperwork would tie me up for days."

Andi looked up at her, and as Carly stepped closer, she saw bloodshot eyes and a face with no makeup. "I still have my key and let myself in," Andi explained. "Sorry I woke you."

"I usually work graves, remember? I thrive on no sleep." She put her gun on the kitchen counter and moved to sit on the coffee table in front of Andrea. "What brings you here now? What's wrong?"

"Oh, what's right?" She uttered a foul word. "I've made a mess of things." She leaned forward and put her head in her hands. The despair in her voice broke Carly's heart.

"Did something happen with you and Hal?"

Andi sniffled and shrugged. "Hal was a mistake . . . one in a long line of mistakes."

When she began to cry, Carly put a hand on her shoulder. "Hey, why don't I make some coffee and we'll talk about it?"

Andrea looked up and nodded. "I could use some of your coffee. I miss it. You make the best."

Carly stood and walked to the kitchen, praying for strength and the right words. She'd never seen Andi shed a tear over any guy. Something else was going on, and she wanted to do and say the right things for her friend.

While she started the coffee, Andrea went to the bathroom to wash her face. As the coffee dripped, Carly grabbed a couple of mugs and wiped off a clean counter for something to do. Never having seen Andrea in such a state, she was at a loss. She remembered her mother's words: *She needs to know she's loved. And job or no job, man or no man, Jesus will always love her.*

Carly drank her coffee black but knew Andrea liked flavored creamers. She opened the refrigerator and thanked God there was still some creamer inside. She put it on the counter with the mugs and a spoon. Andi came into the kitchen just as the coffee beeped finished.

Carly filled their mugs and waited at the table while Andi doctored hers. "So what's going on?"

Andi sat down and took a sip. "I was with Hal yesterday when you put out that 998—that you and Nick were shot at." She shivered. "I didn't realize how scared I was that something could happen to you." She choked back a sob. "Oh, Carly, I couldn't bear that, especially with the way I talked to you the other day." The tears fell.

Carly didn't know what to do but let her cry. When she composed herself, Andi looked at her over the rim of her mug and said, "I almost lost everything—my job, my self-respect, and my best friend. You're like the sister I've never had, and I've been so stupid."

"Andi, I—"

She held a hand up. "No, let me finish. I never got over my mom's crash. You remember how she almost died?" Carly nodded, and Andrea continued. "John walked away unscathed. And then he was in church praying for her when it was his fault she was hurt so bad!" She grabbed a napkin and blew her nose. "But you're not John, and I was treating you as if you were. I've always thought Christians were hypocrites, but if I'm honest, I know you and your mom aren't. But I'm reserving judgment on Nick for now, okay?"

Carly relaxed a tad. "Fair enough."

"Bottom line, when you told me you might reconcile, I just panicked. I don't want to live alone. I hate that there isn't someone to talk to when I come home, someone who listens and understands and who doesn't want anything from me. I even hate that there's no dog wandering around getting hair on everything."

She paused but Carly stayed silent, the lump in her throat telling her she'd be as big a mess as Andi if she tried to speak.

Andi swallowed and continued in a broken voice. "I envy what you and Nick have. I know you think I hate him because he cheated. But as twisted as it sounds, I hate him because he might really have changed enough for the second time around to work. When you broke up and moved back in with me, I'd forgotten how great we got along and how good a friend you were. Even though I called you judgmental, you were anything but. You just accepted me, no matter how out of control I got. I—" Her composure broke again, and this time so did Carly's.

Carly got up and grabbed her weeping friend in a hug even as her own tears fell. "Hey, you *are* the sister I never had, Andi. Of course I accept you. I love you."

The two sobbed, and Carly felt Andi's tight grip. After a few minutes, Andi pulled away and reached for the box of Kleenex on the counter. "I have to get through this; I really do. There is so much that needs to be said." She blew her nose again.

Carly smiled and took the box. "You better get it all out. Look what you did to me," she said as she took several tissues, blew her nose, and wiped her eyes.

Sniffling, Andi said, "I'm sorry I stormed out of here the other day. I'm sorry for a lot of things. I may be losing you as a roommate, but I don't want to lose you as a friend. I'll even be nice to Nick."

"Andi, all is forgiven. I was never mad at you—a lot frustrated, but not mad. And I don't want to lose my best friend either. There's just one thing I need to get off my chest."

"What?"

"I really think you should reconsider your relationship with Sergeant Barrett." She made a face and felt the knot in her stomach evaporate when Andi laughed.

"You're so right. There's a lot in my life that needs to change."

Carly refilled their mugs, and they left the kitchen to get comfortable in the living room.

"Tell me about the kidnapper bringing the baby here and everything that happened yesterday."

Carly did. When she finished, Andrea leaned forward, brow crinkled in a frown. "So your pastor is actually the kidnapper's uncle?"

"Yeah, he was scared away from fighting for her ten years ago. His faith failed him. He's really torn up about it."

"But he's still the pastor?"

"Yeah, of course. Why?"

"Well, gosh, Carly, he's the pastor. How can his faith fail? Isn't he supposed to be perfect? That doesn't happen to you and Nick."

Carly put her coffee down. "What do you mean? Of course it does. No one has perfect faith 100 percent of the time, especially not me and Nick." The bumpy road she and Nick had traveled to reconciliation came to mind. "Why would you think that?"

Andi sat back, looking perplexed. "I don't know—you're so good, so noble, not at all like John. I figured to go to your church, to be a Christian, would mean being more perfect than I can ever be."

Carly laughed. "No, no, no. God doesn't ask for perfect people. He doesn't even demand perfect faith. We can't be good enough or perfect enough. We have to trust Christ to be good enough for us."

Andi's expression was one of interest, and that was the opening Carly needed. As they continued to talk, the morning dawned bright and clear, and before the pot of coffee was finished, Carly shared with Andrea about a love that was perfect, that would never leave her or let her down.

33

IT WAS 9 A.M., and Andi had left for a meeting with her union rep over her suspension. Carly was tired but happy that she and Andi had mended their relationship, and she didn't want to go back to bed. She had decided on a swim when her phone buzzed with a text from Alex: NEED YOUR HELP.

As she started to respond, she realized that Alex had not been around any of the chaos she was pulled from bed for the morning before. Maybe he'd sleep through a fire, but if nothing else, the 998 should have gotten him up. As a spark of worry grew, she typed back, WHERE ARE YOU?

HOME. COME HERE.

ON MY WAY.

She'd just put the phone down to take a quick shower when it buzzed again. This time it was Nick calling.

"Glad you're up. I thought I'd come by and take you to breakfast. We can take Maddie to the dog beach after."

She told him about Alex's text.

"Ohhh, I guess food can wait. I'll come get you—we'll go together."

Fifteen minutes later, Carly climbed into the plain car Nick was now driving. She noticed he'd come prepared again. "Glad you don't think I'm overreacting," she said.

"No, you're right. Alex has been all over this from the start. For him to not show up yesterday is odd." He waited a beat, then continued. "After all, he considers you a rock star."

"Ha. You jealous?"

Nick gave her a warm smile. "What? Because he seems to have totally forgotten that I was out there in Riverside too? Nah."

Carly chuckled. As they turned the corner onto Alex's street, Carly saw the black Town Car parked in front of his house. And two men were getting in it.

"Nick."

"I see them," Nick said as he slowed the car.

Carly grabbed the car radio and gave dispatch the information. She was about to read the plate when the car's horn sounded and it started rolling forward.

"He's going to split," Nick said, punching the accelerator.

The car burned rubber and took off down the street.

"We have to check Alex," Carly said, and Nick took his foot off the gas.

Just then a man ran out of Alex's house and across the yard in the direction the black car had gone.

Nick punched it and pulled the wheel to the right to cut in front of the man on the sidewalk. The man slammed into the front fender and rolled over the hood.

Carly's door was partway open as Nick threw the car into park. Both of them leaped out at the same time.

By the time Carly rounded the front of the car, Nick had one of the man's arms. She jumped in and grabbed the other. Together they lifted the cursing man from the ground and bent him over the hood of the plain car. Nick gripped his wrist in a tight control hold. Carly finally heard the sirens of responding officers.

Nick turned to her. "I've got him. Go check Alex."

Carly paused only long enough to grab her backpack from the front seat. Jogging to Alex's door, she pulled her handgun from the pack and held it at the ready when she reached the porch.

The door was open. From the steps she called out, "Alex?"

Fear blossomed in her gut. Sperry was desperate enough to burn down his own apartment building. What would he do to Alex?

Sucking in a breath, she stepped cautiously over the threshold about the same time the sirens came to a stop and she knew backup was there.

"In here."

As she turned toward the living room, her breath whooshed out with relief. Alex was on the floor, one elbow on a chair while the other hand held a cloth over his face, and he was okay.

"What were they after?"

Alex gave a weak shake of his head. "They pushed their way in right after I texted you. Talk about déjà vu—I thought I'd be safe from intrusions like this with Drake and Tucker in jail."

Just then Nick came rushing in. "Do you need medics, Alex?"

"No. I think I'll live, though I probably need a dentist. I think I'll lose a tooth or two." He dropped the cloth from his face and Carly saw that he'd been smacked around. When he started to get up, Carly and Nick stepped forward to help him. "First a shotgun in the face and now a beating in my own living room."

"The uniforms have the guy. Looks like Boxer, one of the three who work for Sperry, but he won't say why he's here. And he wants his lawyer."

"Three guesses who his lawyer is," Carly said in a huff.

"Cynical today, aren't you?" Alex said with a lopsided grin.

"I'm that and more. What's going on?"

"I'll explain. Help me into the kitchen."

Once he was seated in the kitchen, Carly found a plastic bag and put together an ice pack.

"What did they want from you?" Carly asked once Trejo had the ice on his face and they were all seated at the table.

He ran a hand over his puffy face, new bruises forming over old ones, and wouldn't meet her gaze. "I'll tell you about them in a minute, but first I'd better tell you what happened last night. You aren't going to be happy with me, but I saw Mary Ellen."

"*What?*"

"She came here. She got my address from the registration in the glove box, and she came to give me my car back and apologize for taking it—and to ask for my help."

"Alex! Why didn't you call? She's wanted for kidnapping, for heaven's sake—"

"She's a scared kid. She was babbling about a fire and a threat and barely getting away. What would you have done?"

"I would have called the police! We need to get to the bottom of this. We can keep her safe."

He sighed. "Maybe you're right. Maybe I should have done that, but I wanted to find out what was going on, and I thought I could do a better job getting information from her than the cops could." He shrugged and then winced. "The girl is street smart maybe, and definitely a survivor, but at the core she's still a kid. You said yourself that you didn't think she planned and executed the kidnapping on her own."

"I still want her in custody so we can get some answers! For two cents I'd arrest you for aiding and abetting. She gave you your car back?"

"Yeah, it's in the garage. She said she's sorry; she feels responsible for Harper's death, says it was her fault he got arrested. He was the only person she knew she could trust.

As far as the baby goes, she did her best to take care of him. She said she's only one step ahead of Sperry. That unless she gives him back what she took, he'll kill her."

"He'll probably kill her anyway if he has the chance. Did she tell you what she has that he wants?"

He looked away.

"Alex, did she say what she took that belongs to him?"

He sighed. "I hate being a snitch. But yeah, she did say she took something out of his safe. Apparently she had keys that Harper took from Sperry. He had told her once there was something in the safe at the house in Riverside that she could use, something that would be insurance."

"What?"

"I didn't get a chance to ask."

"You guys had a nice long conversation and you didn't ask her what she took?"

"Look, Edwards, I thought about asking and I thought about calling you when she was at my house, but I knew she'd bolt. What was I supposed to do, tie her up? Anyway, I fed her and listened to her tell me what she wanted to tell me and I hoped to talk her into seeing you, but then the storm troopers came."

"The storm troopers?"

"Yeah, Immigration and Customs Enforcement. They came to my house and practically hauled me away in handcuffs for being a victim."

"ICE? Why did they want to talk to you?" Carly wondered if that was why Wiley was so ready to dismiss Las

Playas PD, because ICE was involved. Made sense because of the human trafficking aspect of Sperry's crime.

Alex leaned back, his puffy lip causing him to speak with a sort of lisp. "She'd been here about an hour when two ICE agents knocked on my door and said they wanted to talk to me about what happened out in Riverside. Now, I don't mind talking to them, but Mary Ellen was sitting in my kitchen. Call me paranoid, but I wasn't going to tell them she was there. I tried to get rid of them, put them off until later. I guess they took my attitude as evasive, and next thing I knew they were asking me if I wanted to be arrested. So I poked my head in the kitchen and told her I would be right back, make yourself at home, that kind of thing. ICE kept me four hours, and when I got home, she was gone."

"Four hours? What did they want to know?"

"Every minute detail I could remember about being in that cellar." He moved the ice pack to a different spot on his face. "They wanted to know everything the illegals said, everything Grant said, and everything I saw and heard. I must have repeated the story twenty times before they decided they had it all and let me go."

"And when you got home, Mary Ellen was gone."

He nodded. "I waited, hoping she'd come back. But when I realized she wasn't going to, I texted you to tell you what happened. Then there was a knock, and Boxer pushed his way in. He had a friend with him, a big guy with a gold tooth in the front."

"Just the two of them?"

"Three of them came to the door. The third guy—" he put the ice on his eye—"Gold Tooth called him Casper. He must have been the driver because right after they grabbed me and had me restrained, Gold Tooth told him to go get the car ready. After I told them I couldn't help them, I guess they weren't sure what their next move would be. Gold Tooth left to call the boss and told Boxer to hang on a minute." Alex moaned and again moved the ice pack around his face.

Carly scrubbed her cheeks with her hands and looked at Nick, who had been listening quietly.

"We have to tell Nelson," he said to Alex. "You could be in trouble for not calling when Mary Ellen was here. For all you know, you might have saved yourself a beating."

"I'm a big boy. I can take the consequences."

"She didn't give you any idea about where she'd been staying?"

"I got the impression it wasn't in one place. I asked her about relatives or friends and she just shrugged."

"How is she getting around without your car?"

"I don't know. I told her to go to you; I said she could trust you—after all, she left the baby with you."

Carly's hands flew to her hips. "Yeah, by the way, how'd she get my address?"

"I have GPS in my car. Your address is on it." He hiked his shoulder sheepishly.

Carly just shook her head.

"Did Sperry's goons know Mary Ellen had been here?" Nick asked.

Trejo frowned and then winced. "They acted like they did. I mean, they kept asking me for some package she left me, but . . ."

"But what?"

"Well, I got the impression they were bluffing."

"They weren't bluffing on your face."

"I know, but it seemed like they were trying to find out how much I knew about the girl. The car was in the garage; they didn't know she'd brought it back." He looked from Nick to Carly. "They might be shooting in the dark, trying to find out anything they can. They might visit you next." He pointed at Carly.

Carly glanced at Nick, and she knew from the expression on his face that he was thinking the same thing she was. He spoke it out loud.

"Or they may visit Jonah."

34

"WHO'S JONAH?" Alex asked Carly as Nick pulled out his cell phone to call the station. One of the officers who had responded to their radio call had come into the house, and Carly asked him to do the paperwork to recover Alex's car.

"They may need to take your car to have it processed," she explained. "It will be up to Nelson."

Alex waved his right hand; his left was tenderly testing one of his front teeth. "Who is Jonah?" he repeated.

"He's the pastor of our church, and he's also Mary Ellen's uncle."

"Uncle? She has an uncle you know? You've been holding out on me!"

"Not intentionally. I just never got around to telling you. Besides, it's a long story. He hasn't seen her in ten years."

Alex sighed. "Then she probably doesn't even remember him."

Nick finished his phone call. "Alex, you need to stay here. Nelson and Harris are on the way over. They need to talk to you and check out the car. And a unit found the black Town Car—it was abandoned about a mile away."

"No sign of the occupants?"

"Nope, that car was burned. We had the plate, and everyone knew what to look for. It's a rental anyway, so it makes sense for the goons to hop to another set of wheels."

"If I'm staying, that means you're leaving," Alex said.

"We're going to see Jonah. I tried calling but didn't get an answer. Since it's lunchtime, everyone might be out, but I want to be certain." He started for the door and waved for Carly to follow.

"Sounds like the story is where you're going."

"Sorry, Alex, but you need to wait here and face the music." Carly smiled grimly and followed Nick out to the plain car.

• • •

"On the phone Nelson told me that ICE plans to set up on the church," Nick said as he put the car in drive and made a U-turn. "They could be there shortly. They think Sperry might want to talk to Jonah. There might be more going on than we know for ICE to be so aggressive. I'm surprised they jumped Alex like they did."

"Sperry took a chance sending those three here to rough Alex up."

"And at least partially failed because we have another one of his employees in custody. But it tells me there's an urgency in his search for Mary Ellen."

Something in his voice made her turn and study his profile. "You're worried because Jonah didn't answer."

Nick nodded. "Someone should be there; someone should have answered the phone."

"We'll be there in a minute." She reached over and squeezed one of his hands on the steering wheel.

Though the ride was over quickly, Carly found herself worrying as they pulled into an almost-empty church lot. She figured at the very least, the construction workers should be there. One of the buildings adjacent to the sanctuary was being remodeled into a coffee shop, bookstore, and fellowship hall.

"Do you want to call for a unit?"

Nick hesitated. "No, he might be in the prayer room. He wouldn't answer the phone if he was there. Let's check that first."

They got out of the car, and Carly slung her backpack over her shoulder. Together they walked toward the sanctuary. They reached the door as Veronica came out.

"Veronica, where is everyone?" Nick asked.

"Jonah canceled construction today. He's been in prayer

all morning." Her face took on a pained expression. "He's fasting for his niece. You're not here for prayer?"

"Not exactly," Carly said. "We wanted to talk to Jonah."

"You'll find him in the prayer room. I'm on my way to pick up some supplies. I'll be back in a few."

They thanked Veronica, then headed down the sanctuary aisle to the small room at the left of the stage and found Jonah inside. He looked as though he hadn't slept.

He brightened when he saw them. "News?"

"No. Sorry, Jonah," Nick said. "We still haven't found her, but we have heard from her."

Carly told him about Mary Ellen's visit to Alex.

The pastor looked deflated. "She returned the car and disappeared? I've been here all night, praying for her life, her soul . . ."

Carly reached out and touched his arm. "I thank God she brought the baby back. And I know we'll find her. We came here to warn you." She told him about the apartment fire and Alex's beating. Jonah paled but said nothing. Carly didn't sugarcoat anything. She was certain they needed to find Mary Ellen, and she was also certain Jonah needed to know exactly how dangerous Sperry was in case he did show up at church.

"Thank you both," Jonah said when she finished. "I appreciate it. This is a scary situation—the worst is not knowing. But I agree with you: prayer was answered with the return of the baby. And I'm glad my trust is in an all-knowing God."

"Amen," Nick said. "ICE will be watching the church later. Someone will probably contact you."

"What will you two be doing?"

Nick looked at Carly, and she shrugged. "Officially we're off, but . . ."

"She means that we'll probably be looking for Mary Ellen on our own time."

"I appreciate that. Why don't the three of us pray so this day continues on the right note," Jonah suggested.

They each knelt, and Pastor Rawlings led them in a heartfelt prayer for Mary Ellen and the safety of all law enforcement personnel.

• • •

They left Jonah in the prayer room and walked slowly back through the sanctuary. Carly found she had more respect for Jonah than before. He'd made a hard, shocking choice to let go of Mary Ellen ten years ago, revealing a lack of faith that made him more real, more human in her eyes. *We're all faithless at times,* she thought, glancing at Nick and thinking of their issues, *but the bottom line is that God is always faithful.*

Nick was quiet, but he reached over and grabbed her hand as they walked between the rows of empty seats. Preoccupied, she heard a noise in the lobby and assumed it was Veronica.

It registered too late that Veronica probably wasn't back yet. Nick had just put his hand on the door to pull it open when someone on the other side shoved it with force. The door smacked Nick in the face, wrenching his hand out of hers. He went down hard.

"Nick!" Carly was thrown off-balance, and before she regained it, she was seized from behind and held in a vise-like grip.

35

THE HARD STEEL OF A GUN BARREL pressed into her cheek. She looked in horror as blood poured down Nick's face from a gash the door left on the right side of his forehead.

"Be still." A harsh voice spoke in her ear.

A second man appeared on her left, pointing a gun at Nick, who looked dazed as he stood and brought a hand to his forehead in an effort to stop the bleeding.

"Don't move!" the man ordered Nick. "Slowly take your gun out of the shoulder holster and toss it my way."

Nick's confused gaze flicked from the gun to Carly and back again. He complied, and the man scooped the gun up and shoved it in his pants. When he grinned, Carly didn't miss a gold tooth shining in the middle of his mouth. *This must be one of the goons who attacked Alex.*

"What about you?" the man holding Carly asked. "Where's your gun?"

When she didn't answer right away, he jerked his hand toward Gold Tooth. "Hit him again."

"It's in my backpack!" Carly said as she strained against his grip.

He ripped the pack from her shoulder with his free hand, half-opening it in the process, and then upended it, dumping everything at his feet. He pushed the contents around with the toe of his shoe. She didn't have much: wallet, brush, spare set of handcuffs, and off-duty weapon. He didn't bend down to pick the gun up; instead, he stepped on it. His grip on her did not loosen.

Sour, hot breath assailed her nostrils as he spoke into her ear again. "Now, I'll make this quick because we're in a hurry. My boss has a plane waiting. I want the package, and I want it now."

"What package am I supposed to have, Casper?" Carly asked, shifting a bit so she could see his face.

His eyes registered surprise that she knew his name, and he cursed. Gold Tooth rammed an elbow into Nick's gut, doubling him over. Blood now covered half his face and dripped to his shoulder.

"Hey!" Carly struggled against Casper's grasp.

"I said hurry." The gun barrel dug into her cheek. "Give me the package and I'll just lock you up and leave."

Nick looked up from one knee, blinking as blood ran into one eye, voice breathless after the stomach shot. "If you're after something that would be evidence, what makes you think we'd have it on our person? If we had evidence, we'd put it where it belonged—at the station."

"I'm not stupid. I know the pastor is that little brat's uncle. She must be hiding here, and if she's here, so is the package she stole." He pressed the gun harder into Carly's face. "And if she's not here, I want to know where she is. Now."

Carly leaned back as far as she could from the pressure of the gun barrel. She could see the man holding the gun on Nick from the corner of her eye. She knew that if the tables were turned and they were on the other side of the gun barrels, she and Nick would finally be close to Sperry. But how to get there?

"We don't have your package, Casper." She spit the words out, angry at having a gun in her face and furious that Nick was bleeding and she couldn't help him.

Just then there was a noise from the stage. Rawlings had come out of the prayer room. "What's going on out here?"

Everyone turned toward him. Gold Tooth raised his gun in the pastor's direction, and Nick lunged, hitting him in the midsection and driving him into a row of chairs.

The gun barrel left Carly's face to take aim at Nick, and Casper's grip on her loosened. Free to move a bit, Carly jerked her head back and connected with the bad guy's face, feeling the satisfying crunch of cartilage. At the same time, she reached for the hand that held the gun and grabbed with both her hands. Once she had hold, she jerked his wrist down hard on the back of a chair. The man was forced to let go and cursed as the gun flew toward the door.

Carly drove an elbow into his face and then leaped toward the gun, picked it up, and pivoted to hold it on Casper, who had fallen to his knees and was crawling toward her gun.

"Don't touch it!" she ordered. The man who'd once had her in his grasp stopped moving and looked up at her from the floor, blood dripping from his nose. "Believe me, I will shoot."

Casper was the classic picture of a deer in the headlights. Carly knew then that there was nothing tough about him in spite of his earlier bluster.

"Nick, you okay?" she asked without taking her eyes from Casper.

"I'm good. Jonah is with me. And I have cuffs for this guy."

"I have a pair for Casper."

Nick was at her side a second later. He picked up her gun and then quickly ratcheted her handcuffs onto Casper.

It was then Carly heard the sirens, lots of them. She turned to Nick, who'd just pulled Casper to his feet.

"Sounds like the cavalry," he said as he wiped blood from his eye. "Better late than never. Jonah and I have these guys. Why don't you go check?"

Carly nodded and left the sanctuary. She stepped outside the church to see four black-and-whites, three black SUVs she knew were ICE vehicles, and two plain cars turn in to the parking lot, sirens wailing.

Wondering how on earth they knew they were needed, but

not complaining, she held her gun at her side and raised four fingers on her right hand. The sirens shut down as the vehicles pulled to the sidewalk and came to a stop. Sergeant Nelson jumped out of one of the plain cars with Alex on his heels.

"Everything okay?" Nelson asked. Behind him came Jacobs, Wiley, and a few ICE agents.

"Now, yeah. Nick needs medics for a cut, but we have two in custody. How'd you know to come here?"

"Boxer talked about their next stop," Alex said as Nelson directed one uniformed officer to request medics and another to help Nick and Jonah. "They were to come right to the church and kill the pastor if he wouldn't tell them where the girl was."

Nick and Jonah walked out of the church, the two hand-cuffed Sperry employees between them.

Jacobs walked her way and smiled. "Guess it's getting to be a trend, Trouble. Now you're dragging Sergeant Anderson into things."

Nick answered, "Nah, she doesn't drag me into anything. We just make a good team when stuff comes up."

36

THE GOONS WERE HANDED OFF to ICE, who quickly moved in to take control of the entire situation. One of the agents gave Carly back Nick's and her cuffs as they replaced them with their own restraints. Paramedics rolled up shortly thereafter and looked after Nick. Carly learned from Nelson that as soon as he and Harris had arrived at Alex's house, Boxer started talking.

"He wouldn't shut up. Says he'll testify. It made Wiley and ICE extremely happy."

"Did he say where Sperry is?"

Wiley nodded. "He's trying to charter a plane out of the country. Agents are on their way to the airport as we speak."

They were standing out in front of the church. ICE was impounding a black Cadillac. Carly assumed the vehicle was Casper and Gold Tooth's.

"Not disappointed that the feds are whisking this all away, are you?" Jacobs asked.

Carly sighed. "Frankly, I'm tired. I really don't care who handles this as long as all involved parties go to jail for a long time. The only thing I do have a problem with is that Mary Ellen Barber is still outstanding."

Nelson nodded. "We need to debrief about all of this. I think here will be as good a place as any. Maybe by the time we're finished, Sperry will be in custody." He and Wiley stepped to Jonah to ask him where they could hold a quick meeting.

Carly took the opportunity to check in with Nick, who'd just had his head bandaged.

"You're going to need stitches, I bet."

"Yep," Nick agreed. He asked the medics to stand by in case he needed transport.

She reached out and gently touched his face. "Does it hurt?"

"It smarts a little." He took her hand and brought it to his lips. "I can hear it now—I'll get stitches, and before long my nickname will be Zipper Head."

Carly laughed and grasped his hand in both of hers. "For me it will be *GQ* Zipper Head."

Nelson joined them. "We're going to review the day's events in the church. Why don't you make your way in there?" he said to Carly before turning to Nick. "You go get your head taken care of. Is it bad?"

"I think I just need some stitches." He looked down at all the blood on his shirt, and Carly winced. "It looks worse than it is, Sarge. You know head wounds bleed a lot."

"Even so, get it taken care of. You can file paper later."

Nick nodded, then took off his shoulder holster and handed it to Carly. "Take care of this for me."

"Sure."

Before he climbed into the medic van, Nick squeezed Carly's hand and apologized. "Sorry to leave you here to do all the explaining."

"That's okay. The next big mess we're involved in will be all yours."

"Deal."

With that, the medics closed the door and the van left for the hospital.

Alex joined her as she walked toward the church. "How is it you hitched a ride with Nelson?" she asked.

"It was easy. He didn't want me to slip out of telling him about my visit with Mary Ellen."

"And you're a witness to a big story now. So why do you look so glum?"

"I've had enough ICE to last a lifetime." He shuddered. "They call this a sanctuary, don't they? Think the good pastor will give me sanctuary from the storm troopers?"

Carly laughed. "It doesn't work that way, but sure, give it your best shot." She watched as Alex hurried inside. Things in the parking lot had calmed down a bit. The medics were gone with Nick, but ICE agents were talking to Casper and

Gold Tooth and going through the Cadillac with a fine-tooth comb.

"Trouble."

She looked toward the church door as Jacobs waved her over.

"We'll be ready for you in the office in a few."

In the sanctuary, Alex was sitting about midway down the aisle with Pastor Rawlings. They were speaking in low tones, and Carly found herself praying that Alex was asking questions that would lead him to a saving relationship. She gathered up her belongings and put them in her backpack before she took a seat. As she sat, she realized that the only worry she felt now was for Mary Ellen. Carly was shocked at the thought that she no longer looked at the girl as a suspect but as a victim. Frowning, she wondered if she was being disloyal to Joe. About a minute later, Alex waved her over to where he and Rawlings sat.

"We were talking about Mary Ellen," he told her when she plopped down next to him. "Pastor Rawlings was telling me what you told him—you know, about the process with minors, what happens when they're arrested."

Carly stretched. "Yeah, it's kind of strange. I never thought I'd say I was glad I worked juvenile, but I am because now I know a lot about the process."

"There's a chance they'll go easy on her." Alex looked at her expectantly.

"It all depends on probation's evaluation and if they decide to try her as an adult. But we still have to find her."

"Any idea where she might be?" Jonah asked.

Carly shook her head. "At least the men threatening her are in custody." Even as the words left her mouth, she noted that worry and remorse still hung around Jonah like a shawl.

"Odd, huh."

"What?" She turned to Alex.

"She kidnapped a baby from your partner, stole my car, and left me to get beat up, and still we feel sorry for her. Go figure."

Carly set Nick's shoulder holster on the seat next to her. "I can't figure, Alex. I want to be mad at her, but I can't. I find myself hoping that when she's caught, she'll get a little leniency. From what Joe has told me, he and Christy might be leaning the same way."

"The fact that she kept the baby safe probably carries a lot of weight."

Jonah noticed blood on the carpet from Nick and left to get something to clean it.

Alex watched him walk away, then turned to Carly. "So this is your church, huh?"

Carly nodded and yawned as she experienced an adrenaline crash.

"Maybe I'll come here sometime, check the place out."

"You'll be welcome."

Jacobs stepped into the sanctuary. "Carly, we're ready for you."

"Okay." She got up and followed the lieutenant into Veronica's office, where everyone else was seated.

"Edwards." Wiley handed her a cup of coffee. Obviously

someone had made a 7-Eleven run. "You look like you could use this."

"Thank you." Carly took the coffee as her stomach reminded her that she'd had nothing to eat all day. She and Nick had never made it to breakfast.

"Your timing for this little incident was impeccable," Nelson said. "I was with Wiley, and ICE said they were just about ready to set up on the church. Then we heard the news that you caught Boxer at Trejo's. By the time we got there we had to slow him down, he was so eager to talk."

"And you saved ICE a surveillance team," Wiley said. "It looks as if Sperry's desperation played right into our hands. Thanks."

"Really, good work, Trouble. Chaos seems to become you," Jacobs said. His phone rang, and when he looked at the caller ID, he cursed. "Garrison." He and Nelson shared a look Carly pretended not to see. "I'd better talk to him." He left the room to take the call.

"Why don't we have a seat and piece this thing together." Nelson pointed to a chair, and Carly sat.

"Still no word from the airport," he said, answering her unasked question. "But Casper has stated unequivocally that Conrad Sperry ordered the attack on Trejo as well as the trip here to bully Jonah Rawlings."

"Glad he isn't screaming for a lawyer."

"A lot of people are. He's corroborating much of what Boxer had to say. What happened here?" Wiley asked as he clicked on a recorder.

Blowing out a breath, Carly started from the beginning with Trejo's text message and attack. Once or twice Wiley asked questions, but Nelson was quiet.

"Conrad Sperry will be charged with ordering the assault on Nick and me and probably a lot more charges ICE will add, right?"

Wiley and Nelson exchanged a look she couldn't decipher before Wiley spoke up. "Yeah, ICE and the bureau both have a list of charges. Especially after Riverside. What has surprised everyone is how long Sperry has been at this."

"What you may not remember," Nelson said, "is that before Sperry was forced to quit the reserves, there was suspicion building that the reason he wanted to be a reserve was so he would have access to law enforcement–only information. We couldn't prove it and then didn't have to when he got caught red-handed tampering with evidence."

Wiley continued. "There were signs of Sperry's activities back then that federal investigators missed, and as a result, a lot of people have been victimized by the man. We could have prevented a lot, so right now ICE and the task force are committed to building a solid, ironclad case."

"So Sperry will go away for a long time."

"Yes, and though it hasn't gone out to the press yet, we found another underground area, right on the border."

"Sperry's?"

"Yep. He dug right under the border fence. This wasn't just a hole in the ground; it was a sophisticated underground highway."

"ICE calls Sperry a modern-day slave trader," Nelson added. "He brought people in, used them at his businesses, and also sold people to others just as exploitive as he is. ICE knew his operation was big, but the scope is staggering."

Carly's mind raced to keep up. She knew human trafficking was modern-day slavery. She'd even rescued a woman once who had been brought across the border illegally and forced to work in prostitution. The human trafficker often promised foreign-born individuals legitimate work to get them across the border. But once the workers arrived, the trafficker would take all their IDs and threaten them with jail—or worse—if they tried to escape. The trafficker instilled in them a fear of police and sometimes forced them to live in squalid conditions. It had been heartbreaking to rescue the one woman and to hear what she'd been through. To think that Sperry had brought thousands across the border to live in servitude made Carly sick to her stomach.

"How do the diamonds fit in?"

"That gets murky," Wiley said. "We think he was trying to fence them, but he also used them as bribes—or, as it turns out, the promise of bribes. I think he knew we were closing in on him. He paid off two border patrol agents in San Diego, near where we found the tunnel, to throw us off the scent. People had to look the other way for him to get out of the noose we were closing around his neck, and the sparkle of diamonds turned heads. He was set to make a payment yesterday. But we showed up instead and have the two agents in custody, caught waiting for their payoff."

"As far as Harper goes, he just had rotten luck. He obviously misinterpreted something Sperry said about a baby. What he did may have been bad for A.J.," Nelson said with a shrug, "but it threw Sperry off his game, especially when his keys disappeared."

"They were safe keys."

"Right. Apparently Sperry thought the remote location in Riverside was the best place for his most important safe. And when the keys disappeared, he panicked. He wanted them back, and that's why Caswell showed up so fast. When they realized that Harper didn't have them when he was booked, they just wanted him out of jail and out of the picture as soon as possible."

"And they needed the keys. That's why they snatched Mary Ellen and took her out to Riverside, not because they wanted the baby. She said she didn't have them, which was a lie," Wiley said with a smile. "She must have been smart enough to realize that once they had the keys, she was dead. It was a stroke of luck that reporter showed up when he did." He looked out the window at the parking lot. "Hopefully Sperry will be in custody by the end of the day. ICE thinks he hoped to have the diamonds with him when he fled the country."

The agent leaned back in his chair. "We've kept a lid on the tunnel for as long as we could, but it's going to be all over the news later today. Indictments are coming down against Sperry and company when we hold the news conference."

Jacobs had come back into the room, and he nodded. "Sperry may be slime, but he's smart. And he hired a slick lawyer to work all the angles. Thomas Caswell is as slick as they come."

"And Caswell may go down with his client," Wiley said. "I can't divulge everything, but from what ICE has collected, Caswell was in the thick of things."

"I knew that guy was dirty." Nelson shook his head in disgust.

Carly drained her coffee. "What about Mary Ellen?"

"Good question. She must have the diamonds," Nelson said. "What do you think she'll do with them?"

"I don't know—I'm not sure she knows what she has." Carly stood. "But as long as Sperry is loose, she is in danger."

Wiley shook his head. "Sperry's on the run. I don't believe he can hurt her now. Maybe we should ask her uncle to do some kind of televised plea, asking her to turn herself in. It's probably safe now for her to raise her head."

"That will only help if she's somewhere near a television. I want to hike around in the catch basin. Nick and I never made it there yesterday. And Harper's car is still outstanding; that has to be her mode of transport. Maybe we should even keep the catch basin as a DCC."

"I'll make that happen." Nelson cast a glance at Wiley. "What's your game plan?"

Wiley stood. "First things first: we need to thoroughly interview everyone who is in custody."

"I'm sure the ones who won't talk are screaming for Caswell," Carly said.

"Yeah, where is he?" Jacobs asked.

Wiley shook his head. "I've paged him twice. He may be our next BOLO."

"Then I'll check the catch basin on my way to the station to file my report," Carly said.

Nelson gave her a mock salute. "We'll tell DHS to expect you in a bit."

37

AS CARLY WALKED BACK to the plain car, her backpack in one hand and Nick's shoulder holster in the other, she felt the excitement of an investigation coming to a close, of loose ends being tied up. *Surely when Mary Ellen learns that the man threatening her is on the run and his goons are in jail, she'll surface.*

At the trunk, she pondered the equipment she had available to her as she thought about what she should carry down into the catch basin. She had her gun and Nick's, the cuffs they'd used on Casper and Gold Tooth, and her cell phone but no radio. Looking down at her small off-duty weapon and Nick's 9mm, she decided that while she didn't expect any trouble, she wanted to look official. She shortened the straps on the shoulder holster and slipped it on, then clipped her badge to a hook on the left strap. After locking her gun in the trunk, she turned as she heard Alex protesting the fact that DHS wanted to talk to him some more. He cast a glance her way as if asking for help, but she shrugged, then got in her car and left.

This time Carly made the turn to the catch basin without the drama of any other vehicles barreling her way. As the plain car bounced down the bumpy road, Carly's mind wandered a bit. She found herself thinking about Nick and how normal things were between them. A smile played on her lips as she realized he'd stopped pushing her away and had instead become a partner of sorts over the last couple of days. With a sigh, she wondered how many stitches his head wound rated.

Once stopped at the gate, she pulled out her phone to call him and ask. His voice mail kicked in right away, and she knew he'd probably turned the phone off at the hospital. She left a message, telling him where she was and to call if he needed a ride from the hospital because she didn't think she'd be long. Next she sent dispatch a message, informing them of her location as well.

Carly pulled Nick's keys out of the ignition, knowing he'd have a gate key on his ring. All officers were issued an SM6 key, a master key for all city-owned padlocks in Las Playas. She fumbled for it as she climbed out of the car. Holding the key, she grabbed the lock, but it came open in her hand. It had been put through the chain and made to look secure but hadn't actually been latched.

She frowned. No wonder the homeless got in so easily if public service didn't bother to lock up. She unhooked the lock, pushed the gate open, and returned to the car. There were about five hundred more level feet, and then the road dropped to go down to a footpath that led under the bridge. She'd started down the hill before she saw the other car. It was a brand-new BMW with paper plates parked at the beginning of the footpath.

There was no dope to be scored down here. Besides that, it was broad daylight. Carly parked behind the BMW, got out of the car, and looked around. She didn't see anyone, only a lot of tall weeds. *Maybe this car belongs to public service,* she thought. *A supervisor coming to check things out. That would explain the open gate.* Whoever owned the car had to be a city employee to get the lock open without cutting it.

Carly checked the car out but couldn't see much because of the tinted windows. As she was about to continue past it, she heard the hum of a Chevy motor. A black-and-white pulled in behind her plain car.

Thinking it was a unit here for a DCC, she started back to greet the officers. But only one man got out of the car: Captain Garrison. Carly stopped between the BMW and her car and faced the scowling captain.

"What are you doing here? I thought you were at the church."

Carly took a deep breath. If this had been Jake, the banter would have been friendly and upbeat. But she had no clue how to talk to Garrison other than "yes, sir" and "no, sir." "I finished there. I came here to double-check for Mary Ellen."

He seemed to consider this as he hitched up his gun belt. He rarely wore a duty belt. Carly could only remember seeing him with a belt holster.

He gestured toward the BMW. "Do you know whose car this is?"

She shook her head. "No plates."

"It belongs to Thomas Caswell."

Carly looked from the car to Garrison. "What is he doing here?"

"Good question." He stepped closer. At six-four, he towered over Carly. "I know you don't like me, and I have a problem with the fact that you have a tendency to disobey orders, but something is amiss with Caswell and I plan on finding out what."

Carly thought she managed to keep her jaw from dropping. "Do we need backup?"

"No, I'll handle this. I need to handle this. You just stay quiet and follow my orders; clear?"

Nodding, Carly said nothing. His tone made her angry, and she didn't want to say something that would get her in trouble. All the negative things she'd heard about Garrison in the course of her career came roaring into her thoughts. *Pompous, not a leader, arrogant, self-serving . . .*

When he moved past her to continue down the trail, she

followed, praying he knew what he was doing, but more importantly for protection in case he didn't.

The area under the bridge was clean as a whistle, as Pete had said. There wasn't even much paper trash lying around. She knew there were some hiding places that would be dark in spite of the daylight, and she wished she'd brought a flashlight. Still, hearing nothing but the sound of traffic on the overpass above, she was inclined to believe no homeless had set up camp yet. Neither was it likely that Mary Ellen was here.

"It's been years since I've been down here," Garrison said, and Carly wondered if he was talking to her or himself.

They were almost to the other side of the bridge when she heard voices. The captain must have heard them as well because he stopped.

"He's not alone," Garrison whispered. He looked at Carly, and for the first time she could remember, his eyes were cop eyes—flat, appraising, alert, not a trace of arrogant condescension. "I'm going to take the direct approach. You circle around." He gestured left. "I don't know what we have here, but you be ready for anything."

Carly bit her tongue and nodded, thinking he almost sounded like a partner but wanting to call for backup just the same. He turned away before she could bring it up. Garrison made noise as he pushed through the growth; it was mostly bamboo, thick and green, and the scraping of his large body moving through it was plain. She took advantage of the sound to split left quickly.

She could hear the voices but couldn't make out what was being said. The brush all but swallowed her up, even though there was a path of sorts through the growth. As she crouched low and made her roundabout way to the voices, she understood why homeless and runaways and people hiding liked it in the catch basin. It was a way to escape prying eyes.

The direction of the path led farther down, into the flood control. Abruptly, the foliage ended and the path opened into a clear spot where another car was parked. She stopped and could only see the top of the roof. Looking right, Carly realized this car had come through the same gate she had, but the driver had continued on, probably driving part of the way on the concrete banks of the flood control since there didn't appear to be any way through the brush. A gutsy person determined to hide.

Carly moved closer for a better view of the car, then stayed still. Now the voices of Caswell and another were clear. She listened and studied the car. It was a two-door compact, and both doors were open. Debris was all over the ground as if it had come from the car. There was a man halfway inside the car while the lawyer stood just outside. Garrison hadn't yet made his presence known. Carly realized they probably hadn't needed to worry about stealth—Caswell and his associate were involved in a heated argument and oblivious to what was going on around them.

"Where else would she hide it?" the somewhat-muffled voice of the man inside the car said.

"How should I know?" Caswell sounded petulant. "I'm not a mechanic! Get someone down here to take this piece of junk apart if you don't know where to look."

She heard the other man curse. "I've trusted too much to people who work for me lately." He stood and smacked the car's trunk hard enough to make Carly flinch. But he was facing the opposite direction, so she couldn't see his face.

"That stupid girl must have it with her." When he turned, Carly gasped. It was Conrad Sperry. His face was red, either from anger or exertion. He was a tall man shaped like a pear; four years ago, when she worked with him, Carly had wondered how he'd ever passed the physical agility portion of the reserve test. Obviously he hadn't done any working out since she'd seen him last.

Carly dropped to one knee, holding her breath and hoping she wouldn't be seen if the men looked her way.

"She's not as stupid as you seem to think. She's eluded capture this long." Caswell's tone was almost taunting.

"What's that supposed to mean?" Sperry's red face was nearly purple now.

"Just that I warned you about hiring Harper. And I suggested a safe-deposit box for your valuables."

Carly saw Garrison step out of the brush, but Caswell's back was to him.

"Speaking of the failings of people who work for me, if you'd gotten that thief out of jail, none of this would—" Sperry saw the captain.

Caswell turned, following Sperry's startled expression.

"Norman, what on earth are you doing here?" The lawyer was clearly as surprised as Sperry.

"I could ask you the same question." Garrison gestured toward the car. "That's a wanted vehicle, and you two are destroying evidence."

Carly's gaze went back to the car. He was right—it was Harper's car with the plates Mary Ellen had stolen. Fear grabbed her by the throat. Where was Mary Ellen?

Sperry's hands went to his hips. "I'm looking for what's mine."

"Norman," Caswell spoke, and his voice was soothing, the voice he used to convince juries to pity his clients. "It's just a car. A car once owned by a dead thief. Surely you can overlook Conrad's pursuit of his own property?"

"What property? The keys or the diamonds?"

She couldn't see Caswell's face, but the shock on Sperry's shone like a beacon. He sputtered, "How . . . uh, who told you about the diamonds?"

Garrison cursed. "I'm not the fool you took me for. That's right; I know you stole the diamonds, and I know he had your help, Thomas."

"You'll never prove that. Besides, what diamonds? No evidence, no crime." Caswell's tone was superior, and he spread his hands out.

"The girl will surface with the goods, and when both of you are in jail, I'm sure it will just be a matter of time before you're ratting each other out. You both have made me look bad, and I'm done. Conrad, get away from the car.

You're coming with me. I think ICE has questions for you and Thomas."

Carly's hand was on her gun; she wondered why Garrison hadn't drawn his if he was going to take these two into custody. But she hesitated to make her presence known unless Garrison gave her a sign.

"Hold on, Norm." Sperry held both his hands up. "No harm, no foul. I didn't find the keys or the diamonds. Surely we can talk about this."

"Enough is enough. You two have played me, pretending to be friends, upstanding businessmen, the targets of baseless smears. It proves to me that I've been sitting on my butt behind a desk for too long that I even believed you for a second. Now, because of it, I'll be sent to babysit old women in records." Finally he drew his weapon and assumed a confident stance.

But Carly saw the flaw in the captain's officer safety: he was in between Caswell and Sperry, so one or both of them could easily distract him. She unsnapped her own gun and tensed. Everything depended on whether or not the two men complied.

"You two are under arrest. We're going back up to your car, Thomas."

"Wait just a minute," Caswell blustered. "You have absolutely no probable cause to arrest me."

"You forget—the last time I was in patrol and made an arrest, we booked first and found a reason to make it stick later." Garrison motioned with his gun. "Stand over with Thomas, Conrad."

Carly saw the glance Sperry shot Caswell and she was moving. But everything happened so fast. Conrad started toward Caswell, crossing in front of Garrison. She leaped to her feet a split second too late. Sperry dropped his shoulder and rammed the captain.

The gun fired, Sperry screamed, and they went down in a heap with Caswell moving in. With a swift kick, he knocked Garrison's gun from his hand, sending it flying toward the car, and landed a second kick to the captain's head.

"That's enough. Stop right there!" Carly pointed her 9mm as a shocked Caswell jerked around to face her.

Sperry was moaning, but she couldn't see how badly he was hurt. Garrison brought a hand to the side of his head where he'd been kicked and seemed dazed. Carly kept her attention on the lawyer.

"I've got more than enough probable cause to arrest you now, Caswell. Step away from the captain."

"What an odd pair you two make." He stood up straight and looked from Garrison to Carly. "But I'm not going to jail." His hand jerked from his pocket, and Carly saw the gun, pointed straight at Captain Garrison's head. "You drop your gun or Norman is a dead man."

38

"**PLEASE, I NEED A DOCTOR,**" Sperry moaned, writhing in the dirt that Carly could now see was being stained red.

"Shut up, Conrad," Caswell said, his eyes pinpoints of fury. "The gun, *now*, Officer Edwards." He had a revolver—Carly guessed it was a .38—and cocked it.

Her pulse jumping, Carly made no move to comply, fighting to think of how to gain the advantage.

"Don't do it," Garrison said, sounding woozy from the kick to the head. "That's an order."

Bam! Caswell fired a round into the dirt, right next to Garrison's head. Carly jumped.

"Are we clear now? Throw your gun this way."

Carly swallowed and fought panic. Giving in to panic would only cloud her thinking.

"All right, all right." She held both hands up, then tossed her gun toward him. "But backup is on the way."

Caswell smirked. "I won't be long. Just one question before I end your life: Where is the girl? Norman was right about one thing—I want those diamonds. Thanks to the good captain, Conrad is out of the running for them."

The gun was now pointed at her.

"I . . ." Carly saw a golf ball–size rock sail through the air and hit Caswell in the right temple.

"Ow!" he yelped, cringing. Carly lunged for her gun and toward the cover provided by the car.

Caswell fired, and she felt the sting of a bullet burn her thigh. She had the gun in her grasp and was behind the car as another bullet pinged the fender. Caswell was after her; he had moved from Garrison's head and was focused completely on her.

As she turned to face the lawyer, another bullet zinged by. But Garrison was moving as well. Now behind the lawyer, he twisted and reached out with his long arms, grabbed Caswell's leg, and jerked it out from under the man.

Caswell screamed. The gun flew from his hand as he tried to break his fall.

Carly jammed her gun into its holster and went for the attorney. She grabbed an arm in a control hold as he tried to push himself up from the dirt. Garrison moved to sit across Caswell's legs and keep him down.

Glad she'd thought to bring the handcuffs, she pulled out a pair and prepared to apply them when Garrison caught her eye.

Clearly enjoying the fact that he had the struggling, cursing lawyer restrained, he smiled and held out his hand. "Please, allow me."

• • •

Once Caswell was cuffed and seated against the car's rear wheel, Carly secured Caswell's gun, then checked Sperry while Garrison radioed for help. Sperry had been hit in the midsection and was going into shock, but there was nothing Carly could do for him but keep him still until medics came.

She had to suppress a smile as she listened to Garrison on the radio because she heard the unspoken question in the dispatcher's voice at the captain calling for help from the field. Captains worked behind a desk; they didn't roll around in the dirt with bad guys.

"Are you okay, Captain?" she asked after he told her that help was on the way.

"Only my dignity is bruised." He looked her in the eye, and Carly saw none of the rancor that had framed their relationship for years. "Thank you, Officer Edwards. You came through at precisely the right moment. I owe you my life."

"I don't know about that." She turned to look at the brush where the rock had come from. She saw nothing and wondered if Mary Ellen was there. A thought occurred to her, and she pulled out her cell phone and made a quick call to Jonah.

By the time she disconnected, she could hear sirens. When the sirens came to a stop, the first person to burst through the brush was the person Carly most wanted to see: Nick.

•••

"Fat, dumb, and happy."

"Excuse me, sir?" Once Sperry had been assessed and whisked away by ambulance, Carly and Garrison were escorted up out of the catch basin to a paramedic rig. Medics examined her leg and the captain's head. Caswell's kick had broken the skin above Garrison's ear, and the cut was being cleaned. He wouldn't need stitches, but Carly's bullet graze near her hip was likely to need a few. Nick had hovered with her until Jonah arrived, and then the two of them had gone back down to where Harper's car was parked, leaving Carly in the company of the captain.

"It's what an old training officer said to me, years ago," Garrison explained. "He said that it was dangerous for a cop to take a desk job. If they weren't careful, they'd become fat, dumb, and happy."

"I've heard that expression as well," Carly said, a little amazed that Captain Garrison was talking to her as if she were an equal as they sat together on the back of the medic rig.

"I'd forgotten it, and that is exactly what happened to me:

I lost the cop edge and became an administrator." He spit the last word out as if he were spitting out an unpleasant taste. "I should have woken up after Drake and Tucker."

Since he started it, Carly got brave. "Can I ask what was going on with you and Caswell and Sperry?"

"At first, we just caught up. We were friends years ago. I was the one who suggested Conrad hire Thomas when Conrad's son got into trouble. He called me after you arrested Harper, to complain. At first I thought it was just a simple case of Thomas mad because you showed him up, so I listened to him vent. But when the baby was kidnapped and he called asking about the investigation, I knew something else was up." He paused and sipped some water. "Maybe it's time for me to retire. Here I was, ready to chat with a thief as if he weren't a thief."

"Maybe you just wanted to believe the best in someone you once knew."

"If only it were that easy."

Carly almost felt sorry for the man. For most of her career, he'd seemed larger than life, but not in a positive way. Now that he'd been cut down to size, she saw a flawed man who'd probably used the arrogance to cover his insecurities. She realized he'd no longer be a nemesis, someone she couldn't talk to, and for that she was glad.

He pointed. "Look what Sergeant Anderson found."

She turned and saw Nick and Jonah walking their way, between them a small girl wearing filthy jeans and a tank top but smiling as she looked up at Jonah. Nick was carrying a grimy backpack. Carly wondered if it contained the diamonds.

"Mary Ellen?" she asked as she stood to greet the trio.

"Yeah," she said.

"Did you throw that rock?"

"Yes, I threw it. I hate that lawyer. He had Stanley killed."

There was a commotion behind Nick. Wiley and another agent were walking up the hill with Thomas Caswell between them.

"I had nothing to do with the human trafficking—nothing," he was saying.

Usually the first thing a lawyer told his client was to shut up. Carly thought it ironic that Caswell obviously couldn't take his own advice.

He broke off when he saw Mary Ellen; then he cursed. "Just tell me one thing," he said, dragging his feet as Wiley tried to move him along. "Do you have the diamonds?"

Mary Ellen looked away. "Some of them."

"Some?" Caswell's eyes got wide, and he stopped, staring at her.

Mary Ellen smiled. "I traded some for money to buy food and gas."

"We have what's left safe and sound," Wiley said with a snicker.

Carly thought Caswell was going to choke. He began rambling almost incoherently about how much money the diamonds were worth and how this street urchin had squandered them. Then Carly was surprised by a sound she'd never heard. Garrison was laughing.

"Well, what do you know? Who played whom? Looks like a little girl got the best of both of you. While you were killing for those stones, she used them to stay alive."

39

CARLY FOUND HERSELF off work for the rest of the week. Four stitches in her thigh also meant no swimming for at least a week. For the first time she could remember, she was glad she was off work involuntarily. Sperry was recovering from his gunshot wound in the jail ward of County General, reputedly looking for a good defense attorney. Sperry's and Caswell's arrests, stolen diamonds, and human trafficking brought the case national headlines. She'd learned from Wiley that the rest of the diamonds had been recovered at a pawnshop in downtown Las Playas. The package of diamonds would be returned to the rightful owner. Cable news outlets descended on the city, but she wanted no part of any of it.

There were plenty of other people in the city for the news outlets to pounce on. Alex was trying to be a reporter but was actually part of the story for his role in uncovering the smuggled Mexican nationals. Jacobs had been promoted to captain when Garrison quietly retired.

Mary Ellen was also somewhat of a story. Jonah had been interviewed about her and his fight to see that the court went easy on her as he submitted a petition to have her released into his custody. Joe and Christy had even lined up with him—which only sensationalized the headline—thankful no harm had come to the baby and that Mary Ellen had brought him back safe.

With all the high-profile news outlets in the city, Carly had been happy to hide in her apartment for two days. But now she was ready to venture out again. Nick was taking her out on a date.

For reasons she couldn't put her finger on, Carly felt bound up with nervousness as she dressed for the big occasion. She stood in front of the mirror, working to get the curling iron positioned correctly in her hair, acutely feeling Andrea's absence. Andrea knew fashion and hairstyles, she knew makeup, and she knew how to put together outfits. As it was, Carly had actually gone shopping earlier with her mother, something that hadn't happened in years.

She tilted her head as she regarded her reflection in the mirror. The bruises around her eyes weren't quite gone, so she still needed a layer of foundation. She was happy that it didn't take much to give her eyes a normal look.

Maddie was back with her since she was off, so in a telltale sign of stress, she talked to the dog.

"It's been such a long time since I've gotten dressed up to go on a date. I really feel awkward." She fumbled with the curling iron for a few more minutes; then she unplugged it and moved to the brush. A few minutes with that and she stopped, finally satisfied with what she saw.

Carly studied the reflection staring back at her, not completely convinced it was herself she was looking at. The hair was neat and stylish, and the smallest bit of eye makeup accentuated her brown eyes. Her lips glowed a soft red. She affixed her earrings—small pearls, a gift from Nick on their fifth wedding anniversary—and added the matching pearl necklace. The new green summer dress her mother had helped her pick out clung just the right way to her athletic physique and made Carly sigh. "I hope he likes it."

A knock at the door caused Carly to turn and her stomach to lurch.

He's right on time, she noted as she glanced at the clock. "Be right there," she called out. Quickly she got her purse together, dumping out her backpack on the bed and transferring what she needed to a small clutch that matched her dress. Her hands trembled and her stomach was awash in turbulence, as if she were on a code 3 run. *This is like a first date! I need to calm down.*

She smoothed her dress one last time, gathered up her purse, and took a deep breath before striding into the living room and opening the door.

Nick stood in the doorway, looking every bit the *GQ* hubby in spite of the row of stitches on the side of his forehead. It took Carly's breath away. He stood ramrod straight and broad-shouldered, his short blond hair shone, and the blue suit jacket brought out the deep blue of his eyes. Carly admired him for a few seconds before he cleared his throat and handed her the roses in his hand.

"H-h-hello, Carly. You look great." He stammered a bit, and Carly relaxed when she realized he was as nervous as she was.

"You look pretty good yourself." She stepped forward to take the roses, pausing to inhale their scent. "You know I love roses. Thanks." She stood on her tiptoes and kissed him on the cheek. The familiar smell of his aftershave made her tingle.

"Yeah, I remember some things."

They stood and stared at one another for a moment before Nick spoke again. "We should probably get going."

"Yeah, yeah," Carly laughed. "Let me put these in water." She hurried to the task and then turned back to Nick.

"Place looks empty," he observed.

"Yeah. Andi has a lease, so she won't be back except to visit. A lot, I hope."

He held out his hand, and Carly placed hers in it.

His grip was warm and strong, and Carly felt her tension fade. "Thanks. I'm ready."

They left the apartment and walked to the plain car Jacobs was letting Nick drive until his truck was repaired. As Nick and Carly settled in, anxiety fled, replaced by companionship and comfortable familiarity. Nick took her to the best restaurant in Las Playas, the Bay Room at the Hacienda. The Hacienda was the oldest resort in town, a beautifully restored enclave overlooking the water. They were led to a window table, and conversation flowed easily.

"So," Nick said as they finished dessert and lingered over coffee, "in all the excitement lately, we haven't really had time to talk about stuff other than work. I was wondering, are you still planning on doing the channel swim?"

Nodding, Carly smiled. "Yeah, I sent my application in months ago. I just made the cutoff for the solo swimmers."

"Great. I was afraid because of the way I've been acting you'd decided not to go. You really are in super shape, and I know how much you've wanted to do that swim. And I look forward to being in the guide boat cheering you on."

"I guess that's fair. You let me cheer you in therapy. By the way, how is that going? You've been walking better lately, so what's the word?"

"We're still working on range of motion." He fidgeted a little bit, and Carly wondered if he was in a hurry to leave. "But you're right; my hip has loosened up a lot. Keith just says, 'I told you so.' My kind of injury takes time, and I was being impatient. I'm not 100 percent yet, but I will be."

He shook his head ruefully. "I have to apologize again for being such a jerk these last couple of months. I feel as though my eyes have been opened after a long blindness. I've been so wrapped up in the fear I couldn't be a cop anymore that I didn't like myself much. I couldn't imagine you liking me. I saw a career I've loved slipping away, and it was scary."

"It's all water under the bridge. I can accept anything as long as I know you are as committed to me as I am to you."

"Know it." He reached across the table for her hand. "This was all I prayed for, the year we were apart. You've always been the only one for me. I'll earn the second chance you've given me. I won't mess it up."

"I don't want to dwell on the past. I want to concentrate on our future. I couldn't imagine life without you."

The waiter refilled their coffees, but the pair barely noticed.

"I have one more important question to ask you." Nick slid his free hand into his pocket and pulled out a small velvet box. Carly's heart leaped in her chest, and her hand squeezed Nick's.

"There's no one else I want to spend my life with. I asked you this once, and then I broke my vows. Can I ask you again? This time I promise to keep all my vows and cherish you forever. Will you marry me?" He opened the box, and to Carly, the sparkle of the beautiful new engagement ring outshone the candles on the table.

"Of course I'll marry you!" Carly wiped away happy tears with her napkin. "You even got a new ring. I hadn't really thought that far . . . I mean, I knew I wanted this, but I hadn't thought ahead to rings and ceremonies. This is so beautiful." She'd tossed her old ring into the ocean and realized she'd never told him that. Now, gazing at the beautiful new diamond, she didn't think she'd mention it unless he asked. Like the sins God tosses into the sea and leaves there with No Fishing signs posted all around. She wasn't going to go back and dredge up memories of how their first marriage ended.

"Yes. A new ring, a new beginning." Nick grasped her hand and slid the ring on. "We are new in Christ. There will be a new and firmer foundation to this marriage, so I want what symbolizes my pledge to you to be something new." He smiled, and Carly saw his eyes fill with tears. "Once we're married, you can move home. You don't need to worry about another roommate. And I was thinking, since the channel swim is two months away, how about we plan quickly and honeymoon there in Maui?"

Carly laughed, feeling giddy. "I didn't want to admit it, but when I sent in my application, that thought was in the back of my mind. I think that would be an awesome honeymoon."

She loved the way her hand felt in his and only now realized how much she had missed this closeness. She never wanted to lose it again. "I love you, Nick. We will make it this time and grow old together."

Epilogue

KA'ANAPALI BEACH

THEY FINISHED THEIR WALK and stopped on the beach near the finish line. The race was tomorrow, but the finish chute had already been marked off with flags. The sky blazed with swirling colors of pink, orange, and red—a glorious Hawaiian sunset. Carly sighed with contentment as she leaned against her husband's shoulder.

He kissed her head and whispered, "You nervous about tomorrow?"

"No, not at all. I'm ready."

In the distance she could see the island of Lanai, the starting point for the 9.5-mile channel swim. Tomorrow morning the escort boat would pick Nick and Carly up around six and take them across the channel to the starting line. The gun would go off around eight, and she'd plunge into the water with the other swimmers—most swimming in relay teams,

but a few doing the whole distance solo like Carly—to com-
pete in a swim that would likely take several hours. But she
didn't consider herself to be swimming solo. Nick would be
in her follow boat, watching, shouting encouragement, next
to her the whole way.

"Not worried about sharks, jellyfish, or currents?"

She smiled, squeezed his waist, and then looked into
his warm eyes. "Jellyfish may sting, but I'll take my allergy
pills to prevent a reaction. As for the current, well—" she
shrugged—"that's what all my training was for, right? And
sharks? I've got you in the follow boat. You'll make sure I'm
safe from any sharks. I trust you."

He smiled, and she felt the warmth down to her toes.
"You got that right. No sharks will come close to you. Enjoy
the swim and do your best."

They shared a kiss. As Carly hugged her husband of two
days, she knew they were a strong and committed team. With
God at the center of this new marriage, Carly found that trust
was not an impossible action where Nick was concerned.

About the Author

A FORMER LONG BEACH, CALIFORNIA, police officer of twenty-two years, Janice Cantore worked a variety of assignments, including patrol, administration, juvenile investigations, and training. She's always enjoyed writing and published two short articles on faith at work for *Cop and Christ* and *Today's Christian Woman* before tackling novels. A few years ago, she retired to a house in the mountains of Southern California, where she lives with three Labrador retrievers, Jake, Maggie, and Abbie.

Janice writes suspense novels designed to keep readers engrossed and leave them inspired. *Abducted*, the sequel to *Accused*, is the second book in the Pacific Coast Justice series, featuring Carly Edwards. Janice also authored the Brinna's Heart series, which includes *The Kevlar Heart* and *A Heart of Justice*.

Visit Janice's website at www.janicecantore.com and connect with her on Facebook at facebook.com/JaniceCantore.

Discussion Questions

1. How do you respond during crisis situations? How does God's supernatural peace affect crises in your life?

2. Nick begins distancing himself from Carly during his long recuperation. What do you think of his reasons for pulling away? How should he have handled their relationship?

3. Joe and Christy go through a terrible ordeal, wondering whether their son will ever be recovered. Has anything precious ever been taken from you? If you are able, share the circumstances, along with how you responded and what the outcome was.

4. Throughout the story, Carly struggles with her roommate, Andi, especially when Andi lashes out in anger. What are some of the things Carly does well in her relationship with her roommate? What could she

have done better? What lessons can you take away from
their interactions and apply to relationships in your
own life?

5. Think of a time you've felt distanced from someone
you cared for. How did you respond to the situation?
When is it right to let a relationship dwindle, and
when is it appropriate to fight to maintain it?

6. What is your take on Alex's pursuit of Carly? Did
he conduct himself honorably? Did Carly respond
appropriately to Alex?

7. At the end of chapter 10, Carly asks herself if she'd
"somehow tied God and Nick together so getting one
meant getting the other." Do you think, at that point
in the story, she believed her desire for Nick was part
of God's plan? Is there something in your life that you
desire but that God might be telling you to let go of?
What steps can you take to evaluate that desire in light
of God's will for you?

8. Andi lashes out against Carly's newfound faith because,
in her past, people who professed to follow Christ had
deeply wounded her. Is there anyone in your life who
has suffered similar hurts? What can believers do to
love such wounded people and heal the damage?

9. Pastor Jonah Rawlings is devastated when he realizes
his connection to the kidnapper and remembers their
shared history. Were you surprised when you read

about his secret? Why does Jonah feel so much guilt? How might you have reacted if you were facing a similar situation?

10. What did you think of Mary Ellen's actions near the end of the story? What is motivating her? If you were a judge or jury member helping to determine her future, what kind of recommendation would you give? Would you follow the letter of the law or show some grace?

Turn the page for a look at Janice Cantore's

BAM! The door to the van slammed shut.

Diondre struggled to sit up, spitting out blood. He'd bitten his tongue when the Ugly Dude shoved him in the van. *He never even said what it was he wanted.*

Next to him, Rojo cursed. On the other side of him, Crusher sobbed; Diondre could tell by the smell that he'd wet his pants. The Ugly Dude was Crusher's friend, his new supplier, so this was his fault, and Rojo swore at him.

"Crush," Diondre said when Rojo finished. The van moved, jerking Diondre into his friend. "Come on, man. We got to get out of this. What does this guy want?"

"Us dead," Rojo hissed with heat.

Diondre ignored him. "Crush, talk to me." As he spoke, he tried to loosen his hands and felt the plastic cuffs cut into his wrists.

Crusher sniffled. "I don't know, man. He told me he had stuff for us to move—lots of stuff. He gave me the money for the TV. I swear I thought he was on the level. I don't know why he's trippin'."

"What did Trey say?" Diondre asked about their boss, the OG of the gang. Tough and smart, Trey would be outraged that three of his homeboys were being treated this way.

"Didn't tell him."

This brought more curses from Rojo, and fear erupted anew in Diondre. If Trey didn't know where they were, they were as good as dead. He pushed himself up a bit so he could lean against the side of the van, fighting for control as panic threatened. He thought about what his friend Londy had said to him earlier in the day.

"Man, the gang life ain't no life. It's just going get you sent to jail—or worse, dead."

Londy used to roll with the Ninjas, but no more. He'd been trying to get Diondre out of the gang. Diondre wanted out when he was with Londy, but when Rojo and Crusher came calling, he wanted to be with them. And now he was going to die.

"God is there if you call." Londy's words rang in Diondre's thoughts as loud as if Londy were in the van with him. Diondre squeezed his eyes shut and focused on everything Londy had told him about God. He prayed all the words he remembered, trying hard not to cry.

"You praying, D.?"

Opening his eyes, he saw Crusher looking at him, face dirty with smeared tears.

"Yeah, as best I can, man. As best I can."

"Pray for me too, will you?"

Diondre nodded as Rojo cursed them both in Spanish.

The van came to a stop, and the side door whipped open. Moist, foggy air that smelled like the ocean assaulted his nostrils. Diondre hoped they weren't at the ocean. He hated the ocean because he couldn't swim.

But there wasn't time to consider where they were because the Ugly Dude and his two friends were at the door and they all had guns. Diondre hoped Londy was as right about God as he had been about the gang life.

• • •

Carly and Joe stepped out of the Las Playas police station and headed to the rear parking lot. It was a mild, hazy summer night, the kind of hazy that developed into thick fog as the night wore on. A familiar voice sounded from her left.

"Officer Edwards, Officer King."

Carly turned, and both she and Joe stopped.

"Hey, G-man, Agent Wiley, how are you?" Carly held her hand out to a man in a dark suit, the stereotypical picture of an FBI agent, a man who had helped with the investigation into the kidnapping and rescue of Joe's son. Wiley shook both their hands.

"Good, busy." He turned to Joe. "How's A.J.?"

"Absolutely great and getting bigger every day."

"Glad to hear it. Do you mind if I have a word with your partner?" He nodded toward Carly.

"Not a problem. I'll get us a sled while you talk," Joe said to Carly. He left her with Agent Wiley.

Carly set her kit down and spread her arms. "Well, I knew you'd catch me sooner or later. And I hid the bodies so well."

Wiley cracked a hint of a smile, which was about the most he ever did. "Why don't we have a seat?" He motioned to some break tables on the back patio.

"What's up?" Carly asked as they sat.

"I'm here to talk to you."

"Then I'm all ears."

"I'm heading up a federal task force. We're pulling in good officers from agencies all over Southern California."

"Mission?"

"Homeland security. Under that umbrella we'll work on a lot of different things. There will be travel involved; it'll be exciting, always changing, and infinitely challenging."

"I'm happy for you. But why are you telling me?"

"Because I want you to join us. It's been cleared with your chief, should you decide to hop on board."

Carly stared at Wiley across the table as bursts of blue, red, and amber flashed intermittently when officers checked their vehicle light bars. The sounds of graveyard shift beginning were swirling around them—cops swapping stories, Ford engines roaring to life, and the occasional short blast as a siren was tested.

"Talk about out of proverbial left field. I don't know what to say." The question *What would Nick say?* shot through her mind as she tried to predict her husband's reaction. He thought she needed a change. That a federal task force would be change was an understatement. It would afford her investigative opportunities she'd never see in small Las Playas. But it would also take her away from home a lot.

"I didn't expect you to answer right now." He reached into his pocket and pulled out a flash drive. "Here, take this; study it. It has all the pertinent information about the job. I'll be in town for a while."

Carly took the flash drive and closed her fist around it even as the gravity of what Wiley just offered her sank in and excitement started to swell. This was a huge honor.

"This will take some thought," she said, working to keep her tone noncommittal.

Wiley stood and Carly followed suit.

"You've got two weeks. I'm hoping you'll decide soon, but don't rush," he said. "You know where to find me when you've made a decision." Wiley shook her hand once, then turned and left her standing by the table.

Carly stared at the flash drive for a minute, the rush of such a challenging assignment biting hard. She couldn't suppress the grin as she slipped the drive into her pocket.

• • •

Joe drove their patrol car out to the old marina, where the pier with a boarded-up Walt's restaurant would stay until an environmental impact study could be prepared, outlining the ramifications of its removal. From Walt's north a beautiful new seaside shopping plaza was taking shape. It would be connected to the inland Apex shopping complex by a pedestrian bridge over Seaside Boulevard. Carly told Joe about Wiley's offer as they got out of the car.

"Wow, what an opportunity," Joe said. "You'd learn a lot and you'd get to do a lot." He cocked his head. "Be great experience for a promotion."

Carly rubbed her face. "I don't know that I want to promote, but I'd love the challenge of a task force like that." Her mind raced with everything the job would entail. Homeland security—protecting the nation, not just Las Playas.

"I'd hate to give up our partnership," she said, turning Joe's way. "That's the part that stinks. But maybe I do need a change."

He met her gaze and smiled. "I'd hate to lose it too. But nothing lasts forever, and I would never try to talk you out of a gig like that. To be honest, if it were me, I'd jump on it. Jobs like that don't grow on trees."

"What would Christy say?"

Joe shrugged. "She'd probably be happy to have me out of the car. She worries that uniformed police officers are easy targets."

"If you traveled a lot, that wouldn't bother her?"

He shot her a sideways glance. "Are you afraid of what Nick will say?"

"Not afraid, exactly. Just not sure." She stopped as they reached the stairway leading up to the pedestrian bridge. "I—"

Bang.

A sharp, distinct gunshot, close by, cut her off.

Her hand went to her gun.

Bang. Another sounded and before she could speak, a third.

She looked at Joe, intently peering into the darkness. Carly pulled out her radio to advise dispatch. "Can you tell where they came from?" she asked before she keyed her mike. "You think some nut out here has a gun?"

Joe shook his head. "Sound echoes here, but I think that came from farther out, near the Catalina dock."

Carly keyed the radio. "1-Adam-7, we heard what sounded like three gunshots, possibly from the Catalina dock area. We'll be investigating. Please advise if you get any calls regarding possible gunshots."

"10-4, Adam-7. Be advised, we're getting a call now. Stand by."

They hurried back to the black-and-white. Joe started the unit and turned for the gate. By the time Carly pushed the gate open, dispatch advised that they had one call about possible shots, a complaining party who lived in the old marina. The CP also thought the shots came from Catalina Shores.

They weren't that far away. The new Catalina Shores terminal was attached to the north end of the marina complex but on the other side of Shoreline Park. There was also a large hotel, the Bluestone, between them and the park. It was encircled by construction fencing for the marina renovation and was dark and unoccupied at the moment.

"The CP called from a cell phone." Carly read more information sent from dispatch on the computer screen as Joe made the turn north on Seaside. "From a marina employee. It's Jarvis; he lives aboard a boat. Says he heard three distinct gunshots"

"I know Jarvis," Joe said, making a face. He slowed as they rolled past the park. "He sleeps at work during the day. Why doesn't it surprise me that he's up at this time of morning?"

A longtime marina patrol officer, Jarvis had a well-earned reputation as a slug.

"He doesn't want contact, just called to make sure the beat car checks it out," she read.

Joe sighed.

They passed the Bluestone; the next ramp would be Marina Access Way. They were on the water now and the haze became thick patches of fog hanging in the air. The streetlights gave off the yellow glow of fog lights and the smell of salt water wafted into the car. But other than the hum of the black-and-white and the sound of the water in the distance, the night was quiet.

Carly's gaze roamed and her ears strained for any noise out of the ordinary. When Joe turned left onto the ramp, Carly unsnapped her holster.

Marina Access Way ended at the Catalina Shores parking structure and dock, a business that ferried people back and forth to Catalina, twenty-four miles across the channel. This was the only part of the renovation that had finished early.

Carly picked up the radio to announce that she and Joe were 10-97, on scene. Besides police cars, Carly had seen no other traffic or headlights anywhere. They reached the parking structure attached to the Catalina Shores pier, and again Joe slowed so they could listen. During business hours a parking arm would be down and parkers would have to pull a ticket to get in. At this time of the early morning the arm was up, and from what Carly could see, the lot empty. She knew that a section of the lot on top was marked off for long-term parking, for those people leaving their cars to spend more than a day on Catalina and for Catalina residents who wanted to keep their cars on the mainland. She couldn't see up there at the moment.

The yellow fog lights illuminated a good deal of the area in spite of the haze. Joe cruised slowly. Both he and Carly had their windows down and heavy, foggy salt air swirled in. Joe brought the unit to a stop at the drop-off area as Carly advised dispatch they would be out of the car.

After sliding her nightstick into its ring, Carly waited for Joe to meet her on the passenger side of the car. They both carried flashlights but didn't need to turn them on as they walked up the steps to the ticket offices. Then Carly saw the foot.

Hand out, she stopped Joe. "Here." Sliding the flashlight into her sap pocket, she drew her weapon. The foot stuck out from behind a stone bench.

"Hello?" Carly called as she and Joe separated slightly to come at the person from different angles.

There was no response to her hails.

And as she made her way around the bench, she saw that there wouldn't be.

Three bodies lay partially hidden behind the bench, facedown, hands secured behind their backs. They'd been shot execution style.